PRAISE FOR THE DEAD-END JOB MYSTERIES BY ELAINE VIETS, WINNER OF THE ANTHONY AWARD AND THE AGATHA AWARD

Catnapped!

"*Catnapped!* moves at a brisk pace as Helen learns the difference between pet owners and those who pamper their star felines to the extreme. An intriguing subplot . . . adds an extra boost to Viets's witty story."
— *South Florida Sun-Sentinel*

"Lively. . . . The behind-the-scenes look at the show cat world is worth the price of admission alone in this witty cozy."
— *Publishers Weekly*

"Fun and entertaining. . . . [Viets] has given us yet another wonderful mystery that takes us to sunny Florida."
— Escape with Dollycas into a Good Book

Board Stiff

"Viets's lively plots and broad humor complemented [her] highly entertaining novels while also showing how low-paid employees often are taken for granted. But the gradual sea change in Viets's series has given the series an even more satisfying story line. . . . Viets delivers a unique look at South Florida's tourist industry. . . . For Floridians, *Board Stiff* is a look at home."
— *South Florida Sun-Sentinel*

"Entertaining. . . . Viets shines at evoking Florida's vibrant landscapes and even more colorful characters."
— *Publishers Weekly*

"Moving Helen from dead-end jobs into full-time employment does nothing to stifle [Viets's] quirky good humor."
— *Kirkus Reviews*

continued . . .

"A smart mystery that is fun and very entertaining."
— Escape with Dollycas into a Good Book

"Sassy and super hip, look for *Board Stiff* to make a big splash this summer."
— Fresh Fiction

Final Sail

"One way for a fugitive to hide in plain sight is to work at low-wage jobs, which is what Helen Hawthorne has been doing in Elaine Viets's quick-witted mysteries."
— Marilyn Stasio, *The New York Times Book Review*

"Enjoyable. . . . Viets presents an eye-opening exposé of spoiled yachters and the not so glamorous lives of their crews in this action-filled cozy." — *Publishers Weekly*

"An engaging tale with two interesting investigations. Both cases are well written and fun to follow . . . an exciting thriller." — The Mystery Gazette

"Delightful, entertaining, and truly insightful, *Final Sail* is a sailor's dream." — Fresh Fiction

MORE PRAISE FOR THE DEAD-END JOB MYSTERIES

"Clever. . . . The real draw, though, is Viets's snappy critique of South Florida."
— Marilyn Stasio, *The New York Times Book Review*

"A stubborn and intelligent heroine, a wonderful South Florida setting, and a cast of more or less lethal bimbos. . . . I loved this book."
— #1 *New York Times* bestselling author
Charlaine Harris

"Wickedly funny." — *The Miami Herald*

Catnapped!

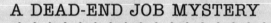

A DEAD-END JOB MYSTERY

Elaine Viets

AN OBSIDIAN MYSTERY

OBSIDIAN
Published by the Penguin Group
Penguin Group (USA) LLC, 375 Hudson Street,
New York, New York 10014, USA

USA | Canada | UK | Ireland | Australia | New Zealand | India | South Africa | China
penguin.com
A Penguin Random House Company

Published by Obsidian, an imprint of New American Library, a division of Penguin Group (USA) LLC. Previously published in an Obsidian hardcover edition.

First Obsidian Mass Market Printing, May 2015

ISBN 978-0-451-46631-0

Printed in the United States of America
10 9 8 7 6 5 4 3 2 1

ACKNOWLEDGMENTS

Catnapped! could not have been written without the help of Tracy Petty, southern region director of the Cat Fanciers' Association, Inc. Cat show judges are natural teachers, and Judge Petty went to great lengths to check the cat facts and explain the intricacies of show judging. Any mistakes are mine, not hers.

There is no Gold Cup Cat Fanciers' Association, and Judge Tracy Petty does not resemble the flashy Judge Lexie Deener except for her uncanny ability to repel cat hair from her black clothes at shows.

Special thanks to Detective R. C. White, Fort Lauderdale Police Department (retired) and licensed Florida private eye, and Houston private investigator and mystery writer William Simon. Poison expert Luci Zahray helped me kill. Fortunately, Luci uses her powers only for good. Chris Byrnes is a fun-loving dancer in Fort Lauderdale. Special thanks to Reverend Karlene McAllister, who ministers to prisoners through Inside Dharma.

Some friends let me borrow their names. Carol H. Berman is not an executive assistant at a financial office but the manager of the J. McLaughlin in Palm Beach Gardens. Valerie Cannata has been transformed into an investigative

TV reporter. Nancie Hays let me turn her into a lawyer. Jan Kurtz does not groom Persian cats. She made a generous donation to charity to have her name in this book. The real Margery Flax is much younger and has been married to Stephen Flax for twenty-two years. She loves purple as much as the fictional Margery.

SmartWater CSI is a forensic coding system being tested by several Florida police and sheriff's departments. Thank you, SmartWater CSI president Logan Pierson, for your help.

Jinny Gender is not the director of the Gold Cup Coventry All Breed Cat Show but a St. Louis friend and devoted dog lover.

Thanks to Molly Weston, Dick Richmond, Mary Alice Gorman, Richard Goldman and MarySue Carl, who teaches at Arroyo High School in El Monte, California.

The Dive Bar in Fort Lauderdale really does have a naked woman discreetly hidden in the mural on its wall. Look for her and her wavy hair next time you stop for a beer and a burger.

Novel writing is a team effort, and I have help from the best: senior editor Sandra Harding, ever-helpful assistant editor Elizabeth Bistrow, and publicist Kayleigh Clark at NAL, as well as my agent, David Hendin, and my husband, Don Crinklaw, an award-winning reporter in Fort Lauderdale.

Boynton Beach librarian Anne Watts lent me her six-toed cat, Thumbs, for this series. As always, I'm grateful to all the librarians who helped with this book, especially the staff of the St. Louis Public Library, the St. Louis County Library, and Broward County Library. Librarians are the original search engines.

I can't forget supersaleswoman Carole Wantz, who could sell snow during a blizzard. I'm grateful to the booksellers who recommend my novels to their customers.

Thank you to the Femmes Fatales. I rely on your encouragement and advice. Read our blog at www.femmes fatales.typepad.com.

Thanks also to the authors at The Kill Zone. TKZ aims to inspire, anger, amuse and entertain readers at killzoneauthors.blogspot.com.

Questions or comments? Please e-mail me at eviets@aol.com.

CHAPTER 1

Monday

The bedroom phone shrilled at five a.m.

Phil Sagemont squinted at the caller ID through bloodshot eyes. "Uh-oh, it's Nancie Hays," he said. "This can't be good."

Helen Hawthorne groaned, reached for the lamp and knocked over an empty wineglass. "I don't want to go to work before dawn," she said.

"We don't have a choice," Phil said. "We're the PIs for her firm." He put the phone on speaker, and they both winced at the lawyer's clipped, brisk voice.

"Helen, Phil, I need you in my office now," she said. The lawyer was barely five feet tall and a hundred pounds, but she had the authority of a four-star general.

"It's a custody case. We think the husband's violated the visitation agreement. We need you to get her back."

"How old is the kid?" Phil said.

"It's not a kid; it's a kitten," Nancie said. "Four months old."

"A kitten!" Phil said. "Call Animal Rescue."

"This isn't any ordinary cat," Nancie said. "It's a pedigreed Chartreux, a show cat owned by Trish Barrymore."

"The socialite married to Smart Mort?" Phil asked.

"His name is Mortimer Barrymore," Nancie said. Helen could almost see the little lawyer fighting back her impatience. Nancie kept her dark hair short and practical. She'd be wearing a no-nonsense dark suit even on a stifling September morning in South Florida.

"Trish says the cat's bloodlines go back to prewar France," Nancie said. "Hers go back a lot further. She's paying and paying well. That cat is her child, and she's upset that her baby has been kidnapped by her husband."

"Oh, please," Helen said. Phil snorted.

"If you two want to keep working for this firm," the lawyer said, "you will take her problem seriously.

"Trish and Mort are in the middle of a bitter divorce. They're fighting over everything: who gets the two mansions, the Mercedes and the Ferrari, even the antique cigar case. It's the biggest headache I've ever handled.

"The only thing they've agreed on is the shared custody of their cat, January's Jubilee Justine. Trish keeps her during the week. Mort picks her up Saturday morning and returns her Sunday night. He gets Justine every holiday. Phil, if I hear another snort from you, you're fired.

"Trish is living at their Fort Lauderdale mansion. Mort's at their estate in Peerless Point, about five miles away. Saturday, he picked up Justine at eight o'clock, like he always does, and took her to his place. He was supposed to return her at seven o'clock Sunday night.

"When Mort didn't show by nine, Trish was frantic. She called the Peerless Point police and wanted them to issue an Amber Alert."

"For a cat?" Helen said.

"That's what the cop said. When he figured out she was talking about a kitten, he laughed at her. Then Trish made it worse and said, 'Do you know who I am?'

"'Yeah, a crazy cat lady,' the cop told her.

"Trish said, 'I'll have your job.'

"'You're welcome to it, lady,' the cop said. 'Have fun dealing with nuts like you.'

"Trish called me and I called you last night. You didn't answer your phone. I lost track of how many messages I left." Nancie didn't hide her annoyance. She expected detectives on retainer to be on call around the clock.

"Uh, we unplugged the phone," Phil said. He sounded sheepish.

"Newlyweds!" Nancie said. "You've been married more than a year. Aren't you over that by now?"

"I hope not," Phil said.

Helen felt her face flush hot with embarrassment in the dark bedroom. She slipped on her robe, as if Nancie could see she was naked.

"Why did they agree on custody of the cat if they fight about everything else?" Helen asked, hoping to distract the lawyer.

"They care about Justine's welfare," Nancie said. "Pet custody is tricky. The court regards pets as property. Some judges won't order visitation for the other pet parent. Get the wrong judge, and it's like asking if you can visit your ex-wife's couch. The judge will think you're crazy."

"I wonder why," Phil said.

"Take this seriously, Phil. Don't you two have a cat?" Nancie asked.

"Thumbs," Phil said. "He's a great cat, but he's not our four-legged son."

Thumbs heard his name, jumped up on the bed and rubbed his head against Phil's hand. The detective absently scratched the cat's ears and said, "Now that your client has destroyed any hope of police cooperation, you want us to rescue the situation?"

"She's *our* client, not *mine*," Nancie said. "Get your clothes on and come straight to my office. Don't bother making coffee. I have a fresh pot and a bag of bagels. Be here before six. I want you to meet Trish, then pick up Justine at Mort's house." She hung up.

"Glad I plugged in the phone at three a.m.," Helen said. She and Phil showered together to save time, but there was no romance this morning. They dressed quickly, and Helen poured breakfast for their six-toed cat. "At least you get to eat," she told Thumbs.

He ignored her and stuck his head in his food bowl.

Phil quietly shut the jalousie door. No other lights were on at the Coronado Tropic Apartments. The two-story white Art Moderne building loomed over the palm trees. Window air conditioners rattled in the soft pre-dawn light. Helen and Phil tiptoed past the turquoise pool. The humid air was so sticky-hot, Helen felt like she was swimming to her white PT Cruiser. She was grateful for the Igloo's air-conditioning.

"I can't believe this," Phil said, as he plopped resentfully into the passenger seat. "Coronado Investigations has solved murders and saved lives, and now we're rescuing kittens."

"Hey, it pays the rent," Helen said, starting the car.

"A kitten!" Phil said. "Not even a cat—or a dog. WWBD? What would Bogie do?"

"Take the job to pay for his scotch," Helen said.

She admired her husband's chiseled profile and noble nose as she listened to him grouse about the kitten rescue. She thought her man looked like a rock star, with his long silver hair tied back in a ponytail. He'd certainly performed like one last night.

She smiled at the memory, then turned into Nancie's parking lot. The law office was a neat, stripped-down charcoal cube with an imposing wooden door. The lawyer's silver Honda was parked in back, leaving the best spots for visitors. A sleek black Mercedes brooded under a palm tree by the door. Helen parked next to it.

Inside, past the foyer, she saw Nancie at her desk. Like the lawyer, the desk was plain, white and strictly business. A pale blonde in a black lace dress sat in the lime green client chair.

"Bogie would definitely approve of our decorative client," Helen whispered, as they headed for the office.

"Helen and Phil, help yourself to coffee in the conference room and join us," Nancie said. "We'll eat after we talk to Mrs. Barrymore. She's anxious to get home in case Mort returns with Justine."

Helen looked longingly at the basket of bagels and bowl of fruit as she poured two black coffees into white china cups. Phil snitched a grape. Nancie introduced them, and the private eyes took the two chairs across from Trish Barrymore.

"Now, tell Helen and Phil what happened this weekend," Nancie said.

"My baby's been missing almost twelve hours," Trish Barrymore said, and dissolved into tears.

Helen Hawthorne watched the woman's well-bred reserve crumble like a hurricane-slammed seawall. She thought Trish was overreacting, but the woman didn't seem to be faking her distress. Her blond hair straggled out of its chignon, and she'd gnawed patches of pale pink polish off her nails.

"You have to find her," Trish said, her voice unsteady. "Nancie said you would." She quit gulping back sobs and unleashed heart-wrenching wails.

"Now, Trish. I said Helen and Phil would *try*," Nancie said, attempting to walk a line between caution and comfort. "Coronado Investigations has had amazing success, but I can only promise that Helen and Phil will do their best."

"Justine needs her mother," Trish said. "She's all alone."

"Trish, you don't know that," Nancie said. "We believe she's with your husband."

"Former husband," Trish said. "Almost former." She discreetly tugged on the hem of her black lace skirt and crossed her legs at the ankles.

"You know Mort would never hurt Justine," Nancie said.

"No, he loves our baby as much as I do," Trish said. "But she's so tiny he could step on her. He walks around the house without his glasses. What if he accidentally hurts her?"

"Justine is a smart kitten," Nancie said. "She won't let herself get stepped on. If something should happen, Mort would take her straight to the hospital."

"He's not cruel," Trish said, trying to reassure herself.

"You and your husband are going through a difficult divorce," Nancie said. "You've instructed me to fight for everything, even your silver pickle forks."

"Those were a present from my great-grandmother!" Trish's temper flared like a lit match. "That Tiffany pattern was created for her. She gave us her silver. Both our homes have been in my family since they were built in 1925. The Barrymores have been social leaders for centuries. Mort came from nothing!"

But Smart Mort knew how to make money, Helen thought. And Trish knew how to spend it. Tastefully. The CPA with the boyishly curly hair and lopsided grin raked in so much cash, Trish could turn her crumbling family mansions into designer showcases—and there was still more to splash around.

"That's why he married me, you know," Trish said. "For my name."

"Oh, I'm sure he married you for more than that," Nancie said.

Helen was, too. Even burdened by grief, Trish had

style. This morning she was mourning her potential loss in a black lace dress that cost as much as a summer vacation.

"You're beautiful," Nancie said. "You're regal. You serve the community. I've lost count of all your civic and charity boards."

"Twenty-three," Trish said. "Mort's last name was Draco! Like a Harry Potter character! What kind of name is that? He used me. He changed his name to Barrymore."

And painted himself with the dull green patina of old money, Helen thought.

"Custody cases are always difficult," Nancie said. "But despite your differences, you and Mort worked out an agreement for Justine."

"We did it for the emotional well-being of our child," Trish said. "Justine has a brilliant future as a show cat. She's a pedigreed Chartreux. They're known for their smoky gray fur and copper eyes.

"Here. See for yourself." She produced a photo from a slim black clutch. The kitten was a fluffy gray cloud with eyes like new pennies.

"That's January's Jubilee Justine," Trish said.

"She's beautiful," Helen said, though she felt disloyal. She knew Thumbs, her big-pawed white and gray cat, wouldn't really mind if she admired another cat.

"Big name for a little cat," Phil said.

"She was born in a *J* year," Trish said. "Chartreux have their own naming system. Their names must start with a particular letter of the alphabet, depending on the year they were born. I'm lucky 2014 is a *J* year. I would have hated it if she'd been born last year. I don't like the *I* names nearly as much."

"So, Mort didn't return your cat on time," Phil said, steering her back to the story. "Did you call him when he didn't show up?"

"I gave him ten minutes' grace time," Trish said, "in case he was caught in traffic. Then I called his landline and his cell phone. He didn't pick up. I called every ten minutes until nine o'clock. Then I called the police. They were no help at all. That's when I called Nancie and she contacted you."

"Do you think Mort left town with Justine?" Helen asked.

"No," Trish said. "Our baby doesn't like to fly and long car trips upset her tummy."

"How do you transport your cat?" Helen asked. "In a pet carrier?"

"We each have a Baby Coach," she said, producing a soft-sided carrier that looked like a small black school bus with clear mesh windows and jeweled headlights. "I brought it for you. She won't go anywhere unless she's in her bus."

She handed the bejeweled bus to Phil, who handled it like a live snake. Helen hid a smile.

"Continuity is so important to help Justine transition," Trish said. "We each have a Zen Cat Tower for her to relax."

"What's that?" Helen said.

"It's a graceful mahogany tower six feet tall with three levels," Trish said, "plus a sisal scratching pad and a hideaway. It has washable suede cushions.

"Justine has the same toys, dishes and food at both places so she will always feel at home. We explained that Mommy and Daddy still love her, but we can't live together anymore. She seems to be coping well.

"We know we're not the only couple in this situation. Britney Spears and K-Fed and Jennifer Love Hewitt and Ross McCall fought over their fur babies."

"So did another Barrymore," Helen said. "I read that Drew Barrymore and Tom Green had a custody dispute over their Labrador."

"Those Barrymores are no relation. They're *actors.*" Trish spit out the word.

"I guess if you don't have children, you have to fight about the pets," Phil said.

"Tell that to Jon and Kate Gosselin," Nancie said. "The reality-show stars had eight kids and still fought over their dogs."

"Please, please bring my baby home," Trish said. "And, if it's possible, try to keep our names out of the media."

"We'll do our best," Helen said.

"Here are the keys to the house where Mort is living and the alarm code," Trish said. "He didn't change them, in case I needed to get Justine in an emergency. Nancie and I agreed it would be better if you picked her up."

"The situation is too volatile at this stage in the negotiations," Nancie said.

"May I go home now?" Trish said. "In case Mort's there with Justine?"

"Of course," Nancie said. "You can count on Helen and Phil to handle Justine's return discreetly."

"Our divorce has already had too much publicity," Trish said.

The PI pair waited until the front door closed before they attacked the bagels in the conference room and carried their plates to the table.

"Is this case for real?" Phil asked, then bit into a garlic bagel slathered with onion cream cheese.

"Very real," Nancie said. "I know you'd rather have a nice clean murder or civil suit. I don't usually take divorces, but Trish and her family are good clients. Pet custody and visitation rights are the hottest area of the law right now."

"But it's ridiculous," Phil said.

"Not to Mort and Trish Barrymore. If you think they're hard to take, you won't believe the Laniers of

Tennessee," she said. "When they split, the wife said she deserved custody of the dog because she kept it away from ill-bred bitches—her words—and made sure the dog went to a weekly ladies' Bible class."

"Was it a lady dog?" Phil asked.

"I have no idea," Nancie said sharply. "Mrs. Lanier wouldn't let anyone drink around the dog. Mr. Lanier said he deserved custody because he taught the dog how to ride on the back of his motorcycle and never drank beer around him. The court gave the couple joint custody. Each spouse got the dog six months at a time."

"I would have bought the dog a beer and given him to someone who wasn't so crazy," Phil said.

Helen saw a frown crease Nancie's forehead. She was running out of patience. "Let's go pick up Justine," Helen said. "What's Mort's address?"

"Forty-two Peerless Point," Nancie said. "Mort and his cat are rattling around in eight thousand square feet of prime waterfront real estate. Call me as soon as you get Justine."

Helen and Phil made the trip in twenty minutes, slowed by morning rush-hour traffic. Peerless Point was an enclave of historic waterfront homes. Mort's estate was hidden behind a ten-foot white stucco fence. Phil punched in the code and the ornate wrought-iron gates swung open.

"Wow," Helen said. "This looks like a silent screen star's house." The two stucco wings were perfectly balanced by a series of arches: arched windows, an arched portico draped with red bougainvillea, and a white arched door.

The pale rose–brick drive wound through a sculpture garden. They drove past time-weathered marble statues of gods and angels.

"Mort's at home," Phil said. "At least his red Ferrari is. It's parked under the arches."

Helen parked behind it and they walked carefully to the front door.

Phil had the door keys out, but Helen tried the massive wrought-iron handle.

"It's open," she said. "What's the dark red puddle on the doorstep? Paint?"

Phil kneeled down for a closer look, but the coppery smell and clouds of flies gave them their answer. He peered inside.

"It's Mort," he said. "He's dead."

CHAPTER 2

Monday

M ort Barrymore died in style, facedown under a
crystal chandelier, his blood spattering the Car-
rara marble foyer. The rusty halo around his
dark hair could have been a decorator's "pop of color."

Helen felt her stomach twist. "His skull is smashed,"
she said, her voice thin and shaky. "What's that wooden
thing on the floor by his head, Phil? A knickknack
shelf?"

"I think that's Justine's Zen Cat Tower," Phil said.
"Solid mahogany. Looks like someone bashed him with
it. There's blood and hair on that cat tower."

Helen shivered. "Poor Mort. Such a waste. I'll call 911."

"Not yet!" Phil said. "We have to find the cat first.
Come in, but watch where you step."

Helen batted away the swarm of fat flies and entered
gingerly. Phil crouched down for a closer look at Mort's
right arm, splashed with dark blood.

"Lucky for us, Mort held up his arm to defend

himself," he said. "He took a direct hit on his watch. It stopped at six p.m."

"How do you know he was whacked last night?" Helen asked. And why was I talking like I was in a gangster movie?

"Because his Rolex shows a.m. and p.m. time," Phil said.

"What's that on the floor beside the body?" Helen asked. "Looks like a round spot of blood, but it's brighter red."

She balanced carefully on one knee to examine it.

"Don't pick it up," Phil said. "It's evidence."

"I wasn't planning to," Helen said. "It's a red enamel medallion with a snarling cat's face."

"That's no house cat," Phil said. " 'Coventry' is printed in gold around the edge."

"Maybe it fell off a necklace. See that brass loop?" Helen said, as she photographed the medallion with her camera phone.

"Do you see Mort's cell phone?" she asked.

"No," Phil said. "Unless he's lying on it, it's not here."

"We'd better find Justine fast," Helen said. "If the police show up and we're chasing a cat through a crime scene, we could lose our licenses."

"How fast can we search eight thousand square feet?" Phil asked.

She glanced up the graceful curved staircase. "The door at the top of the steps is closed," Helen said. "I'll run upstairs and check."

"Take my handkerchief," Phil said. "Don't leave prints on the knob. And don't spend a lot of time up there."

"Won't have to," Helen said. "If Justine is up there, she'll be howling to get out. No cat can stand to be on the wrong side of a closed door."

Helen opened the paneled wooden door and saw no sign of a cat. Back downstairs, she said, "We should look for a cell phone, charger and laptop while we're searching for the cat."

They surveyed the kitchen, a sleek white wilderness. "A gray cat would stand out here," she said. "It's feline free. No phone or laptop, either."

They swept down a picture-lined hall to a sunny salon. Phil whistled at its size. "This room has to be two thousand square feet." He lifted two massive couches and a love seat, while Helen checked under them for crouching cats. There were no curtains to hide behind, and the tables were glass.

"Nothing," she said. "Not even cat hair under the furniture. We've caught another break: The powder-room door is shut. What's in this next room?"

"Judging by the chlorine smell, I'd say it's a swimming pool." Phil's voice echoed in the warm, humid room.

"A vintage one," Helen said. "With a stunning Art Deco mosaic on the bottom of the pool." The light-filled room with the pale blue tiles was a quick, easy search.

"No cat," she said.

"The music room looks like it belongs to someone who played the radio," Phil said. "Just a sound system, a lot of CDs and a grand piano on an acre of white carpet."

"No dust on the piano," Helen said. "Or cat hair. Mort must have an army of cleaners."

Phil lifted two more couches in the room in search of the lost kitten. "Glad I don't have to lift the piano," he said, when he set down the fourth couch.

"That's it for the downstairs," Helen said, as they made their way back to the entrance.

"Wait! Look at that." She pointed to a modern cat flap cut into an antique door behind the curving staircase. The heavy door opened on well-oiled hinges.

"Check this out, Phil. I think I've found the cat's room."

The sunlit space was about the size of a hotel room.

Scattered across the floor were a pink-eared toy mouse and yarn balls. The large window, with a carpeted cat perch for sunning and bird-watching, was surrounded by catnip growing in glazed blue pots.

Two blue bowls were filled with dry food and water.

"The cat hasn't eaten anything in half a day," Helen said.

"Thumbs wouldn't go without eating that long," Phil said.

"If we're late with his dinner, he howls so loud everyone at the Coronado hears him," Helen said. "I'm getting a sinking feeling about Justine. Hey, this is cute. I didn't realize they made feline furniture."

She pointed to a cat-sized red velvet chaise with gold claw feet.

"That cat's a wuss," Phil said. "Our cat wouldn't bother shedding on something so girly."

"Neither has Justine," Helen said. "Do you realize we haven't seen a single cat hair in this house? There's enough of Thumbs's hair under your bed to knit a new cat."

Phil was scanning shelves of cans and bags. "Look at this food," he said. "Savory salmon, shrimp and brown rice. Chicken stew with sweet potatoes and carrots. That cat eats better than I do."

"You don't like carrots," Helen said. "Mort definitely buys the best grade of litter. And washes the scoop, too."

"I wonder why this shelf is completely empty," Phil said.

"I bet that pet carrier, the Baby Coach, sat there," she said, and photographed the empty shelf. "We'll have to ask our client."

A beige wicker chest with an arched opening squatted in the corner. Helen peeked inside. "This is the fanciest litter box cover I've ever seen. The litter is untouched. Someone took Justine, Phil. She'd have used it sometime in twelve hours. It's time to call Nancie and then the police."

"I'm calling the police now," Phil said. "Then we contact Nancie. You know she'll go all lawyer on us. She won't let us talk to the cops until she gets a signed release from Trish. We'll be waiting here all day."

"So?" Helen said. "It will be boring, but we'll get paid."

"The Peerless Point cops and detectives will have to wait, too," Phil said, "and they won't like it. They'll take it out on us—and our client, once they find out who she is. Let's call the cops now and deal with Nancie later."

"We can't," Helen said. "Under Florida law, a PI can't disclose case information unless the client authorizes it. How do we get around that?"

"Easy. We'll simply say we were on a case and came to see Mort. We found him dead, and by the way, the valuable cat is missing. That way, we haven't divulged a thing."

"Why are you so anxious to call the cops?" Helen asked. She heard a noise. Was that a car coming up the drive?

She froze, waiting to see if someone would stop in front of Mort's mansion. A dozen excuses for being in a murder victim's home ran through her mind. None of them sounded good.

"Helen?" Phil cocked an eyebrow. "Are you here?"

"Yes," Helen said. "We need to call the cops now. We've been here half an hour. Someone could show up anytime—the lawn service, the pool service, the housekeeper or the regiment of cleaners who keep this place free of cat hair."

"Now you change your mind. Don't you want to see if Mort's office is upstairs?" Phil said.

Helen shook her head no. "Someone will find us. Call the police. But you'll have to tell Nancie."

And we'll both get chewed out, she thought.

Soon the sculptures in the rose-brick drive were looking down their imposing noses at a fleet of official vehicles. Two Peerless Point uniforms arrived first. Helen and Phil were immediately separated. Helen was sent to the light-filled salon. She paced the room, watching a CSI van arrive.

I wonder if the crime-scene workers will find any cat hair, she thought.

A slender Latina housekeeper showed up next. Her sorrowful cries resounded through the house.

Soon after that, a muscle-bound man marched into the salon. "March" was the only way to describe his stiff, military walk. His dark suit fit poorly, the way suits often did on muscular men. He seemed to have no neck. His head looked like a spit-shined watermelon sticking out of his tight collar. It was a squared-off oval—a squoval, if that was a word. His shiny head was crowned with a grizzled laurel wreath of hair.

The man looked comical, but Helen knew better than to smile.

"Detective Lester V. Boland, Crimes Against Persons, Peerless Point force," he said.

"Helen Hawthorne, partner, Coronado Investigations," she said, then stopped. Was she supposed to say she was a private eye? The answers she'd carefully rehearsed with Phil flew out of her head. She felt queasy every time she thought of Mort's body.

Detective Boland fired questions at her: Why was she here? How did she know Mort? When did she and her partner arrive?

Helen tried to give Boland carefully correct answers, but she was more rattled by Mort's death than she realized.

"How did you get past the gate?" Detective Boland asked.

"Mrs. Barrymore gave us the key and asked us to check on her cat."

"Mrs. Barrymore," he said, rolling the name around in his mouth. "Mrs. Trish Barrymore? The nutcase who called the station and wanted the desk sergeant to put out an Amber Alert for her cat? Hah! Figured it would be the wife who killed him. Usually is."

"What?" Helen said. "You haven't even talked to her yet and you're making her a suspect."

"She was a suspect as soon as I saw her husband's body," Detective Boland said. "A very angry person smashed his head in, and dumped wives are angry."

"But she wasn't hiding anything," Helen said. "She called the police for help. When you turned her down, she called her lawyer."

As soon as the words slipped out, Helen realized her mistake. She'd blabbed too much.

"Smart, isn't she?" he said. "The Barrymores are getting a highly publicized divorce. Mr. Barrymore's death ends the wrangling. Mrs. Barrymore gets the houses, the cars, all the money—and she doesn't have to share the cat."

"What about her call to the police last night?" Helen asked.

"She was trying to give herself an alibi when she said her husband didn't bring the cat back on time, but she didn't fool us," Detective Boland said. "She wanted her husband dead so she could have everything. Divorcing couples fight like cats and dogs. She killed him."

CHAPTER 3

Monday

Phil delivered the bad news to Nancie as promised— but Helen got chewed out.

Detective Lester Boland kept the pair of private eyes four hours. He grilled Helen first. After she let the cat out of the bag, the detective went back to Phil. He shuttled back and forth between the couple until he finally allowed them to sign statements and escape.

Helen gathered her husband didn't give the detective any more information, but she didn't want to dissect her failure. She drove to the lawyer's office in discouraged silence. She'd made a mistake—a big mistake—and she knew it. There was nothing else to say.

Yes, they should have called Nancie. They should have called her after Helen said too much. But they didn't, and now they had to live with their blunder. Helen hoped it wouldn't hurt Trish Barrymore.

The little lawyer frowned when the PI pair entered her office. By the time Phil finished giving her the details,

Nancie was seething. Her tongue-lashing left Helen's hide hanging in bloody strips.

"You told that police detective you were a private eye?" Nancie said, her voice heavy with disbelief. She marched around her office, then raised both hands theatrically, appealing to an invisible jury.

"Why? For the love of God, why?"

"Uh," Helen said.

"You don't have to disclose that information," Nancie said. "You don't have to disclose anything, not even that you and Phil are private eyes. All you had to say was, 'We know Mrs. Barrymore and we were asked to check on Justine if we were in the area.'"

And we just happened to wander over to Peerless Point with the Barrymore security code, Helen thought. But she didn't say it. Nancie didn't stop ranting long enough to let Helen wedge in a word. The lawyer ran her hands through her short, dark hair and circled her desk like a jetliner looking to land.

"You didn't even have to say that Justine was a cat," Nancie said. "You could have just said her name and let it go at that, hoping the cops didn't know what Justine was. That's it. That's all you had to do." Nancie was behind her desk now, pounding on it. "Simple." *Pound.* "Easy." *Pound.* "Legal." *Pound, pound.*

Helen felt each pound as if Nancie had hit her on the head with a hammer.

"You're usually so levelheaded, Helen. What were you thinking?"

"I don't know," Helen said, staring at her shoes.

But she did know. Mort Barrymore wasn't the first dead body Helen had seen, and if she and Phil kept working as private eyes, he probably wouldn't be the last. But Mort's corpse had unnerved her. Even though she'd never met the man, she'd seen his photos in the local papers. She'd watched him accept a civic award on the TV news, and liked him.

Trish was polite, poised and elegant, but Mort was funny, charming and self-effacing. Now he was 170 pounds of spoiled meat, a feast for flies. His murder scene had shaken her to the core. But she couldn't say that to Nancie. Private eyes were supposed to be tough and emotionless.

"Of course, once you started talking," Nancie said, "the door was open for the cops to ask an endless list of questions."

And they did, Helen thought. They were better grillers than chef Bobby Flay. But at least I didn't give them more information. I hoped.

"Here!" Nancie handed the couple two sheets of white typing paper. Each had a large section highlighted in yellow and was protected by a clear plastic holder. "Keep these in your cars. I made them up when Phil called and told me there were problems. This is Florida Statute Four Ninety-three. Next time this situation arises . . ."

Next time, Helen thought. She said "next time." She hadn't fired us.

"Hand this paper to the cops," Nancie said, "and simply say you can't divulge any details of any investigation without the client's express permission—or a court order. And, in my opinion, those details include who the client is.

"Which leads to the most important question, Helen," Nancie said, raising her voice. *"Why didn't you call me as soon as you discovered the body? I would have been there immediately and prevented this debacle."*

Helen had no idea how such a small person could produce such a mighty blast of sound.

Phil stepped in front of Helen. "That was my fault," he said. "I told her that the police would take it out on our client if we waited for you to arrive. I accept full responsibility."

Helen thought her husband looked irresistible when he smiled like that. Nancie did not.

"Good," she said, acid etching her voice. "And how are you going to take responsibility when our client is locked up for murder, Phil? Because you know Detective Boland is going straight to Trish's house to interrogate her. I've warned her to call me the moment he shows up."

The lawyer's phone rang, blessedly interrupting the ferocious harangue.

Nancie checked the caller ID, then said, "It's Trish Barrymore."

She answered the phone, listened a moment, then said, "They're at your home with a search warrant? Trish, you can't do anything about the warrant. But I'm on my way now. Don't say a word until I arrive. Be brave, dear."

After Nancie hung up, she said, "At least someone listens to me. I have to leave. You can go now. Don't let this happen again."

Phil and Helen were out the door before Nancie left her desk. Helen stuffed her copy of the Florida statute into the Igloo's glove compartment, hands trembling.

"Are you okay?" Phil asked, his voice soft with concern.

"I'll survive," Helen said, and shrugged. "I'm surprised I can sit down after she chewed me out. Thank you for defending me."

"That's what husbands do," Phil said, and kissed her on the cheek.

"Only the good ones," Helen said. "Reese Witherspoon's husband threw her under the bus when she was arrested for disorderly conduct."

"Well, movie stars don't have much luck with men," Phil said. "Look at Sandra Bullock and Jesse James."

"I'm no movie star," Helen said, "and I didn't have much luck with men until you. My ex-husband, Rob, would have sold me out in seconds."

"But he's dead," Phil said, kissing her harder. "And forgotten. Let's keep the past buried. Mm?"

Helen realized the front of her blouse was unbuttoned and so were her pants. She removed Phil's hand reluctantly. She wanted hot high school sex right there in the front seat, but for the first time today, her better judgment prevailed.

"Wait till we're back home at the Coronado," she said. "Let's not embarrass Nancie when she comes charging out the front door."

"Uh, right," Phil said, but he didn't sound completely convinced.

"We've got a bed. Two beds. A couch. The kitchen table. The floor. Your desk. My desk. We have two apartments and an office."

After their marriage, Helen and Phil had kept their separate apartments. Both places were small, and the two detectives needed their privacy sometimes.

Helen could almost see Phil trying to figure out his favorite spot. "There's nothing better than love on a lazy summer afternoon," she said, buttoning her clothes. She started the car. "We'll be home in ten minutes and we're free until Nancie calls again."

But the apartment's parking lot was surprisingly busy for a Monday afternoon. A dented white van marked FORT LAU-DERDALE CONSTRUCTION was parked in a guest slot.

"Uh-oh," Helen said. "I wonder what's wrong."

"On a building this old, who knows?" Phil said. "When was it built—1949?"

"That's what Margery told me," Helen said. "It's old; that's for sure."

In the harsh afternoon light, they could see cracks in the white stucco, chips in the turquoise trim, and rust trails cascading down from the rattling window air conditioners.

Helen heard a heavy suitcase rumbling down the cracked sidewalk. Cal the Canadian, brown-haired and bearded, snapped the handle into place and stowed the suitcase in the trunk of his big white sedan.

Helen parked next to his car.

"Hi, Cal," Phil said. "Going on a trip?"

"Going back home," Cal said. "I need to take care of my mother in Toronto. She's too old to be living on her own. I won't be coming back."

"I'm sorry to hear that," Phil said.

Helen was relieved. She'd dated the man long before she'd met Phil. Cal, who was notoriously tightfisted, had stuck her with the dinner tab. Twice. He claimed he'd forgotten his wallet and would pay her back, but he'd done his best to avoid her ever since. It was awkward with him living at the Coronado.

"Can I help carry your things to the car?" Phil asked.

"I'd be grateful for the help," Cal said. "I'm nearly finished. I rented the place furnished, so there's not much more."

"I'll help, too," Helen said. Anything to get you out of here, she thought.

"No, no, there's not enough for you to carry," Cal said. "Just a box each for Phil and me."

Helen peeked into the open trunk and saw a teakettle, a toaster and a coffeemaker wrapped in Margery's distinctive purple sheets and towels. Cal was giving himself going-away presents. Should she say something? If today taught her anything, it was the value of silence.

Cal and Phil returned with two heavy cardboard boxes and stashed them in the backseat.

"Well, that's it," Cal said.

"Want a farewell beer before you hit the road?" Phil asked.

"No, thanks. I should get started before the rush-hour traffic gets bad. I'll say good-bye to Margery and be on my way."

Their landlady was in the backyard, sitting in the

shade of an umbrella table by the pool. She looked like an ad for some summery product: The breeze lightly ruffled her flowing purple caftan and swirled her cigarette smoke softly around her. Margery was seventy-six and wore her wrinkles like stylish accessories.

The meaty, red-faced man wearing khakis and a white hard hat spoiled the scene. He sat across from Margery, talking earnestly and scribbling figures on a yellow legal pad.

Margery kept shaking her head, her chin-length gray hair swinging back and forth like a gunmetal curtain. She lit another Marlboro with her current cigarette, then stubbed out the old one in a tin ashtray. Helen had never seen the unflappable Margery so upset.

No way Helen would interrupt that conversation. But Cal barged right in.

"I'm leaving now, Margery," he said.

"Bye, Cal," she said, absently.

"Uh, Margery, when do I get my security deposit back? Would you like to inspect the place now?"

"No, I wouldn't," Margery said. "I'm in the middle of a business conversation, Cal. I'll inspect your apartment tomorrow."

She turned and looked him in the eye. "I'll also take inventory of all the furniture and household goods. All of them. If anything's missing or damaged, I'll deduct the cost. Got that?"

"Uh, right. Yes. Of course."

Margery must have seen Cal carrying out her kitchenware and linens, Helen thought. Not much gets by our landlady.

"I'll mail you the check within thirty days," she said. "Have a safe trip." She turned back to the man in the hard hat, who showed her another column of figures.

"I'll walk you to your car, Cal," Phil said.

"No need," Cal said. "I, uh, forgot a few items."

Helen saw Cal rummage in his car trunk, then return to his apartment with a cardboard box. When he came back out, he shook hands with Phil, waved good-bye to Helen and drove away.

"Now, let's go find that bed," Phil whispered. "Your place or mine?"

"The bed's made at my apartment," Helen said.

"Let's go mess up your bed," Phil said.

They never made it.

Helen and Phil barely passed the umbrella table when an older man appeared at the back gate. He didn't walk up. He seemed to materialize.

Helen stared at him. He was Margery's match in every way: dramatically handsome with an unconventional edge. Six feet tall, slender, with broad shoulders and thick hair like fine white silk. Blue eyes. So blue Helen could see the color from this distance. He wore Florida dressy casual: crisp, blue fitted shirt, rolled at the forearms, white linen slacks and boat shoes.

His bouquet of purple flowers belonged in an Impressionist painting.

"Margery!" he said, striding toward her with the flowers. "Margery, my darling, I'm back." He kneeled at her feet.

Margery jumped back as if she'd been attacked, and knocked over her chair. Her lit cigarette rolled across the concrete. "You!" she said. Her eyes were fierce with rage.

"I love you, Margery," he said. "I always have. I know purple is your favorite color and brought you these." He held out the bouquet. Helen could see velvety lavender roses, pale, fragrant lilacs and star-shaped asters.

"I don't want your damned flowers, Zach!" Margery said. She hit him in the face with the heavy bouquet.

"Get out!" she said. "Get out and don't come back!"

Monday

Zach had a bloody scratch on one cheek, like a dueling scar.

Even the mystery man's flaws are attractive, Helen thought. Zach ignored the flung flowers and rose gracefully off the grass, without holding on to the umbrella table. He was in good shape for seventysomething.

He stared down the furious Margery and said, "No, I'm not going. Not till you hear me out."

He's her equal, too, Helen thought. Not many people would have the courage to get in a glare-down with our landlady.

"I haven't listened to you since we divorced thirty years ago, Zach Flax," Margery said. "It's one of the breaks I got when we split."

Divorced? Helen glanced at Phil. Her husband looked like he'd been walloped with the flowers. He stared bug-eyed at the warring couple. We thought Margery was a widow, Helen thought, though I wondered why I never saw any photos of her husband. Our landlady never mentioned her ex. Some private eyes we are.

The meaty red-faced guy in the hard hat whose scribbled figures had disturbed Margery watched the scene as if it were a play put on for his entertainment.

"I understand you might be upset," Zach said.

"Upset!" Margery said. "You understand nothing! You never did." She reached for her pack of Marlboros and lit another one. Her hands shook so badly it took two tries.

"I understand how much you love the Coronado," Zach said. "I knew that from the day I met you, when you were eighteen. We got married six months later."

"Please," Margery said. "No ancient history."

"Nineteen fifty-five wasn't that long ago," Zach said. "You wouldn't have the Coronado if it wasn't for me. When your father had a heart attack in 1949, your family had enough money to hang on to these apartments, but not to finish them. I did most of the final work myself, with these hands." He held them up—slender and pale with curiously coarse nails.

"You always were handy, Zach," Margery said, and from her sarcasm, Helen knew she wasn't talking about his construction skills.

"I dealt with the city inspectors, too," Zach said.

"You bribed them," Margery said. Cigarette smoke streamed from her nose and mouth. She was burning with fiery rage.

"I got the place open, didn't I? I paid for the furniture."

"*We* paid for it," Margery said. "You forgot I worked in an office back then, and you tended bar during the season and in the summer took tourists on your guided *fishing* tours."

The way Margery said "fishing" makes it sound like another f-word, Helen thought. What is going on here?

The couple was now eye to eye, two badly wounded warriors fighting a long-forgotten battle.

"We had some good years running this place, Margery," Zach said.

"Yes, we did," Margery said. "Until we needed a new roof in 1978. You'd lost your job at the bar, so you went into the fishing-charter business full-time. At least, that's what you told me."

"I made money, Margery," he said. "I got the Coronado a new roof and a new paint job."

"You didn't tell me you were fishing for square grouper," Margery said.

Drugs, Helen thought. "Square grouper" was the nickname for bales of pot, especially the ones tossed overboard when the Coast Guard was around. Zach might have been running coke, too, in the late seventies and early eighties.

"You didn't mention your little sideline," Margery said. "I found out when a DEA agent came here to question me in December of 'eighty-three. I didn't believe him. Not my Zach. You wouldn't be mixed up in that dirty business. You wouldn't put me at risk by trafficking drugs. It was too dangerous. So I denied that you had any involvement with drugs. I said you made your money as an honest captain. The federal agent laughed at me and said, 'Have it your way, but I'll be back.'

"After the fed left, I got to thinking. Maybe he was right. Suddenly, a lot of things made sense. Now I understood why you put all our assets, including our bank accounts, in my name.

" 'Life at sea is dangerous,' you told me. 'If anything happens to me, I don't want you to have trouble paying the bills while the estate is probated.' "

She breathed out a bitter stream of smoke.

"That's why you leased your boat instead of owning it. You didn't give a flying fig about me, Zach. You didn't want the feds to seize everything we had if you were arrested for drug smuggling."

"Margery, darling, that's not true," Zach said. But Helen could hear his shame. His shoulders were slumped. It was true, and they all knew it.

"I didn't want to believe it," Margery said. "I knew if I asked you, you'd tell me the truth. So after the visit from the fed, I drove to the dock where you kept your boat, hoping you'd be back from your morning charter.

"You were back, all right, and down below. Way down with Daisy Detmer. You didn't even hear me on the boat. I surprised you going at it with the catch of the day—Daisy.

"Daisy! A bleached blonde with bad legs and big tits," Margery said. "The woman who held her own personal Fleet Week for every sailor she met. You cheated on me with the biggest tramp in Lauderdale."

Helen, who'd been married to an unfaithful rat, heard Margery's pain. Zach's betrayal still hurt thirty years later. He'd not only had a fling, but a low-rent one. Margery considered his poor choice a reflection on herself. Zach seemed to realize the magnitude of his error. "Margery, she wasn't worth one hair on your head," he said softly.

"No, she wasn't," Margery said, her voice harsh and hard. "But that didn't stop you from hopping on board, did it?"

Zach hung his head. Phil stood motionless. And Helen suddenly understood the bond she shared with Margery. Her landlady was not only a surrogate mother; they'd also shared similar delusions. Helen had once happily believed she'd had a perfect life in St. Louis. She was on the corporate fast track, living with her charming husband in a McMansion in the burbs. She lived this fantasy until the afternoon she came home from work early and found Rob frolicking with their next-door neighbor, Sandy.

Helen, shocked and outraged, filed for divorce. The judge awarded the unfaithful Rob half of Helen's future income. She swore he'd never see a nickel of her money. Helen fled St. Louis and wound up in Fort Lauderdale, working dead-end jobs for cash under the table. Rob began a relentless search for his money that ended with his death a few months ago.

Now Margery stood face-to-face with her cheating ex-husband and their disappointed dreams.

"Our fine life together was nothing but lies," Margery shrieked. "You repaired the Coronado with your filthy cash. I made the only honest money working in an office.

"As soon as I found out what you'd done, I told you to pack up and get out. And you did. You sailed away with Daisy, and that's the last time I saw you until today."

Helen was confused. If Margery never saw Zach again, how did they divorce?

"Now you show up out of the blue, wanting to come back to me. I'll tell you now what I said thirty years ago: I won't live with a drug smuggler. I won't even have you on this property."

"Margery, sweetheart, I've changed. Can't you see that?"

"I can see you're a hell of a lot older, Zach Flax. Well, so am I. Older and wiser. Smart enough to know that people don't change. We just find out more about them. I know all I need to know about you."

"No, I've really changed," he said. Helen could hear his desperation. "I've reformed. I don't have anything to do with drugs anymore. I'm legit. I'm in the lucrative business of pet furniture. I make custom-made cat houses."

"Figures!" Margery said. Her contempt should have wilted the battered bouquet.

"I mean those kitty towers that cats like to roost in," he says. "Some call them cat condos. The ones with all the shelves and a cat-sized hidey-hole. I always was a good carpenter. I did solid work on the Coronado. Now I custom-make Zen Cat Towers for rich cat owners. They sell for seven hundred dollars each. I use the finest mahogany, sisal for the scratching pads, and real wool carpet."

At the mention of Zen Cat Towers, Helen and Phil looked at each other. Justine the show cat had a Zen tower. Someone had brained Mort Barrymore with it. Was Justine's cat tower made by Zach?

Helen and Phil could both testify that Zach's work was well built and expensive, but they weren't wading into this argument.

"Margery, my business is doing so well, I bought a beachfront condo in Snakehead Bay," Zach said.

Phil raised one eyebrow. That community was as upscale as Palm Beach.

"Hah! Only a tourist thinks that name is cute," Margery said.

"Boca Raton means 'mouth of the rat,'" Zach said, "and it's exclusive."

"It sounds better in Spanish," Margery said. "Most gringos down here are too dumb to know what Boca Raton means. But a snakehead is a predatory fish with a big mouth that screws up its home. It's the perfect place for you."

"That's harsh," Zach said.

"But true," Margery said. "You don't recognize the truth when it's right in front of you."

"Neither do you," Zach said. He tried to take Margery's hand, but she fended him off with her lit cigarette. "I still love you. I've always loved you."

"What about Daisy?" she said.

"She refused to move into my new condo. She stayed in Delray Beach."

"So she wised up, too," Margery said. "Took her long enough. And now that she's left, you come running back to me."

"No," Zach said. "She said she wouldn't live with me anymore because she knew I was still in love with you."

"Well, I'm not and never was," Margery said, with a fierce fervor that made Helen think there was still plenty of heat there.

"There's not enough room in South Florida for both of us, Zach. But your timing is flawless. You picked the perfect day to return. Sal Steer there, head of Fort Lauderdale Construction, just delivered the Coronado's death sentence."

The slab-faced contractor gave an uneasy smile and an odd little wave.

"Sal told me that under that old stucco is rusted rebar. Rebar are the reinforcing bars."

"I know what rebar is," Zach said.

"Then you know that as it rusts, it expands and cracks the stucco and concrete," Margery said. "Sixty-some years of storms and salt air have ruined it. It will cost at least a hundred grand to fix it, and there's no point in spending more money on this old wreck. I'm tearing down the Coronado and selling the land to the developer who makes me the biggest offer."

"No!" Zach said.

No! Helen thought. She shouted the words in her mind, but stood silently by the pool, gripping Phil's arm. They were losing their home and their office. Margery didn't bother breaking the news gently. Their homeless state was casually tossed out as an aside in a scathing fight.

"I can help you," Zach said. "I have money."

"I don't want your money, and I don't want you. Get out. Get out before I call the police and have you arrested for trespassing."

Margery looked so fierce, Zach retreated, tripping over his bedraggled bouquet.

CHAPTER 5

Monday

The sunset salute was a Coronado tradition. Margery, Helen and Phil, Peggy and Pete, and whoever else was at the apartment complex as evening approached gathered by the pool for a drink.

Most sunset salutes were spontaneous celebrations. Margery signaled the start when she arrived with a box of cheap wine. Peggy would drift in after work, with Pete on her shoulder. Pete was a Quaker parrot with a pretty good vocabulary. Peggy was pale as an egret, with an elegant beak and a shock of red hair. They lived in apartment 1C.

Helen and Phil would either come down from their Coronado Investigations office upstairs in 2C or out of their apartments. Everyone swapped jokes, gossip and reports on their day.

But tonight's sunset salute was a wake. When Margery didn't show up with the wine, Helen and Phil brought out Chardonnay with a real cork, a sure sign something was off-kilter.

Peggy was confused. "Helen, where's Margery?" she asked. "Is she sick? Who tossed two hundred bucks' worth of flowers into the Dumpster? What's going on?"

"Nothing good," Helen said. Phil sipped a beer. Helen poured Peggy and herself stiff drinks and delivered the double bad news.

"Awk!" Pete said.

Peggy stayed silent a long time, trying to understand what she'd just heard. Then she reacted like her world was crumbling around her—and if the construction guy was right, it was.

"Margery is divorced?" Peggy asked, and gulped half her wine. "Our Margery? I thought she was a widow."

"She married Zach Flax in 1955 and divorced him thirty years ago," Helen said.

"Bad boy," Pete the parrot said.

"According to Margery, Zach was a drug smuggler," Helen said. "She didn't know he was running reefer until a DEA agent showed up on her doorstep."

"The DEA came here?" Peggy said. Another gulp of wine.

"Right," Helen said. "Margery refused to believe the fed and drove over to where Zach docked his charter boat. She caught him with a woman named Daisy. Margery told Zach to pack up and get out. He and Daisy took off, and she hasn't seen her ex until he showed up this afternoon."

"Woo-hoo!" Pete said.

"Wow," Peggy said. "Just wow. Margery's had worse luck with men than I have—I mean, had. Things are fine with Daniel now. But Margery, married to a liar and a cheat. I thought she was smarter than me."

"Smarter than us," Helen said. "Until Phil, I had my share of Mr. Wrongs and married the worst one. Guess we're all sisters under the skin.

"This afternoon, Zach showed up without warning and

handed her that giant bouquet of purple flowers you saw in the Dumpster. He acted like he'd never been gone and wanted to get back together."

"He's got nerve!" Peggy said. She finished her glass and poured herself another.

"Margery threw his flowers at him, then threw him off her property," Helen said.

"Good for her," Peggy said.

"Sal Steer, the construction guy, sat right where you are, Peggy, watching the whole drama like he had a box seat. She should have sold him a ticket."

"Some people have no manners," Peggy said.

Like Phil and me, Helen thought. We stayed and stared, too. We couldn't tear ourselves away, but Peggy doesn't seem to realize that. "After Zach left, Margery walked into her place and quietly shut the door. We haven't heard from her since."

"We thought it was best to leave her alone until she can absorb everything that landed on her," Phil said. "The clueless construction guy finally picked up his paperwork and left."

"After you stood over him," Helen said.

"About that construction guy," Peggy said. "Is he right? Does the Coronado really need all those repairs? It looks fine to me."

Even the soft blue-shadowed evening light couldn't hide the old building's flaws. This afternoon had opened Helen's eyes. "Does it?" she asked. "Have you looked at this place lately? I mean, really looked? See the turquoise paint peeling off your door—and mine? What about the rust under the window in 2C?"

"That's from the window air conditioner, isn't it?" Peggy asked.

"I'm not sure," Phil said. "I looked it at from the stairs. A chunk of stucco broke off. I think that's rust from the rebar. The stucco needs paint. If you look closely, you'll see more cracks in the building, especially around the stairs and near the roof."

"Oh," Peggy said, a soft, mourning sound. "When you love something—or someone—you don't really notice aging. I always think of my mom as a lively fiftysomething. But the last time I went home, I realized she was nearly seventy-five and starting to look older."

"The Coronado is still beautiful," Helen said, "even if it is showing its age."

"Is Margery really going to tear it down?" Peggy asked, and took another long drink of wine.

"That's what she says," Helen said, between sips of her own wine. "The condo developers have been after this street for years."

"They're after all the good land in Lauderdale," Peggy said. "Condos are going up all around us, but our street is still livable. It's one of the last bits of Old Florida: small apartment complexes with character and pretty Caribbean cottages. If Margery sells the Coronado as a tear-down, that's the end. This street will be one more anonymous concrete canyon."

"She says it's inevitable," Helen said.

"If Margery tears down the Coronado, what happens to us?" Peggy asked, and Helen heard the cry of an abandoned child in her question.

"I don't know," Helen said. "This is the only place I've lived since I moved to Florida. If home is where they have to take you in, then this is home. My mother didn't approve of my divorce. She thought it was a woman's duty to stay married to an unfaithful husband, the way she had.

"But Margery protected me when my ex came looking for me, hosted my wedding, even performed the ceremony. You and Margery helped me when I was in trouble."

"You both helped me when I dated that creep," Peggy

said. "We're family. And now we're going to be separated."

"Good-bye," Pete said.

"We'll never find a place like this again, where we can all be together," Peggy said. She reached for the wine bottle, but it was empty.

"More wine?" Margery asked.

She showed up wearing light mourning—pale lilac—and her strong, springy gray hair seemed wilted. Margery looks old, Helen thought, then realized, Margery *is* old. She's seventy-six.

Their landlady poured more wine for Helen and Peggy with steady hands, but Helen noticed her tangerine nail polish was chipped.

"What about you, Phil?" Margery asked with false cheer.

Phil held up his beer. "I'm fine. Thanks."

Margery lit another cigarette from her almost-finished Marlboro and stretched out in the chaise under a veil of blue smoke. "I assume Helen and Phil gave you the news, Peggy," she said. Her glowing cigarette watched the trio like an alien eye. "Well, what do you think?"

Peggy, perhaps eager to avoid the painful subject of the Coronado's death, said, "I was surprised to learn that you were divorced."

"I got over it long ago," Margery said.

Helen doubted that, judging by what she'd seen this afternoon.

"No man makes a fool out of me," Margery said. "I kicked him out. He took off with Daisy, and that's the last I saw of him until this afternoon."

"How did you divorce him if he disappeared?" Phil asked.

"I got a lawyer and he hired a process server to serve Zach with divorce papers," Margery said. "Hired a good one, too, but Zach had vanished. He still had some months left on the boat lease, and I suspected he was hiding somewhere in the Bahamas. I could have waited until he returned the boat when the lease was up, but I didn't know if he'd default on the lease and steal the boat. I couldn't trust him anymore. I never could, but then I realized how dumb I'd been."

Helen knew how her landlady felt. She also knew Margery would rather have silence than sympathy.

"The lawyer declared Zach a missing spouse, meaning I had no idea how to locate the bastard to serve him with divorce papers," Margery said. "The court requires some sort of service or legal notification, so Zach could be heard. But he was gone. So my lawyer did service by publication. We showed that we'd made a diligent effort to locate Zach—and I had the bills prove it.

"The court agreed, and let me publish ads in the paper, notifying Zach that the divorce was in process. I only had to run them in Fort Lauderdale, but I was taking no chances. I published ads in every newspaper from Key West to Palm Beach. Cost me a bundle."

"Did Zach leave anything behind?" Phil asked.

"A box of old papers. My lawyer published a notice saying Zach could pick them up at his office. He kept the box until he retired and closed his practice. Then the lawyer gave them back to me. I've got the box in a closet somewhere.

"Zach never responded after sixty days, so my divorce was granted as a default judgment. Since all the community property was in my name, that wasn't a problem, either. I was just itching for him to say something about the property, because I'd love to tell the DEA where he got that money. He owed me the Coronado, the car, and every penny in the bank for lying and risking my reputation.

"But Zach never contested the divorce. I assumed he'd sailed away with Daisy. I heard they eventually settled in Delray Beach. Now he shows up in my backyard, and I'm so mad I can barely say his name."

She lit yet another cigarette with trembling fingers. Once its angry orange eye glowed in the dusk, Margery said, "I'm already short a tenant. Cal moved out today. He's no big loss, but he was quiet and he paid on time.

"After I talked to the contractor, I'd thought today couldn't get any worse. The repairs are going to be six figures. For that much, I might as well sell the land to a developer and let him tear down the place for condos."

"No!" Peggy said.

"Good-bye!" Pete said. "Bye!" He paced back and forth on Peggy's shoulder and flapped his wings.

"I have money from the sale of my house in St. Louis," Helen said. "It's enough to cover the repairs. You can have it. No strings."

"You need that money," Margery said. "Even if I fix the Coronado, it will still be an old building, and something else will break down. It will need new gutters next and the sidewalk is cracked."

"You could rent out Cal's apartment," Phil said. "You'd get some rent until you have to make a decision."

"I've already decided," Margery said. "It's hurricane season. One big storm could blow the whole facade off. There will be no more new tenants.

"I can't put you in danger, either. Start looking for a new home."

CHAPTER 6

Monday

Phil's cell phone broke the silence following Margery's bombshell. He checked the display.

"It's Nancie," he said. "The lawyer. Helen and I have to take this call. Sorry."

"Go!" Margery said, waving them away. She seemed relieved to see Helen and Phil leave. Peggy used their departure to excuse herself. No one wanted to stick around for a postmortem.

Phil put his phone on speaker as he walked with Helen toward his apartment. "What's up?" he asked Nancie.

"The kidnapper called with a ransom demand," Nancie said.

"How much?" Phil asked.

"You know better than to ask that on a cell phone, Phil," the lawyer said. "Detective Boland finally released Trish at four o'clock."

"That late?"

"Exactly," Nancie said. "He's gunning for her. We need to meet. Now."

Helen thought she heard an unspoken accusation, but it could have been her own guilt. Her amateur mistake had set the Peerless Point detective on Trish's trail.

"Trish is here at my office," Nancie said.

"We're on our way," Phil said.

They stopped to feed Thumbs. Then, for the third time that day, Helen drove Phil to Nancie's office. Crawled, actually. The highway was clogged with rush-hour traffic.

"How many disasters can we cram into one day?" Helen asked. "In the twelve hours since we've met our client, she's become a widow and a murder suspect, and we're homeless."

"Don't forget Margery's long-lost ex showed up and she chucked him out," Phil said.

"I'm still reeling from that news," she said. "Some detectives we are, overlooking a mystery in our own backyard."

"Why would we investigate a friend?" Phil asked. "Margery's past is none of our business. The subject must have been too painful for her to discuss, even with us."

"I understand that," Helen said. "I don't like talking about my ex, either. I just can't imagine living anywhere but the Coronado."

"Me, either." Phil pointed to a new twenty-story condo on the corner. "Certainly not there, in a pink stucco shoe box with palm trees."

"Didn't that place sue some poor guy because he put up black curtains?" Helen asked. A yellow Hummer trying to make the light cut her off. Helen slammed on the brakes and the burly vehicle blew through the intersection.

"I don't want to deal with condo commandos," she said.

"Yep. The condo rules say all curtains have to be lined in white," Phil said.

"I can't live like that," Helen said. "Besides, most condos don't allow pets. We'd need to find a place for Thumbs." She drummed her fingers impatiently on the steering wheel. "These red lights last forever. No wonder that Hummer ran over me, trying to make it."

"We could get a house," Phil said. "That's a nice one." The sprawling ranch across the street was handsome. Its white tile roof glared in the heat, but the soft lawn was a cool green oasis. "Plenty of room for Thumbs. But I can't see myself mowing the lawn."

"Then we'd have to deal with a lawn service," Helen said. "And hordes of repair people. Every time there's a storm, we'd have to put up hurricane shutters." She sighed. "We can't leave the Coronado, Phil." The light changed at last, and the Igloo crept forward.

"We don't have a choice," Phil said.

"I know. But Margery's made our life there so easy. She manages the property and that gives us time to run our business. Now I feel like an orphan."

"You still have me," Phil said, and kissed her.

She smiled at her husband. "Yes, I do," she said. "And my sister, Kathy, and her husband, Tom, in St. Louis. But the Coronado is the closest thing we have to a family here in Florida. Margery is my mother, Peggy's my sister and Margery's friend Elsie is our sweet, dotty old aunt. Once we move, it won't be the same."

"No, it won't," Phil said.

A sorrowful silence descended while Helen thought about the good times they'd had at the Coronado: the countless sunset salutes, Peggy's schemes to win the lottery, Phil's careful courtship and their triumphant wedding feast by the pool. It was painful to leave the scene of those good times for an uncertain future.

Helen was relieved when she turned into the lot for Nancie's neat cube of a law office. Trish's Mercedes was parked under the same palm tree and Nancie's practical

Honda was still near the back. The place looked the same as this morning, but now everything was different.

Inside, Nancie sat behind her desk, still fresh and energetic. Trish had changed dramatically. Her grim ash-gray pantsuit matched the smudges under her eyes. She'd tucked her blond hair back into its chignon and put on fresh makeup, but she seemed frail and exhausted.

Her eyes were red from weeping. Helen didn't know if she'd been crying over her murdered husband or her missing cat.

"I'm sorry for your loss," she said, hoping that would cover either.

"Mort was a good man," Trish said, sniffling. She reached for the box of tissues that Nancie kept next to the client chair. "He always wanted what was best for our baby. Even though we disagreed about everything, he put Justine's welfare first so we could work out a custody agreement."

She wiped her eyes. "Now I don't know how I'm going to bring her up alone."

Another tear storm threatened, and Nancie tried to hold it off. "We did get some good news," she said. "The catnapper called, so we know Justine is alive."

"Tell us about the call, Trish," Phil said, his voice gentle.

"Well," Trish said, then took a deep breath, "Detective Boland kept me at the police station for hours. Nancie wouldn't let me say hardly anything, and that made him madder. He kept asking the same questions in different ways. When he finally let me leave, I was so tired I could hardly drive home. I'd barely unlocked my door when my cell phone rang.

"A voice said, 'I have Justine. If you want to see her alive again, I need half a million in cash.'

"I said, 'Please don't hurt my baby.'

"The voice said, 'I won't if I get the money. But I'm no cat lover. If I don't get five hundred thousand, she'll go to the pound, and you know what they do to strays.'"

She was crying so hard, Helen had trouble understanding her.

"Trish!" Nancie said. "You have to pull yourself together. For Justine's sake."

"Yes, yes, you're right," Trish said, wiping her eyes. That left muddy mascara smears, but she was too distraught to notice.

"I told him it would take time to get that much money in cash—I'd have to sell some holdings—but I'd get the half million.

"He said, 'You have until next Tuesday. Used bills. Nothing bigger than a twenty. Miss the deadline and Justine goes to the pound—and not one in Fort Lauderdale, where you can find her. She goes to a kill shelter.'"

Trish erupted into fresh tears.

"You keep saying 'he,'" Phil said. "What did he sound like? Is the kidnapper a man? Young? Old? Educated?"

"He used a voice changer," Trish said. "He had a Darth Vader voice. That made it worse. Besides, no woman would be so cruel to a helpless baby."

A vision of Cruella de Vil flashed in Helen's mind. She'd wanted 101 Dalmatian puppies to make a coat. Cruella was fiction, but real mothers beat their babies. Helen hastily banished that thought, as if Trish could read her mind.

She glanced at Phil, and he raised an eyebrow, but neither detective said anything. They both knew men and women could be cruel, but why add to their client's distress?

"We'll get her back," Phil said. He sounds so comforting, Helen thought, and looks so strong and competent, Trish has to be reassured. "And if you decide to give the kidnapper money, we'll get that back, too," he said.

"I don't care about the money," Trish said. "All I care about is Justine. If you do find the money, you can have ten percent."

A fifty-thousand-dollar bonus, Helen thought. Trish casually tossed in that staggering sum as if it were pocket change.

"There's a way to mark the money that the catnapper can't see," Phil said. "SmartWater CSI. It's a forensic coding system. A tiny dab on the money and it will fluoresce under UV black light. I can buy a kit for about two hundred dollars, if you authorize it."

"It's not like those dye packs they put in bags to stop bank robbers, is it?" Nancie said.

"Nope. SmartWater can't be seen without a black light," Phil said. "It's been used in Britain for years."

"No reason the bad guy should profit," Nancie said. "Do you agree, Trish?"

Trish nodded.

Helen jumped in with another question: "Did the kidnapper give any details about what time and where you'll make the exchange?"

"He said he'd call me the morning it's due with the details," Trish said. "He warned me not to contact the police." She gave a delicate, ladylike snort, almost a dainty sneeze. "As if they'd do anything."

"He doesn't want you to make advance plans," Phil said. "Helen and I will be with you that morning. We'll stay the night, if you want. Did the kidnapper say anything else?"

"I tried to tell him what Justine eats and the brand of litter she uses, but he hung up on me."

"Have you filed a police report for your stolen cat?" Phil asked.

"Why? They won't look for her," Trish said.

"Good idea," Nancie said. "We'll need it to claim the cat and go after the catnapper."

"How do we prove it's your cat?" Helen said. "Does she wear a collar and tags?"

"She's microchipped," Trish said.

"Good," Helen said. "What is the kidnapper's phone number?"

"He didn't give me one," Trish said.

"The number he called you from should be in your cell."

"Oh. Right," Trish said. "I didn't think of that. Here. You look. I'm afraid I'll hit the wrong button and wipe it out."

She handed Helen her cell phone, and the detective checked the incoming calls list. "There's a call at four seventeen p.m. today with a 713 area code," she said. "It's your only call after you called Nancie at eleven fifty-six."

"That's a Houston area code," Phil said. "Do you know anyone in that city?"

Trish looked puzzled. "No," she said. "I don't know anyone in Texas."

"My guess is the catnapper's cell phone is a throw-away," Phil said. "To know for sure, we'd have to get the records from the cell phone company, which takes a court order or a subpoena."

"Don't you know a friendly cop who can check for you?" Trish asked.

"That only works in the movies," Phil said. "The laws and department oversight have been tightened. Now cops risk their jobs for a stunt like that."

"Let's assume we have a sensible catnapper who used a burner phone," Nancie said. "We have more important things to investigate. Find the kidnapper and you've got Mort's killer."

Trish melted into tears again. "Mort loved Justine," she said. "He wouldn't let anyone take our baby. He fought for her to the death."

Murder has transformed Mort into a saint, Helen thought. We need some information before Trish completely canonizes him. "Who would want to kill your husband?" she asked. "Did Mort have any enemies? Maybe an unhappy client?"

"I don't think any of his financial clients were unhappy. I didn't understand the details of what he did, but he made lots of money."

"What about his love life?" Phil said.

"Mort is—I mean, was—seeing two women. One is Jan Kurtz, an assistant for Deidre Chatwood. Dee breeds and exhibits prizewinning show cats—Persians. Her cattery is called Chatwood's Champions. She's had at least one national champion in the Gold Cup Cat Fanciers' Association.

"Mort's other girlfriend, Amber Waves, calls herself an actress," Trish said, and sniffed. She wasn't crying, she was sneering. "Some career. She had a scene as an extra in the movie *Rock of Ages* with Tom Cruise. That was filmed in Fort Lauderdale, you know. Amber was in the pole-dancing scene.

"Two seconds of show business went to her head. Now she wants to open her own studio. She tells everyone, 'Pole dancing is a respectable fitness workout, and I'm an actress. Did I tell about my scene with Tom Cruise?' Whether you want to hear it or not, she'll give you the details."

"Is Amber Waves her real name?" Phil asked.

"Nothing on that girl is real," Trish said.

"Mort was also giving financial advice to an important cat show judge, Lexie Deener. He thought it would help Justine win in the big Gold Cup Cat Show. I said Justine would win without bribes, but he insisted, and I figured it couldn't hurt. Mort knew money. Besides, if Justine does lose when that woman judges her, well, I'll be able to appeal her decision."

Do cat shows work that way? Helen wondered. Now wasn't the time to ask.

Trish lowered her voice. "Mort said he knew a major

secret—a very damaging secret—about Lexie, but he wouldn't use it."

"What kind of secret?" Helen asked.

"He wouldn't tell me. For all his faults, Mort wasn't really a bad guy."

"Was he keeping it in reserve, in case his financial advice went bad?" she asked.

"Mort didn't give bad advice," Trish said. "He almost never failed. That's why people fought to be taken on as clients."

Phil tapped his cheek, a signal he was asking a tough question.

"And who are you seeing?" he asked.

"Why is that important?" Trish hissed. Helen expected her to swipe at Phil with her pink claws.

"An attractive woman like yourself might incite jealousy. It's important to know about your life as well as Mort's if we're going to save Justine."

"I can't see why you need to know, but I'm dating an attorney, Arthur Goldich," she said. "But only after my husband moved to our other residence. Everyone likes Mort and he's successful, but an attorney has more prestige."

She's said "attorney" twice, Helen thought, and that so-called prestige is debatable.

"What kind of lawyer?" she asked.

"Arthur specializes in foreclosures."

"Oh," Helen said. After Florida's real estate tanked, foreclosure lawyers were as prestigious as roaches.

Trish heard her disapproval. "Don't believe what you see on TV," she said. "The media likes to show veterans and old people getting thrown out of their houses. The truth is, most people who lose their homes are gamblers, flipping property for profit. Arthur says they should honor their financial commitments."

Helen bit back a reply. Nancie saw the fire in her eyes

and stepped in quickly. "I've already discussed my concerns with Trish about the police. I've tried to prepare her for the worst, though I hope it won't happen. There's still a chance that Detective Boland will come to his senses or the prosecuting attorney will say there isn't enough evidence."

"Mort knew the prosecutor," Trish said.

And that could work against you, Helen thought.

"Yes, well, there's a possibility that you could be arrested, and I don't think you'll get bail," Nancie said.

Trish's control cracked. "Then how will I get my Justine back?" she wailed. Helen felt her heart contract. Trish might be a snob, but she loved her cat.

"The catnapper will know if you've been arrested," Phil said. "He must be watching you. He knew exactly when you got home.

"Coronado Investigations has a dummy number on a cell phone. We can set it up to forward your calls to us and have you record a voice mail message. We'll screen your phone calls. If the catnapper calls, I'll say I'm your office assistant."

Trish hesitated.

"Someone on your level should have an assistant," Helen said.

"I'll do it," Trish said. "You have to get my Justine back. For her sake. There's a big Gold Cup show in June and I know she'll win. But what will you and Phil do until the catnapper calls next week?"

"I'll be your office assistant and monitor your calls," Phil said. "And I'd like to trace that red cat medallion we saw near Mort's, er . . . near Mort. I think it may lead to the killer."

He called up the photo on his cell phone. "Ever see this before?" he asked Trish.

"No," she said.

"It says 'Coventry' in gold around the edge. Does that mean anything?"

"That's in England, isn't it? I think there's a big cat show in Coventry, but I'm not familiar with the international shows," she said. "But if you think it's important, you should investigate it. Will Helen help you?"

"No," Nancie said. "Time is limited. Justine is a show cat. Helen needs to get a job in that world. Trish, you're wired into the local scene. Is Dee, the show cat breeder and exhibitor, hiring anyone at Chatwood's Champions?"

"She's always hiring," Trish said. "Dee's a difficult woman and her staff rarely lasts longer than a month. Jan's managed to hang in there six months, which is a record. I'm sure Helen could get a job at her cattery. Persians require lots of brushing and bathing. I'll give her a reference and say you worked with Justine. You have a cat, right, Helen?"

She nodded, too discouraged to speak. Phil would be answering the phone and she'd be up to her elbows in cat hair.

Nancie passed Trish a sheet of expensive plain cream stationery. "Write the reference now," she said. "Helen can look for a job first thing tomorrow."

"You'll have no problem getting hired," Trish said. "Dee goes through employees like cats go through litter."

Terrific, Helen thought. We all know what happens in a litter box.

CHAPTER 7

* * * * * * * * * * * * * * * * * * *

Tuesday

D ee Chatwood's door belonged on a fortress. Helen lifted the snarling lion's-head door knocker carefully—it looked like it might bite her. A uniformed Latina maid answered.

"I have a job interview with Ms. Chatwood," Helen said.

The maid nodded. "Ms. Chatwood is taking her morning swim," she said. "I'll take you to the pool."

Helen felt like she'd been swallowed by a leopard. The walls of the vast entrance hall and living room were a dizzying display of animal-print paper, reflected in the shiny black marble floor. Palms lurked in the corners. On a sleek black couch, a Persian cat with ebony fur and gleaming copper eyes looked down its short nose at Helen.

"Beautiful cat," Helen said.

"His name is Midnight," the maid said. "He's a stud."

A stud? Oh, right, Helen reminded herself. Dee runs

a cattery. Stud is Midnight's job. She was glad she didn't
say anything dumb.

She followed the maid past a wall of oil paintings, all
Persians with flat, haughty faces. The cats seemed to disapprove of Helen and her bloodlines. The portrait of a
silver-haired Persian, labeled CHATWOOD'S SILVER SHADOW —
CAT OF THE YEAR, 2008, hung over a case crammed with
huge ribbons, the coveted cat-show rosettes. The shelves
held dizzying numbers of framed photos of longhaired
cats, plaques and trophies. They weren't bowling trophies,
either. Each had a figure of a cat, and some could have
been sculptures.

The hall led to a screened-in pool the size of a lake, with
a view of the Intracoastal Waterway. The house shouted
money. The mustard mansion was built around a swimming
pool with a bell tower. Yeah, a bell tower, a phallic object
that thrust up from the edge of the deep end, where a div-
ing board would be. The tower was taller than the house.
The morning sun shining on the bell blinded Helen.

Then she saw a big-boned blonde in a leopard-print
retro bikini doing the backstroke near the bell-tower end.
Dee Chatwood.

When she reached the edge of the pool, Dee climbed
out, toweled off her short platinum hair and asked,
"You're Helen Hawthorne?"

"I'm here for the job at your cattery," Helen said.
"Trish Barrymore recommended me."

Up close in the bright light, Helen could see that Dee
was fifty, fighting to look forty. Her waist had thickened,
but the swimming kept her fit. She had skin like fine
brown leather and long red claws. Her Botoxed forehead
was frighteningly smooth and her collagened lips were
overripe, but the effect was curiously attractive.

Dee slid into a black caftan with feline grace and settled herself at a wicker patio table. Helen half expected
her to lick the stray water droplets off her arms.

The maid came back carrying a tray with two silver pitchers and glasses. "Water?" Dee asked. "Orange juice?"

"Water, thank you," Helen said.

"Sit down," Dee said. "Trish speaks highly of you."

"I've heard good things about your cattery," Helen said. "Congratulations on your Cat of the Year."

"We're small but choice. We have five cats: three breeding queens, one stud and a spay." Dee gulped her water thirstily, and poured herself a glass of orange juice.

"Is the stud Midnight?" Helen said. "I saw him in the living room. He's gorgeous."

"He knows it," Dee said. "None of the females are in season right now, so he has the run of the house.

"I'm campaigning two this year," she said. "Are you interested in breeding cats?" Her green eyes narrowed and she studied Helen carefully.

She's on the alert for something, Helen thought. All I can do is tell the truth and hope it's what she wants to hear. "No," she said. "I like cats. I have a rescue cat, Thumbs. He has six toes and he's neutered."

"Good," Dee said, nodding approvingly. "Polydactyls should be altered. Their offspring have a higher incidence of birth defects.

"I'm glad you don't want to be a breeder. I got burned once. Now I make my employees sign an agreement that they won't breed or show cats for five years after they work here."

"Fine with me," Helen said.

"I'm not going to hire and train my competition. Breeding cats is a labor of love. I'm lucky if I break even. Persians require constant care." Dee downed half her juice.

"Lots of brushing?" Helen asked.

"Combing. Daily," Dee said. "Their fur mats easily. My cats must be bathed once a week, more if they're going to be shown."

"Do your cats like baths?" Helen said. Thumbs would claw off her arm if she tried to bathe him.

"Love them," Dee said. "I start bathing them when they're babies. They learn to enjoy them. The process takes hours, but the cats find the experience pleasant—and if they don't, they'll let you know."

She swiped her red-tipped nails at Helen's eyes, and Helen jumped back.

"Good," Dee said. "You have quick reflexes. You'll need them.

"We're extra busy this week. I'm showing Red and Chessie at the regional Gold Cup show in Plantation on Saturday and Sunday, and my other girl up and quit. Walked out on me with no warning. Really, people have no work ethic. They're bone lazy."

Helen's antenna went up. In her experience, employers who complained about lazy staff were cheap and demanding.

"What do you pay?" Helen asked.

"My wages are very generous," Dee said. "Eight-oh-four an hour." She said it with a flourish, as if she doled out bags of gold.

The cats aren't the only queen around here, Helen thought.

"What are my duties?" she asked.

"You'll change ten cat boxes daily—five in the cattery and five around the house. Gabby, the maid, will show you where the others are. You'll have to wipe their eyes daily and keep their noses and bottoms clean. You'll help with the grooming and bathing.

"During the shows, as well as the day before and after, you'll be expected to work eight to ten hours."

Helen knew the answer to her next question, but asked anyway. "Do we get overtime?"

"Of course not!" Dee sounded so shocked, Helen feared she'd lose her chance for the job. "I'm paying you eleven cents above Florida minimum wage. And don't ask for sick leave. I don't pay people to lie around in bed."

"What about benefits?"

"You'll get one major benefit," Dee said, and smiled. "A regular paycheck. Every Friday. You'd be surprised how few people appreciate that."

Dee stood up. "Jan Kurtz, my head girl, is working in the cattery now. I'll take you back."

Finally, I get to meet Mort's girlfriend, Helen thought. She's why I'm cleaning ten cat boxes a day.

Dee padded down a back hall to a large, sunny room with pearly white walls. Helen saw a pair of blue-eyed beauties at a waist-high white table. Jan looked like she'd stepped off a romance novel cover, with her creamy skin and what could only be called raven tresses tumbling down her back. She should wear a silk skirt and a bustier, not a pink polo shirt, white shorts and flip-flops, Helen thought.

Jan was combing a white cat's back, while the cat stretched luxuriously and rumble-purred.

"This is Jan Kurtz and my beautiful baby, Chessie," Dee said. She scratched the cat's small, delicate white ears, and Chessie yawned in her face.

"Jan, this is your new assistant," Dee said. "I'll be in my office."

"Boy, do I need you," Jan said. "Can you start work right now?"

"Absolutely," Helen said. She felt a surge of triumph. This was easy. "What do you need?"

"Clean the ten cat boxes," Jan said.

"Scoop them?" Helen asked hopefully.

"No, they have to be emptied, washed and dried."

Helen's surging triumph deflated like an old balloon.

"But first, come meet the other cats."

The floor-to-ceiling glass windows facing the water

had a series of white carpeted shelves. A longhaired orange cat lounged on the lowest shelf. "That's Red," Jan said. "She's a spay. She's being campaigned for a national win this year."

On the next shelf was a cat whose glowing coat was a river of hot fudge.

"This is Chocolate, and her deep, rich brown looks good enough to eat," Jan said. "Her coat is dark, long and thick, even in the summer when some Persians blow their coats."

"Is she a breeding queen?" Helen asked, proud that she knew the term.

"A real queen mother. Choc is bred twice a year and produces the most beautiful kittens. She's a good mother."

"Doesn't that come naturally?" Helen said.

"It should, but it doesn't. Red showed little interest in nursing and nearly ate one of her last kittens. She was getting a little old for breeding by then, and Dee had her spayed."

Choc licked Jan's hand with her pink tongue. "She's grooming me," she said, scratching the cat's ears. "Good girl."

She patted Chocolate's broad head and moved to the cat on the next shelf, a soft, pale gray cloud. "This is Mystery," she said.

"Such a pretty shade of gray," Helen said.

"Blue," Jan corrected. "Pedigreed cats are blue, not gray. Mystery is a laid-back kitty. Most Persians are."

With that, all three cats sat up, ears alert, short tails lashing, avid eyes on the scene outside. Mourning doves and tiny yellow-breasted finches fluttered around a bird feeder heaped with seed. The cats chirped and squeaked.

"Cat TV," Jan said. "The birds are quite safe—this bunch never ate anything that didn't come off a store shelf—but the Audubon Society here loves watching their feathered friends."

Helen pointed to the barbed wire twined around the feeder's pole like a deadly vine. "What's that for?"

"It's Dee's squirrel deterrent. It doesn't work. They still steal the birdseed. We wash the cats in that sink there," she said, pointing to the long, deep metal sink on the wall near the grooming table.

Next to it were two more grooming tables and a shelf of thick white towels. Along the far wall were five wire cages the size of bedroom dressers. Each held a plush bed, a cat-sized hammock, a carpeted shelf and a rainbow of toys—mice, balls, catnip pillows.

"The cage doors are open," Helen said.

"When they're not in season, the cats have the run of the house," Jan said. "I'll say this for her: Dee socializes her cats. Some catteries confine them in cages, but Dee's cats love people. Makes them good pets and good show animals. Midnight likes the front of the house, but the queens hang around here for their baths and cat TV."

In the corner of each cage was a small litter box.

"There's your first chore," Jan said. "There's a stack of plastic litter boxes over there. Next to it, in that big green plastic garbage can, is fresh litter. The old litter gets dumped in the big metal can with the lid on it.

"Fill ten new boxes first, then collect and clean the used ones. Wash them in the porcelain sink by the litter supply. Meanwhile, I have to bathe Mystery and comb Red."

Helen and Jan worked for the next hour. Jan groomed both cats, talking to them softly. They rubbed their heads against her hand and begged for scratches. She played with them, waving a wand with shiny Mylar strips and teasing them with feathers.

"I'm not goofing off," Jan said. "This is how the judges get the cats' attention at the shows. It's also exercise for them."

Helen's job wasn't nearly as pleasant. She filled the fresh

boxes with litter, emptied the used ones in the cattery, found Gabby Garcia, the maid, and then carried five more fresh boxes—two to upstairs bathrooms, one in a guest bathroom, two more in a utility room off the kitchen—and removed and cleaned the old ones. Then she swept up cat hair in the cattery, wiped down the grooming tables, and tossed loads of wet towels into the washer and then the dryer.

By four o'clock, her arms ached and her nose itched from the cat hair, but her work was done and so was Jan's.

"Tonight we can leave on time," Jan said. "It will get hectic in a few days."

Jan looked surprisingly fresh after a day of bathing and combing cats.

Her dark hair held its curls and her skin was still creamy and makeup free.

"I'm so glad you're here," Jan said. "This has been a hellish week. My assistant, Petula, quit, Dee went on a rampage and yesterday was worst of all."

"What happened?" Helen asked.

"My—my fiancé was killed," Jan said. "Murdered, actually. I found out about it on TV. Last night on the ten o'clock news."

"How horrible," Helen said.

"It was," Jan said. "I cried all night. Mort was a lovely man, and we planned to marry as soon as his divorce was final." She wiped away more tears.

"I'm very sorry," Helen said.

"I didn't want to come in today, but Dee said she'd fire me if I didn't. I can't afford to lose this job. The kitties are a great comfort, and work helps me forget a little." She sighed and said, "Well, you don't want to hear me talk about Mort."

"Oh, but I do," Helen said.

CHAPTER 8

Tuesday

Helen, grumpy, hot and cat-hairy, was glad she didn't run into anyone back at the Coronado. She went straight to her apartment, showered, changed into clean clothes and poured herself a glass of white wine.

After a few sips, she was ready to talk with Phil. She found him typing furiously at his computer in their second-floor office. She paused a moment to study him. She liked his silvery hair, and his slightly crooked nose gave him an offbeat handsomeness. He had a cute little wrinkle in his forehead when he was working intensely.

He looked up and said, "Helen! You look nice." He got up and kissed her.

"I didn't ten minutes ago," she said. "I've been slaving over a hot cat box—ten cat boxes—while you're working on a nice, cool computer.

"Any interesting calls come in today on Trish's phone?"

"One from the Police Benevolent Association," he

said, "and two from her boyfriend, Arthur. He was surprised to find his fiancée had a secretary."

"So they're engaged," Helen said.

"That's what he said. She didn't mention it. I've been hard at the computer. I've had a breakthrough in the case."

Helen sat in her black-and-chrome partner chair, and Phil rubbed her neck and shoulders. "You're tense," he said. "I'm glad you got the job, but it must be rough."

"I can whine later," she said. "Tell me about the breakthrough."

"I think the red medallion by Mort's body is from the Gold Cup Coventry All Breed Cat Show," he said. "It's a big-deal show in Britain."

"That's no cute kitty," Helen said. "Why the ferocious feline?"

"Cat shows will sometimes rent a big-cat mascot," Phil said. "A panther, a tiger or a leopard, and then give out medallions with its image. I was at a cat show in Fort Lauderdale that had a cougar."

"Brilliant," Helen said.

"My middle name," Phil said.

"Now we have to figure out who went to the Coventry cat show."

"Already did that," Phil said. "I did some research on Arthur, the boyfriend."

"The foreclosure lawyer," Helen said. "I couldn't believe Trish said he had more prestige than Mort. I wanted to tell her about the classy foreclosure lawyer who put *Su casa es mi casa* on his yacht."

Phil kissed her again. "I admired your fortitude," he said. "Arthur is even richer than Mort, and he is prestigious, at least in his profession."

"Humph," Helen said. "I have more respect for garbage collectors. They serve society."

"Okay," Phil said. "I agree, but the faster we solve this case, the faster you're away from those reeking cat boxes.

Arthur has an impressive Web site, and he bragged he was a guest lecturer at the Mapesbury Comparative International Law Seminar in Stratford-upon-Avon."

"Shakespeare's hometown," Helen said.

"And a major tourist center. The Stratford seminar was the same weekend as the Coventry cat show, and Coventry is a little over twenty miles away."

"You think Arthur went there?"

"I called Trish and she said yes," Phil said. "His lecture was early in the morning; then he went to the show to get pointers for Trish. They have big plans for Justine. Trish thinks she can be an international star. A British show win would be an important step in Justine's career.

"I think there's something off about this kidnapping, Helen."

"Off how?"

"I think that Trish faked it and stole her own cat."

"How could she do that?" Helen asked.

"Easy. Arthur did the catnapping. Why would a kidnapper wait eight days for the money?" Phil asked. "The longer the wait, the easier it is to catch the kidnapper."

"If Trish kidnapped her cat, do you think she killed her husband?" Helen asked.

"Well, it would be convenient for her," Phil said.

"Can't see it," Helen said. "Murder would mess up her designer dress. She's too girly."

"Don't underestimate her. Did you see the muscles in Trish's arms?" Phil said. "She's strong, but I don't think she walloped Mort with the cat tower and walked off with Justine. She stayed safely at home and called the cops to set up an alibi."

"That didn't work," Helen said.

"Right. The cops think like I do," Phil said. "Trish set up her alibi and then her boyfriend did the dirty work. Arthur doesn't look like a desk jockey. I saw his picture on his Web site. He'd have no trouble killing Mort."

"Why would he bother? Trish is getting a divorce," Helen said.

"And it's taking forever," Phil said. "The money's being eaten up in legal fees, and the publicity is brutal. Arthur knows the longer a high-profile divorce drags on, the more likely one party will say, 'Take everything. I don't care anymore. Just cut the knot.'"

"And Trish, who's engaged to a rich guy, is more likely to cave first," Helen said. "But Arthur is already rich."

"And greedy," Phil said. "He's a foreclosure lawyer, remember?"

"I'm not convinced Trish is a black widow. She seemed genuinely upset."

"I used to work insurance cases," Phil said. "You'd be surprised the frauds so-called solid citizens try. You'd also be amazed at how good they are at acting. Trish may be one of those undiscovered acting talents. And she does have real reasons to be upset. The cops suspect her. Her alibi didn't fool them and she could be arrested anytime. If her scheme unravels, she goes to jail for murder one."

"So Arthur kills Mort," Helen said, "and steals the kitten. What did he do with her?"

"He takes Justine to his home. Trish said Arthur has two cats of his own and 'he's a good father.'"

"What's that mean?" Helen asked.

"She told me, in great detail. If you want to lose an hour or two, talk to Trish about cats. Arthur comes home every night at seven to feed both cats and play with them. One's a Russian Blue kitten and the other's a big Maine Coon."

"I love Maine Coons," Helen said. "They're big, furry teddy bears."

"Trish said Arthur often works twelve-hour days, but he insists on being at home at seven, no matter what. If it's not raining, he feeds his cats by the pool and then plays with them. He makes sure they have a half hour for dinner and quality time."

"Does Arthur live in Peerless Point?"

"No, near downtown Fort Lauderdale. A waterfront house in Rio Vista."

Helen raised an eyebrow. "He's definitely got some bucks."

"It's after six," Phil said. "Wanna go catnapping with me? You can drive the getaway car. I'll swipe the cat and we'll drive it to Nancie's office."

"How are you going to see Arthur's backyard?"

"A former client lives on the same street. She's a snowbird, and I still have her security code. Arthur's the only year-round resident on that block. I'll get in through her back gate and make my way down the seawall. You'll wait in the car with Thumbs's pet carrier."

"Okay," Helen said. "But I still think Trish isn't guilty."

"So noted," Phil said. "Now think about never seeing those steaming cat boxes if I'm right."

"Let's go," Helen said.

Even in rush hour, Rio Vista was only twenty minutes away. The pricey neighborhood along the Intracoastal Waterway was built during the roaring twenties. Helen could see Scott and Zelda playing in a tiered fountain, and Gatsby gazing wistfully out an upstairs window.

Phil had changed into his disguise—board shorts, a T-shirt and sneakers. "I'll wade into the water first, so if I'm caught, I can say I fell in and lost my paddleboard."

"Yuck," Helen said. "That water's nasty."

"But it gives me an excuse to carry a towel so I can wrap up the cat," Phil said. "That way Justine won't claw my arm."

At twenty after seven, Helen dropped off Phil half a block from Arthur's home, a three-story mansion with a fountain. They could see a long, shiny black Mercedes in the curved drive.

"I'll be back in fifteen minutes or so," Phil said. He reached in back for Thumbs's carrier and left it on the front passenger seat with its door open. "Keep driving around until you see Arthur's car leave, then park back here."

He left, the towel slung over his shoulder.

Helen toured Rio Vista's tree-lined streets, waiting for Phil. Many of the stucco mansions had yachts docked in the back and exotic gardens, but she couldn't enjoy the sights. Helen was sure the Neighborhood Watch program would report her.

At least I'm a white woman, she thought. That means I look harmless to these homeowners.

Helen was relieved when Arthur's Mercedes backed out of the drive. She drove around one more time, then parked at the drop-off, drummed her nails against the steering wheel and checked her watch. "Come on, Phil," she muttered.

Finally, Phil jogged out of his former client's backyard, singing loudly to cover the howls coming from the towel-wrapped bundle in his arms. Helen opened his door, he tossed the bundle into the carrier and climbed in. He was soaked, and his wet tennies squelched.

"Go!" he said.

Helen wasted no time. On the short drive to Nancie's law office, Phil called the lawyer. As they expected, she was working at her desk.

"I think our client is scamming us," he said. "Helen and I are bringing you the proof. Once you see it, you may not want to take the case."

"I'll make that decision after I talk to you," Nancie said.

At the stoplight, Helen noticed a long, bloody scratch down Phil's arm. "You're hurt," she said.

"Justine has a set of steak knives on her paws," Phil said. "Arthur has a screened-in cat run in the backyard, with a cat door so his pets can come and go as they please. The people door on the run wasn't locked, so I walked in. The big, fluffy brown cat was asleep in the corner. Little Justine put up a fight, but I threw the towel over her and legged it out of there. Nobody saw me."

"Thank goodness," Helen said.

"Ouch!" Phil said. She heard a loud, snaky hiss.

"What's wrong?"

"I opened the cage to take the towel off Justine and she clawed me again." He wrapped his pocket handkerchief around his wounded hand.

Phil insisted on carrying the pet carrier into Nancie's office, even though he'd bled through his handkerchief.

"I want her to see I was wounded in the line of duty," he said.

"Your blood, your story," Helen said.

Phil made a dramatic sight with his bloody, bandaged hand and the blood-spattered carrier. Nancie listened patiently to his story, then said, "If Trish is in on the cat-napping, I won't represent her if there's a criminal case. Let's see Justine."

She cleared her papers off the desk, then opened the carrier door. An indignant gray kitten tested the desk with one paw, then eased out its round gray head, and finally its whole body.

The cat hissed, lifted its leg and whizzed all over Nancie's black leather desk pad.

Helen and Phil couldn't understand why Nancie was laughing. "That's no Justine," she said. "This angry gentleman is an unneutered Russian Blue. I believe Phil's kidnapped Arthur Goldich's kitten, Misha. I'd get him back before the lawyer has you both arrested."

"I—I thought Russian Blues would be blue," Phil said.

"They're slate gray," Helen said, using her newfound knowledge.

"And they have green eyes," Nancie said. "Justine's

eyes are copper. Now get this cat out of here, will you? Cat pee stinks. I have to clean up my desk. I'll deduct the new desk pad from your bill."

Phil shoved the snarling, hissing kitten back into the carrier and earned another vicious scratch. "Ow!"

"Hurry!" Nancie said. "Get him back home before I have to bail you two out of jail."

As they ran for the Igloo with the furious feline, Phil said, "Don't say it."

"Say what?" Helen asked.

"I told you so."

"Don't have to," Helen said. "You just did."

CHAPTER 9

Wednesday

"So far, the police have made no arrests in the brutal murder of Peerless Point financial advisor Mortimer Barrymore," said Channel 77 investigative reporter Valerie Cannata.

Helen and Phil had flipped on the TV in Phil's living room to catch the morning news over a hasty breakfast. Mort's murder was still the lead local story.

"Damn, she looks good at seven in the morning," Phil said.

Helen felt a sharp sting of jealousy. Phil and Valerie had had a fling years ago. Helen knew it was over. She also knew Valerie was exceptionally well turned out. The reporter's yellow dress hugged her curves, and her dark red hair glowed in the morning sun.

Helen felt frumpy in shorts and a T-shirt that would soon be covered with cat hair.

"Full makeup," Helen said. "I'm impressed."

Lock away the green-eyed monster, she thought. Phil's

no hound, and Valerie brings Coronado Investigations lots of business when she covers your cases.

On-screen, Valerie was standing outside Mort's wrought-iron gate. The TV camera panned the marble statues and the bougainvillea-draped mansion, then focused on the front door. "Mr. Barrymore was battered to death inside this historic mansion, where he had been living since separating from his estranged wife," the reporter said. "We are expecting a development later today. Peerless Point Crimes Against Persons detective Lester V. Boland has called a press conference for three o'clock this afternoon, and reliable sources say an arrest may be imminent."

"What do you bet that reliable source is Detective Boland himself?" Helen asked.

"You're so cynical," Phil said. "And so right." He kissed her, a lingering kiss that made Helen wish they could go back to bed.

"To be continued," she said. "I have to run to work or I'll be late."

She fished her tennies out from under the couch and the phone rang. "It's Nancie," Phil said, and put the phone on speaker.

The lawyer sounded clipped, quick and urgent. "I only have a minute," she said. "Trish is being arrested this morning. They're charging her with first-degree murder."

"We just saw Valerie's story on TV," Phil said. "Does Boland have a case?"

"If he wore anything that flimsy, he'd be arrested for indecent exposure," Nancie said. "He says Trish's DNA and prints are all over Mort's front door and the murder weapon, and Trish's tire tracks are in the driveway."

"So?" Phil said. "She used to live there and still visits regularly. She has a key."

"That's what I said. Boland said only someone Mort knew—or someone with a key and the security code—could get through the gate, and he says that's Trish. They found hair and fibers from the pantsuit Trish said she wore the night of the murder in the hall, but she wears it all the time."

"Any blood on it?" Phil asked.

"Boland says she got rid of the outfit she really wore."

"Can't have it both ways," Phil said. "What about bloody fingerprints? Blood on her shoes? Any witnesses see her at the scene?"

"No, no and no," Nancie said. "But the cops did find out she'd been to the Coventry cat show with Arthur. They made the same connection about the cat medallion that you did, Phil."

"Clever," Helen said.

"Not really," Nancie said. "A uniform worked security at the Lauderdale cat show when he was off duty. He remembered the cougar."

"Trish never told me she went to the Coventry show with Arthur," Phil said.

"Me, either," Nancie said. "When the cops told me, I chewed her out. Trish said she was embarrassed because Mort hadn't moved out of the house when she went to the UK with Arthur."

"If she's worried about embarrassment," Phil said, "wait till she's strip-searched in jail."

Helen shuddered. Fragile, elegant Trish had some ugly shocks waiting.

"So, Trish was cheating on Mort?" Phil asked.

"It was mutual. I think they were both seeing other people before they called it quits," Nancie said. "Mort had two girlfriends, and Trish has Arthur. She's the kind who won't leave a man unless she has another waiting for her."

"Did Trish have a Coventry cat medallion?" Phil asked.

"She says she has no idea what that is," the lawyer said. "She swears there were only show cats, not cougars, panthers or wild cats, at the Coventry cat show. But since she lied, the cops don't believe her."

"Are Trish's fingerprints on the medallion?"

"No," Nancie said.

"Someone else's prints?"

"I won't find that out until discovery," Nancie said.

"So why are they arresting her?" Helen asked.

"She's rich, she lied about a silly nothing and here's her real crime: She tried to pull rank and get the Peerless Point police to find her cat," Nancie said. "I told her to be brave and get through this. When I finish with Peerless Point, Trish will own the city."

That wasn't an idle threat. Nancie had taken on a bumbling detective and the town that hired him. By the time the town settled, she'd nearly bankrupted it, and the detective took early retirement.

"I'm surprised the DA is going ahead with it," Phil said.

"He was Mort's golfing buddy," Nancie said. "Mort filled his ear with anti-Trish propaganda every Wednesday afternoon."

"And left out his own transgressions," Helen said, tying her tennies.

"Old boys will be old boys," Nancie said. "I've warned Trish she probably won't get bail with murder one, even with these trumped-up charges. With her money, she'll be considered a flight risk."

"But she'd never leave Florida," Phil said. "Not without Justine."

"I know that, but these cops don't get cat lovers," Nancie said. "I worked out a deal to take Trish to the police station at eight this morning. That's all I can do — save her the shame of a public arrest. She wants you to do two things."

"Name them," Phil said.

"Handle the kidnapping negotiations for Justine," Nancie said. "She's worried sick about her cat."

"I'm on the case," Phil said.

"And find the catnapper."

"I got the job at Chatwood's Champions," Helen said. "I'll be working with Mort's fiancée, Jan Kurtz. There's a cat show Saturday and we'll be working overtime. Lots of opportunity to talk."

"Good. Report as soon as you learn something," Nancie said. "Phil, I need you to contact someone at the Coventry show and find out about that medallion."

"Will do," he said.

"And call me the moment you hear from the kidnapper," Nancie said. "When you find him, we'll have the killer, and Trish will go free. Gotta run." She hung up.

"Me, too," Helen said. "I'm going to be late." She kissed Phil good-bye. "Love you." Thumbs stood in her way, demanding a scratch. She gave him a quick pat and bolted for the Igloo.

She would have made it, except for a traffic accident on Federal Highway. Helen was five minutes late when she knocked on Dee's front door. Gabby Garcia met her and said, "Mrs. Chatwood wants to speak with you in her office."

"Is something wrong?" Helen asked.

"Not sure," Gabby said. She seemed reluctant to say more. Helen followed the slender Latina maid to Dee's office on the east side of the pool, with another stunning view of the Intracoastal.

"She's in there," Gabby said, and nearly ran back down the hall.

Helen was mesmerized by the majestic white yachts churning past the window. They were much better-looking than the tiger-striped wallpaper. Midnight, the Persian stud, lounged on Dee's black marble desk. Dee paced her office in a black halter and tiger-print clam diggers, her bloody claws clenched.

Uh-oh, Helen thought. She's ticked. She could almost see the frown trying to burst through her boss's Botoxed forehead, like a newly hatched alien.

"You wanted to see me?" Helen asked.

"Five minutes ago," Dee said. "You're late."

"I—"

"Don't waste my time with explanations. I'm docking you a day's pay. I'm doing this for your own good. It's not about the money."

It's always about the money, Helen thought, as resentment burned through her like a lightning strike. I'd love to tell you what to do with this job, but I need it.

"I'm sorry," she said, forcing herself to sound contrite.

"Next time, you're fired. And from now on, use the servants' entrance on the side, behind the travelers palm. That's the tree shaped like a fan."

Helen nodded, too angry to speak. The servants' entrance. A day's pay docked. Welcome to your new workplace.

Dee pressed an intercom button and shouted, "Gabby, come here. I need you to witness a contract."

"Right away, Mrs. Chatwood," Gabby said.

Gabby didn't seem surprised by the request. She reappeared, slightly out of breath, and stood near the desk, head down and hands folded in front of her. Her forehead was smoother than Dee's and her natural beauty made Dee look grotesque.

"Helen, you must sign this employment agreement to work for Chatwood's Champions," Dee said. "I want to make sure you understand the noncompete clause."

While Helen scanned the one-page agreement, Dee brought out a small recorder. She recited the date and time, then said, "I'm speaking with my new employee, Helen Hawthorne, in my office at Chatwood's Champions. Ms. Hawthorne, do you know you're being recorded?"

She stuck the recorder in Helen's face. "Yes," Helen said.

"In your own words, can you tell me what the noncompete clause says?"

"I cannot show or breed pedigreed cats of any variety for five years in the state of Florida after I leave this job."

"Or?" Dee demanded.

"Or I'll have to pay all your associated legal costs plus fifty thousand dollars."

"Are you signing this of your own free will?" Dee asked.

"Yes. Right now," Helen said, and signed the paper with a flourish. She wondered if the recorder picked up the pen scratches.

"Gabby, you sign, too, as a witness." Gabby did.

"You can leave now," she said. "You, too, Helen. Jan's going to show you how to bathe Red. That old sweetie is one of my favorites."

I bet, Helen thought. Two cannibal queens.

She fumed all the way to the cattery, but her anger melted when she heard giggles and meows. She stood in the doorway and watched Jan play with three Persians. She waved a long, flexible wand with feathers on the end. Chocolate, a glossy swoop of deliciously dark fur, stood up on her hind legs and batted at it. Chessie, the snowy contender for national winner, chased the feathers as fast as her short, sturdy legs could move. Red bounded over Chessie, chomped the feathers and pulled one out. She triumphantly chased her prize across the white tile floor.

Helen enjoyed the three show cats and the showy, dark-haired Jan.

Jan saw Mystery lounging on a carpeted window shelf, watching the fluttering, feeding birds on cat TV. "You need your exercise, too, lazybones," she said, and shook the wand at the fluffy pale gray cat. Mystery took a lazy swipe, then yawned.

The other three cats, looking like conspirators, gathered at Jan's feet. *"Merorower,"* they said.

"Sorry, kitties," she said. "Playtime's over. Red needs her bath." She scooped up the flame-colored Persian and saw Helen.

"What's wrong?"

"Nothing," Helen said.

"Dee chewed you out, didn't she?"

"I was five minutes late," Helen said. "I got caught in traffic. She docked me a day."

"I should have warned you," Jan said. "She's a stickler about time. I bet she also told you to use the servants' entrance."

"She did," Helen said.

"She should install a revolving door for that entrance. Gabby and I have stayed the longest. I hope I don't lose you. I'm taking off for Mort's, my fiancé's, funeral, even if she fires me."

"When is it?" Helen said.

"I don't know yet. The story has been splashed all over the media, but so far I haven't heard anything about the funeral. I only took this job to help Mort. He had big plans for his cat, Justine. I wanted to know the important players in the show world."

"What kind of cat is Justine?" Helen asked, proud she remembered she wasn't supposed to know about the kidnapped cat.

"A pedigreed Chartreux," Jan said. "French cats with copper eyes, round bodies and short legs. Some call them potatoes on toothpicks, but their eyes are hypnotic and they're so lovable. They're thick-coated shorthairs with smoky blue fur. Mort is—was—in the middle of a divorce. He and his wife, Trish Barrymore, disagreed about everything, but they worked out joint custody of Justine. Trish believes her cat will be a national winner."

"Do you?" Helen asked.

"She has the potential," Jan said. "She's beautiful, sweet and has great conformation. But Trish treats her like an only child. Kittens need to get used to the noise and smells and commotion of a show hall. Trish doesn't understand that show cats need to be around other cats and other people, or they can come to hate the show scene.

"Trish keeps Justine in her own room and caters to her every whim. I warned Mort and Trish that Justine is too isolated, but Trish won't listen to me. I'm just the Other Woman.

"Well, not my problem. Not anymore. Not with Mort gone."

She buried her head in Red's soft fiery fur. "I miss him," she said, hugging the cat. Red patted her with a velvet paw.

"Who do you think killed him?" Helen asked.

"I don't know. Mort was a financial adviser and a good one. A real people person. He made you feel he was genuinely interested in you. It wasn't an act, either. It's one reason why I loved him."

"Ever hear of Amber Waves?" Helen said, tossing out the name of Mort's pole-dancing lover.

"The TV movie with Kurt Russell?" Jan asked.

Did she know about Mort's other girlfriend? Helen wondered. Is Jan lying? She has her head buried in Red's fur and I can't see her eyes.

Jan lifted her face, and Helen saw that she'd been crying again. Her blue eyes were almost as red as the cat's fur. "I'm supposed to show you how to wash this beauty," she said, sniffling. "I feel better talking to you about Mort, but we have to get to work, or Dee will have a fit."

"Right," Helen said.

"I'll tell you who I think did it," Jan said. "Trish. She'd do anything to get control of that cat."

"The socialite?" Helen said.

"Wouldn't be the first woman to think she can buy her way out of trouble. There was also something funny going on with Mort and a Gold Cup judge."

"Funny how?" Helen asked.

"I'll tell you after we start the cat bath," Jan said.

CHAPTER 10

Wednesday

*There was also something funny going on with Mort
and a Gold Cup judge,* Jan had told Helen. Then,
as if she were waving the cat teaser at Helen, she
dropped the subject and prepped Red for her bath.

Jan carried the Persian to a grooming table next to a
deep, double stainless-steel sink, filled one side with
warm water, then plunked a plastic gallon jar labeled
ORVUS into it.

"I'm warming the shampoo," she said. "No cold soap
on that pretty coat, right, Red?"

Helen struggled to pay attention, but her mind was
racing. She knew the Gold Cup Cat Fanciers' Association was a prestigious cat registry, on a par with CFA, the
Cat Fanciers' Association, and TICA, The International
Cat Association.

The associations recognized and set the breed stan-
dards. Cat shows don't have big-money prizes like horse
races, but grand champions or national winners would

produce kittens worth hundreds or even thousands of dollars. As for the male cats, boy toys would envy their stud fees.

So what was Mort doing with that Gold Cup judge? Helen wondered. Giving her financial advice? Or something more personal?

Jan was cooing to the big orange cat. "We'll need lots of towels and a washcloth for her face," she told Helen.

"First, we comb Red. Unlike ordinary Persians, Dee's show cats get combed daily. You have to groom long-hairs every single day. When I worked at a grooming salon, I'd see Persians who didn't get combed by their lazy owners. Their poor hair was so matted, I'd have to cut it and risk a hole in those gorgeous coats."

"Don't you brush the cats, too?" Helen asked.

"Never. A brush doesn't do a darn thing for long hair. We use metal combs. This wide, long-toothed comb is for her coat, and this smaller one is for her head, legs and feet. You start at the head and neck and work down the body."

Red stretched out perfectly still as Jan combed her thick, glossy coat into a rippling river of fire. Then the cat rolled over and presented her tummy.

"Good girl," Jan said. "The belly and under the legs are the most sensitive spots, and most cats hate that part. But you're no ordinary cat, are you, gorgeous? The fur is fine here and tangles easily."

Helen could almost see Red's long, silky hair tying itself into knots.

Jan kissed the cat on her broad head, and Red nuzzled her. "Pretty girl," she crooned.

"Red seems to love the attention," Helen said. "My cat wouldn't sit still for this."

Jan gently combed the fluffy fur on Red's belly.

"I can't believe this sweetie ate her own kitten," Helen said.

"Tried to," Jan said. "We stopped her in time. It's rare, but it happens. Red produced spectacular kittens, but she wasn't a good mother. Dee bred her the same time as Chocolate, who's a terrific mom. Red had small litters—usually two kittens—and Chocolate would nurse her kittens, too."

"And Red didn't mind?" Helen said.

"She was happy to let Chocolate do her work," Jan said. "Motherhood isn't natural to all humans, either."

"I'm not interested in babies," Helen said, "though I enjoy my niece and nephew."

"You were smart enough not to breed," Jan said. "Red didn't have a choice."

Helen was a bit startled by Jan's analogy, but she understood it.

"Now, lazy old Mystery there"—Jan pointed to the soft, pale gray Persian sleeping on the window shelf—"is a good mom, and she'll play auntie to the other cats' new kittens."

"What's that mean?" Helen asked.

"Mystery will groom them, play with them and, when the kittens get older, let them jump on her tail and pretend it's a snake.

"The real surprise is Midnight. Our handsome stud is a good daddy. He'll visit his kittens and groom them. He looks a little startled when they try to find a nipple to nurse, but he's no tomcat."

"Does he hang around with Dee?" Helen asked.

"Mostly. Or reigns in the living room."

Red patted Jan with her paw. "Sorry, girl," she said. "We should focus on you. Next, check the nails. Red's were clipped yesterday. I even remembered the little dewclaws on her front legs. Unclipped claws can really slice.

"Now use the ear-cleaning solution on cotton makeup rounds."

"They look like the ones I buy at the drugstore," Helen said.

"They are," Jan said. "And you're a good kitty." Red sat still while Jan delicately cleaned her small, feathery ears.

"She doesn't like getting her teeth brushed. This cat toothbrush is smaller and softer than a people brush. Its pointed end can reach in back. I load it with chicken-flavored toothpaste."

"You don't use people toothpaste?"

"Never," Jan said. She held Red firmly and gently scrubbed her teeth. "Good girl."

"Can you show Red if she loses her teeth?" Helen asked.

"Depends on the association," Jan said. "Some cat owners get dental implants."

Red shook her head impatiently and Jan said, "There, pretty baby. Almost done."

She gave Red a Greenies dental treat. "She loves those," Jan said. "Now comes the fun part: degreasing."

Jan filled the empty stainless-steel sink with warm water, then gently lifted Red into her bath.

"She's not fighting or scratching," Helen said.

"You have to start when they're young," Jan said. She scratched the beauty's broad head, then pulled out a gallon jug of Goop, pumped a generous handful and smeared the creamy gunk all over the cat's fur.

Helen stared. "That's a hand cleaner for mechanics."

"Yep. Works for cats and dogs, too." Jan worked the Goop into the coat. The fluffy fur was now a flat, sticky mess.

"You're kidding me," Helen said. "Thumbs would amputate my arm."

"She learned to like it as a kitten," Jan said. "Persians have thick fur, and nature intended cats' coats to protect them from rainy weather, so you have to work to get them wet. The challenge is getting the water through the dense fur all the way to the skin. If you don't wet the cat thoroughly, the shampoo won't get there, either. So you start with the Goop, working it into the coat with water. The Goop washes the cat, and then you have to wash out the Goop.

"Notice how much smaller she seems when her fur's wet."

"But strong," Helen said. "She has a proud chest and sturdy legs."

"Red has good muscle tone," Jan said. "She's a little jock. Don't forget the tail and the back end." She rubbed more Goop on the cat's hindquarters, and Red's tail plume deflated into a straggle of white-smeared fur.

"Now rinse her completely. Any residue attracts more dirt and her fur will look cruddy."

Red rested her head on the edge of the sink and closed her copper eyes while Jan rinsed the cat with the warm spray.

"Why did Dee make a big deal out of my noncompete contract?" Helen asked. "She recorded me and called in Gabby as a witness."

"She did the same with me," Jan said. "When Mort and I got engaged, I also had to sign a pet-nup—a pre-nup agreement that if we split, Mort would get custody of any pets he owned prior to our marriage. He didn't want a repeat of his expensive fight with Trish over Justine. I like Chartreux, but I really want to breed and exhibit Persians. We agreed I could keep any Persians we acquired during our marriage."

"Were you planning to open a cattery in Lauderdale?" Helen asked.

"Yes," Jan said. "Mort said he'd cover any legal costs if I wasn't willing to wait five years. Well, those plans are gone. Just like Mort."

She sighed and kept working her fingers through

Red's wet fur, gently massaging her and getting out the Goop. A tear slid down Jan's creamy cheek and splashed in the water.

"Dee's cautious because she was badly burned by a former employee, Vanessa, who never told her she planned to show Persians. Vanessa quit without notice at the start of the show season. Mystery was on her way to becoming a Gold Cup national winner. But Vanessa's Elusive Elsah, another Persian, kept racking up more points. When the show season ended, Elsah was the national winner. Vanessa had worked for Dee long enough to learn her tricks, and Vanessa's nice, besides."

"What does Dee do that's so good?" Helen asked.

"Lots of little things," Jan said. "See the scratching posts?"

She pointed to the slim metal poles. The tight sisal wrapping started about a foot off the floor. "When the cats are small, Dee wraps the bottom of the columns and trains them to use it as their scratching post. As the cats get bigger, she raises the sisal and the cats have to stand up full-length to sharpen their claws.

"Ever see a cat-show judging table?"

"No," Helen said.

"It's actually a rectangle about the size of a restaurant table for two," Jan said. "The judging table sits on a bigger folding table draped with a skirt for the show. Many judging tables have two posts holding up a fluorescent light fixture. One post is usually wrapped with sisal. The judges love it when the cats stretch their full length to claw that sisal. They can see their bodies easier. That's a risky move for short-bodied Persians. Stretching up a pole can emphasize a fault. Since so few Persians do it, it may catch the judge's attention and show Dee's cat has a well-shaped body."

"Clever," Helen said.

"So are Dee's pet carriers." Jan pointed to the row of

ordinary beige plastic carriers. "Bet you use the same one for your Thumbs, and he fights when you put him in it."

"Like a wildcat," Helen said.

"Dee keeps her carriers out with the doors open. Inside are comfortable cushions, toys and treats. The cats go in and out. The carriers are their caves."

"So they don't fight the carriers," Helen said.

"Yep. Dee also uses water bottles instead of bowls," she said.

Above each metal food dish hung a plastic water bottle with a long thin tube. "See Chessie licking water from that tube? The bottle keeps her fur nice and clean. Persians put their flat little faces in bowls and get their fur wet.

"All the Goop's gone, beautiful girl," Jan said to Red. "Now for the nice warm Orvus." Jan plastered the cat with the shampoo, then rinsed her again.

Helen was getting bored. "Is that it?" she asked.

"Oh no," Jan said. "Next she gets washed with Tropi-Clean papaya and kiwi shampoo and conditioner."

"Two shampoos and conditioner?" Helen said. "I don't use that on my hair."

She caught her reflection in the window, her dark hair limp and frizzed. "Of course, my hair doesn't look as good as the cat's."

Helen tried to hide her impatience when Jan lathered Red's sunset orange coat with the sweet-smelling shampoo. "Use the warm washcloth on her face. Be sure to get the gunk out of her eyes and nose."

After rinsing the cat for the third time, Jan said, "Now we float the coat."

Tonight, Thumbs gets all the treats he can eat, Helen thought. I had no idea he was so low maintenance.

"Helen, warm those towels in the dryer, will you?"

Jan washed out the sink, filled it again and carefully placed the clean, damp Red in the warm water.

"See how her coat floats? Now I gently squish it and check for bubbles. That means there's still soap in the coat. Good! It's gone."

"Mrreorrrr," Red said. It sounded like a complaint.

"I know, baby girl, this is taking too long," Jan said. "I need a towel, Helen."

Jan wrapped the cat in the warm towel, and the Persian gave a full-body purr.

"Now do you hit her with the hair dryer?" Helen asked hopefully.

"At last," Jan said. "We use special dryers for cats." She squeezed the water out of the cat's coat with a warm towel. "The coat needs to be blown out to separate all the hair and get it standing away from the body. A Persian coat is too thick to air dry. In warm, humid Florida, we have to dry Persians quickly and thoroughly. Otherwise, we risk ringworm. Besides, a wet cat licking her coat would smear our work with saliva. Red's rough tongue can pull out her fur, and when she swallows it, that leads to hair balls."

"Yuck," Helen said. "How long does the drying take?"

"Almost as long as the bathing," Jan said.

Helen tried not to sigh.

"If you do it right, the cat enjoys it," Jan said. "A cat hair dryer isn't as hot as a people dryer. Start with her tummy and feet, combing and drying, then slowly work up the cat's body, blowing against the lay of the fur, and combing to separate the hair."

The furry sybarite lay on her back, paws flung out, while Jan carefully combed her legs and dried her tummy.

"That is one trusting cat," Helen shouted over the dryer roar.

"That trust had to be earned," Jan said. She gently turned Red over and began blowing out her fur. Soon her long coat was a blazing mix of red, orange and brick.

"With her copper eyes, she looks like a bonfire," Helen said.

"She's gorgeous, no doubt about it." Jan turned the dryer down a notch. "Now, when I do her face, I have to be extra gentle so I don't dry out her eyes."

Red shut her eyes, like an actress facing into the wind. "We're almost finished." Helen wasn't sure if Jan was reassuring her or the cat.

"Why do you think there was something funny going on with Mort and a Gold Cup judge?" Helen asked. "Did he date her?"

Jan laughed. "Lexie Deener? No, she's about twenty years older than Mort. She's divorced and splashes money around on clothes, boy toys, a classic Jaguar and her pedigreed Persians.

"Last January, we were out of Orvus and the next shipment wasn't due for two days. I picked up some at a pet store. Who did I see two aisles up but my Mort with Lexie. I recognized her from past shows and wondered if he was seeing the glamorous judge. I slipped into the next aisle to listen.

"I heard her say, 'It's serious. I need at least five thousand dollars to save Blackie.'

"'I can make you a lot more than that,' Mort told her. 'You'll be able to keep him in style.'

"'You'd better be right,' Lexie said. 'I love him. He's part of my image.'"

"So Blackie is a cat?" Helen asked.

"That's my guess," Jan said. "Cats can run up huge medical bills. Dee spent nearly ten thousand dollars when a Chatwood cat developed polycystic kidney disease."

"Does Lexie live near here?" Helen said.

"No, she's an eastern regional Gold Cup judge, but this region covers most of the East Coast. Lexie lives in North Carolina. Cat shows often bring in judges from other parts of their region. That way they don't socialize on a daily basis with the exhibitors and breeders."

"So what was Lexie doing in Fort Lauderdale?" Helen asked.

"On vacation, probably. A pet store is a safe place to meet. But you can see why I thought it was funny."

CHAPTER 11

Wednesday

Helen came home looking like something a cat dragged in—but not a Chatwood Champion.

Those pampered Persians wouldn't touch anything as bedraggled as Helen. Her shorts were smeared with suspicious brown streaks. Her pink T-shirt was damp, wrinkled, and dotted with clumps of Red's hair. Her body ached from lifting and bending, and her nose itched. She felt cat hair clinging to unseen, unreachable places.

She parked the Igloo in the Coronado lot, brushed more cat hair off the seat and saw Margery in the backyard on her knees, ripping out weeds and cussing.

"Come on, ya buzzard," she said, yanking on a green, stringy plant with silver-dollar-sized leaves. Her purple gardening gloves were streaked with sandy mud.

Margery looked up, wiped the sweat off her face and asked, "Since when did you start accessorizing with cat hair?"

"Since you started giving yourself mud facials," Helen said. "You've got dirt streaked on your face and forehead." She handed Margery a tissue from her purse. It felt good joking with her landlady after their last, dramatic encounter.

"Thanks, but I'll finish pulling out this patch here and then clean up," Margery said.

"What are you doing?" Helen asked, hoping she sounded casual.

"What's it look like?" Margery said. "I'm not on my knees, praying for rain. Damned dollarweed thrives in wet lawns. This summer's rains have turned my yard into a swamp."

My yard, Helen thought. That's encouraging. "But it hasn't rained for four days," she said.

"Too late," Margery said. "The dollarweed moved in and put down roots. Now it's nearly impossible to get rid of. It has seeds and runners—rhizomes, I think they're called—that dig in and spread all over. Usually, I can pull weeds by hand, but I'll have to use weed killer on this menace."

"Poison?" Helen said hopefully. This was a good sign.

"Something nice and lethal," Margery said. She grinned. "I want to watch it die, slowly and painfully."

"But why do you care?" Helen asked. Please, please give me the reason I want for your weed whacking.

"What do you mean?" Margery reached for her Marlboro, balanced on the sidewalk by a puddle. The cigarette was nearly lost in her muddy purple gloves, but she managed a puff.

"If you're selling the Coronado to a developer, why are you pulling weeds?" Helen asked.

"I changed my mind," Margery said, and blew out a blue cloud of smoke.

"You did?" Relief flooded through Helen. She wanted to sit down, stand up, shout, sing, find Phil and celebrate. Their home was safe!

"I'm getting the rebar work done on the Coronado," Margery said.

"Why? How? Where'd you get the money?"

"I'm cashing in a CD," Margery said. "I told myself I was saving it for my old age. Well, I looked in the mirror. It's here. When I started cleaning out more than fifty years' of junk in my apartment, I knew I didn't want to move. Where would I go? Assisted living? The work starts tomorrow."

"That's wonderful! Let's drink to that. I'll tell Phil."

"He's upstairs in his office," Margery said. "I've got no business criticizing your clothes when I've been rooting in the mud, but you may want to change. How's the cat house?"

"Cattery," Helen said. "Full of spoiled cats. They're better groomed than an actress on Oscar night. I'm going to reward Thumbs for being an easy-care cat."

"Tell him to shut up," Margery said. "He's been howling since Phil went upstairs to his office."

Thumbs is kind of loud, Helen thought, as she unlocked Phil's door. "Hi, bud," she said. "Did you miss me?"

He shut up and bumped her hand. Helen gave Thumbs a serious scratch while he sniffed her thoroughly.

"I know," she said. "I smell like foreign cats. Will Greenies help you forget I was unfaithful?"

The big-eyed cat chomped three Greenies, then groomed his fur. "As a self-cleaning cat, you deserve an extra treat," Helen said. She found a pound of shrimp in Phil's freezer, defrosted two shrimp for Thumbs, then poured his dry food.

"Time to groom me," she told the cat. Half an hour later, Helen had showered and washed and dried her hair. It's almost as glossy as Chocolate's, she decided. And I'm comparing myself to a cat. How pathetic is that?

She put on her slim white pants, turquoise silk blouse, heels and lipstick. There. She was ready for Phil. She skimmed upstairs to the Coronado Investigations office.

Phil whistled when he saw her. "You are a mirage in the desert," he said, and kissed her.

She kissed him back. "Is that a gun in your pocket?" She giggled. It seemed right to say that under his framed poster of Sam Spade.

"No," he said. "I'm really happy to see you. We never finished what we started this morning."

"Why are we waiting when there's a perfectly good couch?" she said.

Phil picked her up and carried her over, while Helen sighed. "My hero."

He unbuttoned her blouse, she helped tear off his shirt and the rest was a hot frenzy of lovemaking. Much later she was resting in his arms, the tension from her long, cat-hairy day gone.

"I didn't tell you the good news," Helen said. "Margery's going to fix the Coronado. We'll still have our home. We're supposed to celebrate with her."

"Let's go," Phil said, buttoning his shirt. While they dressed, Helen told him about Lexie, the cat-show judge.

"No calls from the catnapper," Phil said, "and the time-zone differences in England are making it hard for me to track down the cat-show people. I'm supposed to get a call from the organizer about seven tonight. Let's go enjoy this sunset salute."

Out by the pool, Margery looked fresh and relaxed in purple clam diggers and a pale lavender off-the-shoulder blouse. Her silvery gray hair had a springy swing.

"Well, I see you two started celebrating early," she said. Helen blushed and looked down at her shirt. "Everything's buttoned," Margery said and smiled wickedly. "You two have that glow."

"Where's Peggy?" Helen asked, awkwardly changing the subject. "I know she'll want to hear the good news."

"Daniel's picking her up after work," Margery said. "Wine?"

They toasted Margery, the Coronado, even the contractor, and were starting on a second glass and another round of toasts when Margery's friend Elsie toddled through the gate. Helen hadn't seen Elsie for months. The Coronado's honorary aunt seemed older than Margery, possibly because of Elsie's slightly dotty manner.

Elsie, who was pushing eighty—and it was pushing back hard—had a festive attitude toward fashion. Today's outfit came straight from the pages of *Seventeen*. Helen was sure she'd seen that same style on a magazine model who looked like preppie Cher Horowitz in the old *Valley Girl* classic *Clueless*, except Elsie's short, fluffy hair was Jell-O pink.

Elsie's plaid miniskirt, white blouse, navy blazer, and Mary Jane platforms looked creepy. School uniforms do not mix with cellulite and varicose veins, Helen thought.

"Am I interrupting?" Elsie asked in her soft, quavery voice.

"You're always welcome, Elsie," Margery said. "Interesting outfit."

"I'm glad you like it," she said. "I promised my son I'd dress more conservatively."

"He can't argue with a navy blazer," Margery said. "Join us for wine?"

"I was hoping I could invite you to dinner. My treat. I know it's short notice, but I have reservations at Beachie's."

"The restaurant on the water in Fort Lauderdale?" Phil said.

"You and Helen will join us," Elsie said. "Please?"

"Love to," Helen said.

"I'm supposed to get a phone call shortly," Phil said. "Can we meet you there?"

"I have a table on the water," Elsie said.

Phil's phone rang as Margery's white Lincoln Town Car was backing out of the driveway.

"Is this Mrs. Jinny Gender, director of the Coventry All Breed Cat Show?" Phil asked. "Oh, her secretary. How long will she be gone? I see. Did you attend the show? You like dogs. I see. Is there someone else I could speak to?" Silence. Then, "I understand. Volunteers do move on. Well, I'll wait until she returns. Thank you for getting in touch with me."

Phil hung up. "Gotta wait till Monday for more information on the medallion," he said. "Let's go see Margery and Elsie."

"I'll drive. It's too hot in your un-air-conditioned Jeep," Helen said. "Wonder why Elsie is inviting us all to dinner?"

"It's Wednesday? She got a check? Elsie never needs an excuse. But I sure could use a dozen Beachie's oysters."

"Keep up your strength," Helen said, and winked at him.

"Any complaints about my prowess?" he said.

"Absolutely none," she said. "I want you to maintain the same high standard."

Beachie's was an old fish shack that kept expanding. After thirty years, it was a jumble of additions, painted white, green, pink and turquoise, sprawled along the Intracoastal Waterway. The coveted seats were on the screened-in porch.

Helen found a parking space. She and Phil sidestepped a colony of fat cats that hung around the fish-house Dumpster. At the entrance, they ran into a wall of sound and a line that wrapped around the building. Inside, the dark restaurant was lit by glowing beer signs.

"I see our party out on the porch," Phil said to the hostess. "The lady with the pink hair."

"Elsie," said the hostess said. "She's so cute. Here are your menus."

Helen and Phil threaded their way through the tables, dodging servers with loaded trays.

Margery and Elsie were drinking wine at a table for five.

"Helen, dear, sit by me," Elsie said, "and Phil, you sit near your honey." That left the chair next to Margery empty, but there was a glass of white wine on the place mat.

Is someone else here? Helen wondered. Before she could ask, the server arrived. Her name tag read PEG.

"Can I get you two drinks?" Peg asked. She was fifty-something with straight brown hair, a little overweight and comfortable-looking.

Phil ordered a beer and Helen wanted Chardonnay. "I'll have another wine," Margery said.

"Ready to order?" Peg asked.

"As soon as our other guest joins us," Elsie said. "Why, here he is now. Hello, Zach."

Margery's dramatic-looking ex approached the table with an expansive wave, like a B-list celebrity. "Hi, everyone. I'll have another white wine, sweetheart," he said to Peg, and sat down next to Margery. She froze, like a child playing statue. Her hand stayed wrapped around her wineglass. Her smile was painted on.

Zach chugged his wine.

"What the hell are you doing, Elsie?" Margery asked, through gritted teeth.

Elsie began fluttering and flapping like a wounded bird. "Now, Margery, don't get upset. You know we've been friends since we were girls. I was there when you first met Zach. You were crazy in love with him."

"That. Was. A. Long. Time. Ago," Margery said.

Elsie should have had frost on her pink hair, but she rushed on sweetly, recklessly, desperate to make her case. Margery looked ready to explode.

"At least hear Zach out," Elsie said. "For my sake. I know you still love him."

"You know nothing," Margery said. "Nothing at all. About Zach or me or what happened."

"I know you were terribly disappointed," Elsie said. "I think when Zach showed up at your home recently, you were taken by surprise. You were in shock. Now that the shock is over, you need to listen to him. He's sorry, Margery. And he's changed. Completely."

Zach had a smug grin, as if no woman could resist him. This time, Helen thought he wasn't as handsome as he first appeared. Yes, his white hair was thick, but his eyes were slightly yellow, his nails were rough and coarse, and his skin was way too pale under his fake tan.

"Zach change for the better? I doubt it," Margery said, her voice dangerously low. "But I'll listen. You've got two minutes."

"Margery, I did it all wrong when I came to our apartment house," Zach said.

"My apartment house," she said.

"I shouldn't have surprised you," he said. "I should have called you first, but I was afraid you wouldn't speak to me."

"You got that right," Margery said. She took out a cigarette, then seemed to realize she couldn't smoke in the restaurant. She kept rolling it back and forth between her fingers.

"I love you, Margery," he said. "You're the only woman for me."

She crushed the cigarette flat. "What about Daisy?" Margery asked. "The woman you've been living with for thirty years."

"She means nothing to me," Zach said.

She ripped the crushed cigarette in two. "You spent a long time with someone you didn't care about," Margery said.

"Yes, I did," Zach said. "That wasn't fair to her or to you."

"Oh, don't worry about being fair to me," Margery said. She stripped the paper off the cigarette and took the tobacco apart. "I got what I wanted—the apartments, the car and the divorce. I also thought I saw the last of your sorry ass, but now you're back like a senior stalker."

Margery was getting angrier as she talked. She crushed the torn-up cigarette in her hand. "We're finished, Zach. I never want to see you again. Leave me alone."

Peg was back with the wine. "Here you go," the server said, handing Helen and Phil their glasses. She set one at Zach's place and gave the last one to Margery.

"Anything else?" Peg asked.

"Yes," Zach said. "I want you to be my witness."

Peg stared while Zach slowly knelt in front of Margery on the sticky tile. Diners at nearby tables gaped. The noisy restaurant grew quiet. "Peg! Order's up!" someone yelled in the kitchen.

She stayed rooted while Zach said, "Margery, I love you. Come back to me. I'll love you for the rest of my life."

"With any luck, that won't be long. Get up, you grandstanding fool," Margery said. She was shouting now, and the restaurant was ominously silent. "I don't love you. I never have. Get out. Stay away."

"But," Zach said.

She picked up her wineglass and tossed the wine in Zach's face.

"And in case that didn't convince you, remember this." She dumped Zach's wine on his head. "Now go away and leave me alone. *Up! Out! Never let me see you again!*"

Peg, an unflappable veteran of the restaurant wars, rushed over and helped Zach to his feet. She wiped his face with a napkin. "Are you okay, sir?"

"I'm fine, sweetheart," he said. "I won't be having dinner. I don't feel so good. My stomach's acting up."

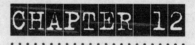

CHAPTER 12

Wednesday/Thursday

Zach lurched through the silent restaurant, clutching his gut. Near the hostess stand, he stumbled and started to fall. A worried Peg, who'd been walking beside him, caught Zach and guided him out the door.

Maybe he really is sick, Helen thought. He did look pale.

After Zach left, the show was over. The restaurant resumed its noisy hum.

Margery hissed at Elsie, "Thanks for the surprise party. I'm leaving. Find your own way home. You're good at arranging things."

Elsie reached for her friend's hand. "Margery, please forgive me," she said. Tears streaked her face. Her cheerful cherry pink frizz had flattened into sad strings.

Margery slapped away her hand like it was an annoying insect, then stomped out.

"I didn't mean it," Elsie said, her face crumpling. Phil hugged her and let her cry on his shoulder.

"If you could have seen Margery and Zach when they were young," she said. "They were so in love, they had a . . . a radiance. I know Zach was wrong when he took up with Daisy. He knows it, too. When he called me, he sounded so contrite."

"He called you?" Helen said. That rat, dragging soft-hearted Elsie into his mess.

"He came by my house and told me everything," Elsie said. "I told him he shouldn't have surprised Margery at the Coronado. The shock of seeing him after so many years was too much. He suggested meeting her at this restaurant. They used to come here when they were courting. I thought if Margery would listen to him, they'd get back together."

Poor Elsie, Helen thought. Along with her schoolgirl outfit, she had a girlish faith in true love. She didn't understand Zach's betrayal had burned away that incandescent love.

Helen did. She still remembered the white-hot hate blasting through her when she'd caught her ex with another woman. That savage rage had consumed her love for Rob.

Elsie sat up, sniffling, and Phil handed her his pocket handkerchief. "Such a gentleman," she said, dabbing her damp eyes. "Thank you."

"Elsie, it's over," Helen said softly. "Zach and Margery are different people now. They can't get back together. Would you like a cup of tea?"

"No, thank you," Elsie said with great dignity. "I'd like to go home, please."

Helen left enough cash to cover their drinks, plus a generous tip.

"Do you think Margery will forgive me?" Elsie said. "We've been friends since we were girls, almost seventy years."

"Give her time to cool down," Helen said.

Phil helped Elsie toward the door. She seemed sad and crushed. Her sagging bosom strained her white blouse, her short plaid skirt clashed with her varicose veins and her stylish Mary Janes showcased her bunions.

Cruel snickers followed Elsie. Helen glared at the woman's tormentors. Elsie's friendship with Margery stretched back to when they both wore schoolgirl clothes without the sneery comments.

Helen and Phil made sure Elsie was settled at home. "Poor Elsie," Helen said, as they drove to the Coronado. "She meant well. What do we say when we see Margery?"

"Let her set the tone," Phil said. "She'll discuss it when she's ready. Margery's had too many people trying to tell her what to do lately."

Back at the Coronado, the lights were on in Margery's place. Helen and Phil hurried inside his apartment, grateful they didn't run into their landlady.

"How about if I defrost those shrimp and make scampi?" he asked.

"Yum," Helen said. "I'll chop garlic and do the salad."

They worked together quickly and well and dinner was soon on the table. "What are you doing tomorrow, besides waiting for the kidnapper to call?" Helen asked, as she sampled her plate of garlicky, buttery shrimp. "This scampi is fabulous."

"I want to track down Amber, Mort's other girl-friend."

"The pole-dancing actress? I wish I could see that one," Helen said.

"You could," Phil said. "I can video it on my phone."

"Isn't that illegal?"

"I'll have her consent," Phil said. "I'll tell her my partner loves *Rock of Ages*. You want to see one of the pole dancers from that awesome scene in the club."

"I do?" Helen said.

"Yes. That's why you insist that I record the interview. You're such a fan."

"I'll really be a fan if you get her to talk," Helen said, stifling a yawn.

He took her plate and kissed her cheek. "I'll clean up. Go to bed."

The next thing Helen knew, Phil was shaking her awake. "Helen! Get up! It's after seven!"

"No! I'm fired if I'm late." Helen sprang out of bed and threw on shorts, shirt and sandals. "Good thing I don't have to be as well-groomed as the cats," she said, as Phil gave her an energy bar and coffee and pushed her out the door.

At Dee's she raced into the cattery, slightly out of breath. Jan looked at the clock. "Relax. You have five minutes to spare," she said. "Dee's in a foul mood. Keep out of her way. It's bath time for Mystery. I'll supervise."

Helen picked up the sleepy smoky gray Persian and started to hold her against her chest. "No, she doesn't like to be carried that way," Jan said. "Stretch out your arm."

Helen held out her right arm and Mystery rode it, her chest in Helen's hand, her legs dangling. "Show cats are trained to be carried that way," Jan said. "The exhibitor can keep one hand free. Also, it doesn't mess up their fur as much."

Helen walked gingerly to the grooming table. "She's such a pretty shade of gray," she said.

"Blue," Jan corrected. "Pedigreed cats are blue, not gray."

Helen stared at the fur, but it looked gray as a rainy day. "Do you have a cat at home?" she asked.

"No," Jan said. "After waiting on these babies, I don't have time for one." She scratched Mystery's ears. "I get my feline fix at work. Don't forget to lay out your tools. I'll keep you in warm towels."

The sweet-faced Persian didn't seem to mind Helen's

bumbling bathing. She stood patiently while Helen combed her long, thick coat. "Is Dee married?" Helen asked.

"Sure," Jan said. "To a real sweet guy, Justin Chatwood. He's got the money. He's in Brazil now. Justin travels a lot, which, I suspect, is the only way to stay married to Dee."

She lowered her voice and turned on the water in the other sink. "Justin had an affair with Trish."

"Mort's wife?" Helen asked.

"I think someone at the country club told Dee. She was livid. I went looking for Midnight about a month ago and heard Dee screaming at Justin in the living room. She shouted that she was leaving for good. He begged her—I mean literally—to forgive him. Swore it would never happen again. Dee said she wanted to think about it, but she took him back."

"Did she really forgive Justin?" Helen said. "She doesn't seem the forgiving type."

Jan shrugged. "Maybe she did. Maybe she took a long look at her bank account. She can't keep these cats on the money she makes. But I don't think she'll ever forgive Trish, who's younger and better-looking."

"What would Trish see in Justin?" Helen asked.

"Oh, you've never met him," Jan said, and smiled. "He's older, but he's sexy and suave, as my mother would say. Same social background as Trish. She likes money, and Mort had plenty of it, but Justin has more. Trish kind of looked down her nose at Mort. That hurt him. Eventually, he had enough and turned to me." She smiled at the memory, then looked stricken. Mort was gone, along with their life together.

"Do you think Dee framed Trish for Mort's murder?" Helen asked.

Jan paused for a long moment. "She's devious enough. At first I thought Trish killed him. But now I remember how mad Dee was at her cheating husband.

"After a day or so, they were all kissy-kissy, walking around here holding hands. But when he wasn't around, she lashed out at everyone. She went through three assistants in three weeks. One afternoon, she ordered me into her office. I figured she was going to chew me out again. She did, but first she made me stand by her desk while she talked on the phone. She had the new issue of the *South Florida Society Chronicle*."

"The glossy mag that's all society parties?" Helen asked.

"That's the one. It was open to a story about some charity ball, featuring Trish in a black diva dress. While she talked on the phone, Dee stabbed out Trish's eyes."

"What do you mean?" Helen asked.

"She actually punched holes in Trish's eyes with a ballpoint. Gave me the creeps."

Mystery lightly patted Helen's arm with a paw. "Sorry, girl, I've been rinsing you long enough," Helen said. She turned off the water and wrapped the cat in a warm towel. "When I finish Mystery, what's next?"

"Litter boxes and cattery cleaning," Jan said. "Then we can go home at four. We'll work longer hours as we get closer to the show. I need to check on my cat."

Huh? Before Helen could say, "What cat?" Mystery knocked over a bottle of shampoo and she forgot to ask.

Helen came home to construction chaos at the Coronado. The dented white Fort Lauderdale Construction van and two rusty pickups took the guest parking spots. Sal Steer, the slab-faced boss, was directing a hard-hatted crew. Scaffolding covered the front of the building, and a worker with a noisy jackhammer was tearing out part of Margery's wall.

Helen carefully stepped around the equipment and tools and ducked into her apartment to shower and change. She could feel the *rat-a-tat-tat* of the jackhammer through the wall. She wondered how long the Coronado would be torn up. Thumbs must be frantic. She found her cat pacing Phil's apartment.

She soothed him with talk and treats, then went upstairs to their office. Phil was pacing, too.

"Any calls?" she shouted over the jackhammer.

"No," he screamed back, and then suddenly the din stopped. "Nothing from the catnapper. Nancie says our client was denied bail. Trish is having a hard time in jail."

"She must be terrified," Helen said.

"I called Mort's girlfriend, Amber Waves, and she agreed to meet me at the studio where she works part-time, teaching pole-dance fitness."

"You're kidding? Who takes those classes?"

"The women looked like soccer moms with a sprinkling of businesswomen on their lunch hour. Here. I videoed the interview with my iPhone. Amber was changing into her outfit. That's her voice you hear. She's in the dressing room."

Helen watched the grainy video. Phil wasn't in it. He'd aimed the camera at the slatted dressing-room door. She saw a dance floor with mirrors and a ballet barre along one wall. Four poles ran down the center of the room.

"Are you really a detective, Phil?" Amber asked. Her voice was soft and teasing. The hackles rose on the back of Helen's neck.

"Licensed and everything," he said.

"And your partner saw *Rock of Ages* and liked it?" Amber asked.

"Loved it," Phil said. "We both did. The pole dancing at the Venus Club was amazing."

"Well, what does your partner think of this?" Amber said, and threw open the dressing-room door.

"Uh," Phil said.

"It's my movie outfit," she said.

Amber was curvier than Trish. Her honey blond curls swept past her shoulders. She probably had more hair than clothes. She wore a retro black bikini sparkling with sequins, and ankle-strap heels.

"Well?" she asked, thrusting her hips forward. "Do you think your partner would like me in this?" She stuck out her long slender legs, put her hand on her hip and twirled. Most of her well-toned bottom was exposed.

Helen growled.

"Uh, my partner is my wife," Phil said. "She'd look good in that outfit."

"Nice save," Helen said to her husband. Was he sweating?

"Oh. So you're married," Amber said. Helen heard her disappointment.

"Very," Phil said. "I'm investigating Mort's murder. I understand you used to date."

Amber reached into the dressing room for a white terry robe and slipped it on. "I did. Are you going to ask me where I was at the time of the murder, like in the movies?"

"Okay," Phil said, "where were you?"

"Here. Teaching a class for charity." She handed him a flyer advertising the event and a sign-in sheet, dated the day of Mort's murder, with a list of names.

"Thanks. This makes my job easier," Phil said. "Tell me about you and Mort."

"We were going to get married once his divorce was final."

"How long did you go out?" Phil asked.

"You have to understand, I never date married men," Amber said. "As a pole specialist, I met a lot of unhappy husbands at the club where I worked."

"A pole specialist?" Helen said. "I bet."

"Hey," Phil said. "That's what she calls herself. Deal with it."

"Mort came to the club often," Amber said. "He was so generous and so unhappy, well, our love just happened. He knew I wanted to leave the club. He helped pay for my dancing lessons and hired a professional photographer to take head shots that showed my full range. He even paid for a video. He found me a good agent, not some sleaze. That's how I got the part in *Rock of Ages*.

"He wanted to finance my pole-dancing fitness studio. Pole dancing is a difficult discipline. It's Pilates, yoga and ballet all rolled into one."

What position is that hip thrust? Helen thought. She didn't dare say anything.

"Mort was so invested in my career, I thought we'd play house and open the studio once he left Trish. We would have, too, if it hadn't been for that stupid cat."

"Justine?" Phil said.

"Yes. That cat groomer, Jan Kurtz, wormed her way into Mort's life, telling him she could help Justine be a Gold Cup Cat Show national winner. He started spending less time with me, but I didn't notice. I was busy with the movie. I met Tom Cruise when we made *Rock of Ages*. He plays the rocker, Stacee Jaxx. Tom is the nicest man. Those tattoos he wore in the movie were fake and he'd get so sweaty they'd come off. Juli—that's Julianne Hough—she was Sherrie, the small-town girl. She said I was a marvelous dancer."

"So, which pole dancer were you?" Phil said. "There were five."

"Pole specialist," she said. "My part wound up on the cutting-room floor. You're the only person who knows, except for my mom and my agent. I got paid and everything. And there's no shame in being cut. Juli and Tom did an incredible pole dance to 'Rock You Like a Hurricane' that was cut from the cinema release. But you can see it on the extended-cut Blu-ray version."

Phil quickly tap-danced back to the topic.

"Your secret is safe with me," he said. "But while you were working on your career, this Jan Kurtz worked on making Justine into a champion."

"Right. She has a job with a big-time breeder. Next thing I knew, Mort told me he was engaged to Jan. She'd signed a prenup giving him custody of Justine."

Phil made a sympathetic noise. Amber sniffed back tears. A bit too dramatically, Helen thought.

"Mort was a good, decent man. He fell for Jan, and she killed him."

Helen wished she could have seen Phil's face when Amber dropped that bomb.

"Why would Jan kill him?" Phil said. "They were getting married."

"He changed his will," Amber said. "He left half his money to Jan, his future wife. A cat groomer will inherit millions. You do the math."

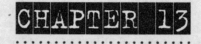

CHAPTER 13

Thursday

"The Coronado is saved. Come on down and celebrate!" Peggy called. Their neighbor knocked on Helen and Phil's office door to invite them down by the pool, the scene of so many sunset salutes.

"Party hearty!" Pete the parrot said. He looked like a feather corsage perched on Peggy's shoulder. She looked relieved and happy.

"I've got wine, cheese and appetizers. It's party time," she said.

"That pink sundress looks stunning with your red hair," Helen said.

"Thanks. Daniel's picking me up in an hour, but I want to celebrate this good news now. Let's call Elsie."

"Not a good idea," Helen said, and told her why. "We're playing it by ear, waiting to see if Margery says anything about forgiving Elsie. Now let's get that drink."

"And the appetizers," Phil said. "I'm hungry."

Margery was already by the pool, loading her plate with hummus, olives, cheese, chips and crackers spread out on the umbrella table. Beer and white wine with a real cork sweated in a tub of ice.

"You look gorgeous, Margery," Phil said, and kissed her cheek.

Their landlady wore a striking, long, lilac tie-dyed caftan and earrings the size of coasters. Cigarette smoke circled her like an enchanted spell.

The hard-frost Margery of last night was gone, but Helen felt the barbed wire and Keep Out signs guarding the subject of Zach and Elsie.

Pete eyed the appetizers and edged toward them.

"Can he have a cracker?" Helen asked.

"He can have a carrot," Peggy said, and handed him one from the hummus platter. "He's an ounce overweight."

Pete dropped the carrot on the concrete.

"Bad," he said.

"I agree," Helen said. "Margery, what's that big brown patch in your lawn?"

"The weed killer worked," she said. "The dollarweed is dead. I still have more to kill under the palm tree. When the construction is finished I'll resod the yard. How are you doing with the cat woman?"

"It's bizarre." Helen cut herself a generous slice of cheddar and slid it onto a cracker. "Trish treats her cat like a kid. No, an only child. The cat has her own room."

"Sad," Peggy said. "I like cats, but they're not children."

"The client knows that," Margery said. "It's just her way of saying, 'I have something in my life that's lots of trouble but makes me happy.' How you and Phil can stand that yowling flea bag is a mystery to me."

"Thumbs is cute and cuddly, but I'd never treat him like a kid," Helen said.

"Oh yeah? You defrosted shrimp for Junior. He

howled all afternoon till you babied him. I don't know which was worse, the cat or the jackhammer."

"Maybe I can take him to work with me," Phil said.

"Aw, what the heck, the construction will have this place torn up for weeks," Margery said. "I'll put up with your cat if you'll put up with the Coronado."

"Deal," Helen said.

"You've saved a bit of Old Florida from the developers," Peggy said. "Thank you!"

"To Margery!" they cried, and raised their glasses.

Their cheers died as a long black shadow darkened their table. A man with a gray suit and a grim voice asked, "Which one of you is Margery Flax?"

He looked like a fire hydrant with a bad haircut—short, stout and no-necked, with bristly brown hair.

"I am," Margery said. "Who are you?"

"Detective Millard Whelan, Crimes Against Persons, Snakehead Bay Police. Do you know a Zachariah Flax?" he asked.

Margery's eyes flashed and her nostrils flared. Uh-oh, Helen thought. She's getting mad all over again.

"He's my ex-husband," Margery said. "What about him?" She blew a cloud of smoke at the detective.

"When's the last time you saw him?" Detective Whelan asked.

"Last night," Margery said.

"Did you have dinner together at Beachie's seafood restaurant?" he asked.

"I didn't intend that. A misguided . . . matchmaker arranged that. Zach had a drink. He didn't stay for dinner. Neither did I."

"Did you have an altercation and throw a glass of wine in his face?"

"Two glasses," Margery said. "I divorced the SOB and never wanted to see him again. I wanted to make sure he got the message. What's he done now?"

Helen sat frozen, wishing she could find some way to shut up Margery.

"Did you kill him?" Detective Whelan asked.

"What?"

Margery's eyes widened. Helen felt like someone had walloped her with the wine bottle. Zach was dead? She didn't dare look at Phil or Peggy.

"You heard me," the detective said. "Did you kill him?"

"No," Margery said.

"He was found dead in his condo this morning," he said.

"Good!" Margery said. "He should have died years ago."

What's wrong with you? Helen thought. Quiet!

"It looks like he was poisoned," the detective said.

"Rat poison, no doubt," Margery said, narrowing her eyes. She stubbed out her cigarette in a tin ashtray. "Look, Detective, if you're expecting me to burst into tears, it ain't gonna happen. He's been out of my life for thirty years. Recently, he tried to worm his way back in, but I made it clear we were through. I don't need a seventy-six-year-old stalker."

"What caused that brown spot on your lawn?"

Helen nearly got whiplash from the abrupt switch in topics.

"Weed killer," Margery said. "Are we finished?"

"For now." Detective Whelan stalked out, leaving the Coronado celebrants stunned silent.

"Bye!" Pete said, nervously patrolling Peggy's shoulder.

"What was that about?" Peggy said.

"Damn Zach. I knew he'd come to no good end," Margery said, trying to light another cigarette with shaking fingers. Phil took the lighter out of her hands and lit the Marlboro for her. She took a deep drag, then said, "Why the hell did he have to screw up my life again?"

Phil refilled Margery's wineglass and said, "Margery, this is serious. Zach was poisoned. They've figured out he was at Beachie's, and you had a very public fight with him there and he walked out."

"So? He didn't eat anything. How could I poison him?"

"He drank that glass of wine," Phil said. "The wine that was sitting at his place for some time. You could have put poison in it."

"Anybody see me?" she said, defiant.

"Maybe not. But they sure as hell saw the fight and the wine tossing."

"Zach didn't look good when he left," Helen said. "He stumbled, and Peg, the server, caught him. I'm sure she told the police."

"That doesn't look good, either. You need to hire a lawyer," Phil said. "I recommend Nancie Hays."

"The hell I will," Margery said. "I'm not paying some shark five hundred an hour."

"Then at least retain us to investigate Zach's murder. That way the police can't question us. Anything we know will be confidential under Florida law."

"You can't beat our price," Helen said. "We're free."

"Oh no," Margery said. "I'm no charity case."

"Give us a dollar to seal the deal," Phil said. "Helen will get the paperwork now. We'll work out the money later."

Helen didn't give their landlady a chance to say no. She ran upstairs for a standard contract and a pen.

"Sign here," she said.

Margery signed, dusting the contract with cigarette ash. Peggy witnessed, then said, "Pete and I are going in. Daniel will be here any minute."

"Night," Pete said.

"Helen and I are starting our investigation tonight," Phil said. "If the detective is asking about weed killer,

I'm assuming he believes that's what poisoned Zach. Who do you think killed him?"

"I haven't a clue," Margery said. "Like I said, he's been out of my life for decades."

"What about Daisy, the woman he was living with?" Helen asked. "He split up with her after thirty years. Would she kill him?"

Margery shook her head and exhaled a long stream of smoke. "Daisy Detmer? I don't think so," she said. "From what I remember of Daisy, she wouldn't touch a fly. Unless it was unzipped."

Ouch, Helen thought. No hurt feelings there.

"Maybe Zach committed suicide after being rejected by you," Phil said.

Margery's laugh was hard and ugly. "Do you really think I'm the kind of woman men die for?" she asked. "Whoever heard of a wrinkled femme fatale?"

"Okay, then tell us who killed Zach," Phil said. "What pops into your mind?"

"One of his drug-dealing buddies," Margery said. "Thick as thieves, and that's what they were. I think he ripped one off when he left town suddenly after the feds showed up here."

"Do you remember their names?"

"Those bums? I went out of my way to forget them."

Helen was frustrated with Margery's stubborn refusal to help. "Do you have any of Zach's things?" she asked. "Didn't you say the lawyer gave you back a cardboard box of Zach's belongings from 1983? One he never picked up."

"That's in the hall closet," Margery said.

"Dig it out," Phil said. "We're driving up to Delray Beach tonight to meet Daisy."

Delray is one of the beach towns dotting South Florida's east coast like a string of pearls. Some forty miles north of Fort Lauderdale, downtown Delray is a pleasant mix of low-rise restaurants and high-end shops, prettily painted and draped with bougainvillea.

Daisy lived in a bungalow about three blocks west of downtown, with an actual picket fence. It was periwinkle, and the cottage was turquoise trimmed in hot pink. Tropical plants and red and yellow flowers rioted in the yard.

"Let's hope she's home," Helen said, and then rang the doorbell.

Daisy answered the door, looking like she'd escaped from her own garden. She wore a long, black sleeveless dress dotted with giant red poppies. She had a pleasant round face, a plump body, and fluffy gray-blond hair. She held a Diet Coke. Helen could hear a television in the living room.

"Well, hello," Daisy said, fluttering her eyelashes at Phil. "What are you doing on my doorstep?"

Daisy might be in her mid-seventies, but she was still a flirt. Phil flirted right back. "I'm glad you're home," he said. "I'm a private eye."

"That's exciting," Daisy said. "I've never met one before."

"Well, now you get to meet two," Phil said. "I'm Phil Sagemont and this is my partner, Helen Hawthorne."

He didn't mention we're married, Helen noticed. He'll probably get more out of Daisy that way.

"Nice to meet you, Helen," Daisy said, but it sounded like "Get lost, will you?"

"I'd like to talk to you about Zach Flax," Phil said. "He listed this as his address."

"He doesn't live here now. Moved out six months ago. Ancient history," Daisy said, making it clear she was free for Phil.

Helen tried to hide her surprise. Daisy didn't know Zach was dead.

"We've been told Zach is well-off," Phil said.

"Zach's good at impressing people," Daisy said. "Not as good at making and keeping money."

"Can we come in to discuss him?"

"It's a nice night," Daisy said. "Let's sit out in the yard."

It was a warm, steamy night, but Daisy was no fool. She wasn't going to let two strangers inside, even a handsome silver-haired one like Phil.

She shut the screen door and led the private eyes to a black wrought-iron table on the lawn. Mosquitoes whined in the sticky night air.

"I haven't seen Zach in a while," she said. "He borrowed three thousand dollars from me, so I don't expect to see him any time soon."

You won't, Helen thought. Ever again.

"He bought an expensive condo in Snakehead Bay," Phil said.

"He's missed two mortgage payments," Daisy said. "He spent the money on a lawyer instead. I gave him the three thou, but that man's in a boatload of trouble." She took a long drink of cold Diet Coke. Helen was thirsty, but didn't dare ask for a drink and interrupt Daisy.

"Isn't his Zen Cat Tower business doing well?" Phil asked.

"It was until he got the cease-and-desist order from the company that made the original version," Daisy said. "He stole his Zen Cat Tower from a design sold by the big-box stores. Copied it right down to the suede cushions, and the company is threatening a suit. The bank is about to foreclose on his Snakehead Bay condo."

"Are you married?" Phil asked.

"No, thank goodness," Daisy said. "I've made a lot of dumb mistakes, but I didn't tie myself down to Zach and his problems. It's bad enough I lived with him all those years.

"He wanted me to move in with him. I have to take care of my Aunt Tillie. This is her home. She's quite old, and I'm her only relative. I can't leave a sick woman. She needs me.

"I kicked him out, and now I'm enjoying being a single lady. Got that big old bed to myself. No old guy shuffling around the house, demanding dinner at six, snoring all night. It's quieter without him. More fun, too."

Fun? Helen thought. Taking care of a sick person?

"I love dancing," Daisy said. "That's my real interest. Do you dance?"

"Sometimes," Phil said.

Never, Helen thought.

"I take ballroom and salsa dancing lessons at the Coral Room, a fabulous ballroom built in the thirties. They say Fred and Ginger danced there. It's worth the drive to Fort Lauderdale. It's my one free night. Aunt Tillie sleeps, and I go with a regular group of women every Friday. Fun-loving women, if you know what I mean."

She winked at Phil and patted his hand. "You should join us. Handsome guy like you would go far."

I bet, Helen thought.

"You'd have a good time, too, honey," she said to Helen.

"You know what I like about dancing? You can rent a good man. Lessons with a professional dance partner cost me a hundred dollars an hour. That may sound like a lot, but I get a man who devotes his attention to me for a full hour. Does whatever I want.

"It's cheaper than living with a man full-time who ignored me. And when I get tired of him, he goes home."

CHAPTER 14

Friday

*B*rat-brat-brat-braaat! Screeech! Screeeeeeeech!

The power tool shriek sent Helen rocketing out of bed. "Construction this early?" she said. "What are those bozos doing?"

"*Merf!*" said a grumpy Thumbs. He'd been sleeping on Helen's feet when she sat up and accidentally booted him across the bed.

"It's six fifty-seven," Phil said. "Almost time for you to get up, anyway. Of course the workers are starting early. It's hurricane season. The contractor wants to get the Coronado finished in case a major storm hits."

"Well, at least I'll get to work on time today." Helen peered through the mini blinds. "Nice sunny morning. Margery's in the yard, spraying dollarweed again. I'll get dressed and take my breakfast outside."

"Make sure she doesn't spray you," Phil said. "I miss our usually cool landlady."

"She's still in love with Zach," Helen said. "She can't admit it, even to herself."

"If you say so, Doctor Phil," he said.

Helen, freshly showered and ready for work, carried her coffee and toast out by the pool. She loved South Florida's soft mornings, with the silvery skies and slightly salty tang of the ocean.

The hard-hatted workers stopped chipping and hammering at the Coronado's cracked and pitted face and stared at her. She waved, and the men went back to their noisy work. Upstairs, she saw Sal Steer, the beef-faced boss, pointing to the cracks around the window in 2C, Helen and Phil's office.

Helen watched their landlady spray the dollarweed with the built-in nozzle on a square plastic jug of weed killer, working with savage intensity. Margery wasn't her usual stylish self. Nobody wore good clothes to kill weeds, but her purple shorts and top had escaped from a rag bag. Her normally shiny, swingy gray hair was flat and uncombed, and she had a cigarette clamped in her teeth. Helen thought she looked slightly demented.

"Morning," Helen said, and took her last gulp of coffee. *Squirt. Squirt.* "Did you see Daisy last night?" Margery asked. "Did you learn anything?"

"She still doesn't know Zach is dead," Helen said. "She tried to hit on Phil."

"As old and wrinkled as she is? Fat chance," Margery said, with a sneer. "What did she say when you told her Zach was dead?"

"We decided to let the police handle that," Helen said. "We learned more this way."

"You two still bent on drumming up business for that lawyer of yours?"

"Nancie doesn't need us to find her work," Helen said.

"You going to offer me more advice for my own good?" It was a challenge.

"Margery, what's wrong?" Helen asked. "Did I say something that offended you?"

"Nothing," she said. "Everything is just— Oh, hell. Here's that snake from Snakehead Bay."

"I'll stay here with you," Helen said.

Detective Whelan moved through the yard like an approaching storm—thick, solid, unstoppable.

"Morning, ladies," he said, and nodded. "Mrs. Flax, I have a few more questions." He took out a small notebook with a pen stuck in the spiral top.

"It's Ms.," Margery said. She plunked her weed killer on the table, dangerously close to Helen's breakfast, folded her arms and glared defiantly at the detective.

"Your husband, Zachariah Flax—"

"Ex-husband," Margery corrected.

"How long has it been since you've seen him?" the detective asked.

"You asked that last night. I kicked him out some thirty years ago, after I found out he'd been running drugs with his fishing charter boat. I got that news from the feds. He took off with some floozy."

Daisy's a floozy? Helen thought. That's harsh.

"I divorced him in 'eighty-four. He didn't show up in court. My lawyer did service by publication. I didn't see him again until this Monday, when he showed up here with a big bunch of flowers, saying he loved me. I threw him out on his posies."

The detective dutifully made notes, then asked, "Have you placed any phone calls to him?"

"Never. I don't have his phone number," Margery said.

Another note. "Then how did you arrange to meet him at Beachie's restaurant Thursday night?" he asked.

"I didn't," Margery said. "I was tricked into that meeting."

"What is your relationship with the person who arranged the meeting?" he asked.

"I've known Elsie since grade school," Margery said. "We're ex-friends now."

"Why would Elsie arrange the meeting?"

"Because she's a meddling old fool," Margery said. "She's going senile. Her son wants to put her in assisted living."

Helen winced. Poor Elsie. She didn't deserve that. Detective Whelan wrote down her answer.

Out of the corner of her eye, Helen saw Phil run upstairs to their office. He talked briefly to the boss and the worker chipping out the rust-discolored stucco under the window. He started to unlock the door, then stopped to watch the detective interrogate Margery instead.

"Now I've got a question for you, Detective," Margery said. "Do you think I poisoned my ex at that restaurant?"

"I never said that," Detective Whelan said.

"A blind woman can see where you're going," Margery said. "I didn't kill him. He's been dead to me for years."

"That's not what Zachariah Flax thought," the detective said. "He wanted to get back with you."

"How do you know what he thought?" Margery said. "He's dead."

Please shut up, Helen prayed.

"Ms. Flax, do you understand how many witnesses heard your altercation at Beachie's? I've talked with four so far, including your server. She says the victim, Zachariah Flax, insisted she be his witness, and he got down on his knees in the restaurant."

Whelan paged through his notebook, then read in a monotone, "'Margery, I love you. Come back to me. I'll love you for the rest of my life.'"

The effect was comical, but Helen didn't smile.

"She says you responded, 'With any luck, that won't be long.' Did you say that, Ms. Flax?"

"I did," Margery said. "I wanted to make it clear to

him that our marriage—and any so-called romance—
was over for me."

"Really?" he said, drawing the word out as if he didn't
believe her. "Because from what I heard, you had a lot of
heat for no fire. You basically told him he should drop dead,
and that night he does. An amazing coincidence."

Margery's eyes glowed with anger, and her words
came fast and furious. "You want to know if I poisoned
him? Go check the restaurant's surveillance video system. Beachie's has to have one. Those cameras are everywhere. You'll see for yourself I didn't poison him."

Silence. Even the construction work was quiet. Helen
studied her toast crumbs and wished Margery could get
control of herself.

"Did you check the surveillance video at the restaurant?" the landlady demanded. "Well?"

"I don't answer questions, Ms. Flax," he said, closing
his notebook. "You do. This interview has left me with
more questions. I'll be back. I promise."

He stalked up the stairs toward Phil. Helen saw her
husband shaking his head. He must be telling Detective
Whelan that he couldn't talk to him and neither could
his PI partner.

"You asked a good question, Margery," Helen said.
"I'll get Phil to check the restaurant surveillance video
for you. Did you find that box of Zach's papers?"

"I dug it out last night."

"I'll carry it up to Phil now," Helen said.

"I can take it myself," Margery said. "I'm no helpless
old lady. You'll have it as soon as that detective leaves."

Helen started up the stairs to the office. Now Detective Whelan was talking to Sal. "That's right, Detective,"
he said. "I'm in charge of this project."

Helen slipped into the Coronado Investigations office, closing the door carefully so the glass slats in the
jalousie door wouldn't rattle.

"Hey, there," Phil said. "How's it going?"

"Just fine," she said. She mimed listening at the door, and they both eavesdropped on Whelan's interview with Sal Steer.

"Yes, I was here on Monday," he said. "My crew wasn't. I'd given Ms. Flax my evaluation of her building's rebar problem. I told her there was extensive damage. The rebar—that's the reinforcing steel bars."

"I know," the detective interrupted.

"This building has been exposed to salty sea air for more than sixty years, and the rebar has started to expand and flake from rust. You can see the damage around the window on this unit here. That's just a small example."

Helen thought she heard the scratch of the detective's pen on his notepad.

"My company is qualified to do the remedial work," Sal said. "Faulty concrete repair can worsen the structural problems, you know."

"Yes," the detective said. He sounded impatient.

"I discussed the corrective measures that we'd need to take. Ms. Flax seemed shocked by the state of the building's deterioration as well as the price of the restoration."

"How much will it cost to repair?" Detective Whelan asked.

"More than a hundred thousand dollars," Sal said. "When I told her that, she said she couldn't afford it. She was going to sell out to a developer. This is a valuable piece of real estate, Detective. They'd have to tear down the building, of course, but land this close to downtown is worth a pretty penny.

"I was concerned Ms. Flax was making her decision too quickly. I wanted to discuss it with her further, but then the white-haired gentleman showed up with an enormous bouquet of flowers, and I stayed, hoping I could talk with her after he left."

And to watch the show, Helen thought.

"She called him Zach, and she didn't seem happy to see him," he said.

"What did they discuss?" the detective asked.

"It was quite heated," he said. "I gathered they used to be married and he'd been gone some time. Now he wanted to come back. Ms. Flax was very angry and the discussion ended violently."

"How?"

"She hit him."

With a bouquet of flowers, Helen wanted to scream.

"He was bleeding," Sal added.

His cheek was scratched! Helen had to fight to keep from running outside and telling Detective Whelan what she'd seen. Phil looked at her and shook his head, warning her to stay out of it.

"Zach said he wanted to come back to her, but Ms. Flax said, 'There's not enough room in South Florida for both of us.' She threatened to call the police, and he left. I left right after that.

"The next day, Ms. Flax called me. She said she'd changed her mind and wanted me to fix the building."

"Did she say why she changed her mind?" Detective Whelan asked.

"No."

"Do you know where she got the money?"

"No. She wrote me a check for half the estimate, fifty thousand dollars. I cashed it and the work started today."

"Thank you, Mr. Steer. That will be all for now."

Helen and Phil heard footsteps on the cracked stairs. Phil looked out the window. "They're both gone."

"That no-good Sal," Helen said. "Twisting Margery's words."

"There's nothing we can do but find Zach's real killer," Phil said. "Did Margery find the box of Zach's unclaimed papers?"

"Yes," Helen said.

"I'd better get it before the detective comes back here with a search warrant for her apartment. And you'd better run. You're going to be late at the cattery."

"I can't believe my job is making me late for work," Helen said.

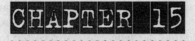

CHAPTER 15

. . . .

Friday

Helen slid into the cattery like a base runner reaching home plate.

"Safe!" Jan said. "But cutting it close. Another sixty seconds and Dee would have flown in here."

"On her broom?" Helen asked.

"Careful," Jan said. "I can't afford to have you fired. I can't do tomorrow's show alone. Not with two cats."

"The traffic gods were with me," Helen said.

"I do have bad news, though," Jan said.

"What?" Helen's voice was a croak. Was she going to be fired after the show, before she learned anything that could help Trish?

"Dee says she doesn't need you Sunday. She and I can handle that day. We will need you to help set up and groom Saturday and come in at six Monday morning to help wash Red and Chessie for the Hasher School Pet Appreciation Day."

"Why the change in the show plans?" Helen asked.

"She saw the entry and judges lists. Dee knows the Sunday judges and thinks her cats will win."

Helen tried to hide her relief. She could help Phil with Margery's case on Sunday. They were sure the police would arrest their landlady any moment.

"Do you know who the Saturday judges are?" Helen asked.

"Sure. Here's the schedule, downloaded from the Internet." Jan handed her a fat printout. "It has the cat classes and breeds."

Helen scanned the list and saw Lexie Deener, the cat-show judge Mort had been giving financial advice to, was judging on Saturday. She had the longhair championships in Ring Two, including Maine Coons and Persians.

"Red and Chessie are entered in the solid-color division," Jan said.

"Dee's going to let her cats compete against each other?" Helen asked.

"No, Red's spayed," Jan said. "Cat shows allow altered adults to be shown in the Premiership Class. Dog shows don't permit that. Their champions are supposed to be breeders."

"So, what's the plan today?" Helen said. After work, she and Phil were going undercover to the Coral Room, where Daisy went ballroom dancing, and she didn't want to be fiddling with cats all evening.

"We'll comb the cats who won't be shown, then pack the van for the show. While you, lucky girl, clean the litter boxes, I'll pick up the cat curtains at the dry cleaner."

"Cat curtains?" Helen looked at the tall windows where the four cats—silvery-soft Mystery, fiery Red, snow-white Chessie and Chocolate, the delicious brown beauty, sunned themselves on their shelves. "You put curtains on these windows?"

"No, these are cage curtains," Jan said. "Start combing Chocolate. I'll take Mystery and explain. Here, little girl." Mystery buried her pale gray head in Jan's thick, dark hair, and Jan carried her to a grooming table.

"*Merp!*" Chocolate protested when Helen picked her up. She didn't like leaving her sunny spot, but soon began luxuriating in the soft strokes of the comb. Chocolate closed her coppery-gold eyes and let Helen groom her.

"At the shows, the cats are displayed in cages on long folding tables—benches—while they wait their turns in the judging ring," Jan said, pulling a clump of gray fur off her comb. "Each cage is like a miniature stage to show off the cats. Most cages are decorated with signs, toys and curtains. Dee's cage curtains are custom-made and have to be dry-cleaned."

"Must be some cages," Helen said.

"They're little jewel boxes," Jan said. "Some breeders rent wire cages, but Dee has pop-up cages with mesh sides. Chessie has a black show cage with blue curtains. With a blue-eyed white, that combination is devastating. It really showcases her eyes. Red has a deep blue cage with copper curtains that make her eyes glow."

"Do the judges like the cages?" Helen asked.

"They never see them," Jan said. "But they're a good way to get your cattery's name in front of the spectators, especially if you're selling kittens or have a stud."

Jan finished combing Mystery and set her on her carpeted shelf. Helen started to pick up Chocolate, but the Persian said, "*Merr?*" and patted Helen's arm with one paw.

"What's she want?" Helen asked.

"She wants to stay on the grooming table and watch you," she said. Mystery jumped off her shelf and patted Helen's sneaker.

"And what can I do for you, Your Majesty?" Helen asked.

"Lift her up and put her next to Chocolate," Jan said. "They like to hang out together."

"She can't jump up?" Helen asked.

"Sure she can, but she'd rather you do it," Jan said.

Helen lifted up the fluffy gray-blue cat, who snuggled in her arms. "You're like a warm teddy bear," she said, scratching her soft silvery ears.

Mystery and Chocolate curled themselves into muffins to watch Helen empty and wash the litter boxes, while Jan had assembled a long row of cat supplies, then packed a soft-sided bag with treats, cornstarch, Q-tips, ear cleaner, tissues, cotton balls and more.

"Now what am I missing?" she said, half to herself.

"Cat litter?" Helen asked.

"No, they'll have that at the show," she said. "I'll load the van, so all we have to pack tomorrow are the cats. Show check-in starts at seven thirty a.m., so be here at six thirty sharp."

Helen tried not to groan. She had no idea how late they'd be out tonight.

"Hey, I have to come in at five thirty tomorrow to feed the cats," Jan said. "I'll get back from the dry cleaner about three thirty today, and we'll bathe both show cats."

"Why so late for the baths?" Helen asked.

"We're lucky Dee's letting us wash the cats the day before the show," Jan said. "Usually she makes us bathe them the morning of the show. That would mean getting here at three a.m."

Helen winced.

"This show is local. It gets really crazy when we have a road trip. You haven't lived until you've washed two cats in a hotel bathroom."

Jan returned from the dry cleaner at three thirty. "Bath time. You take Red," she said. "She's easy to work with. She'll need a vinegar rinse to get out every last bit of shampoo. I'll wash Chessie. Her white coat needs special treatment for a show."

The red Persian was on her window shelf, watching

cat TV, chirping at the birds gathered around the feeder and twitching her tail.

"Sorry, baby," Helen said, gathering the soft, fluffy cat into her arms. "We have to make you beautiful for the show."

"Merrr!" Red said, protesting slightly. Then she buried her soft head in Helen's shoulder and licked her neck with her sandpaper tongue.

"Thank you," Helen said. "So nice of you to groom me first."

She set Red on the grooming table and laid out her supplies, while Jan worked on Chessie. "Her fluffy white coat needs some extras at showtime," Jan said. "She'll get a special whitening shampoo and a vinegar rinse."

"That's a lot of work," Helen said.

"After a while, it becomes routine," Jan said. She worked on the cat with swift, practiced movements. Helen thought the contrast between Jan's black hair and Chessie's snowy whiteness was a picture in itself.

Helen was slower than Jan and had to spend extra time getting the soap out of Red's long fur. The two groomers finished combing and drying their cats about the same time.

The cats were gorgeous—and they knew it. Both posed on their tables: Red, a flaming beauty, and Chessie, a dazzling snowball.

"Look at them," Helen said. "Fire and ice!"

"Now we have to keep those coats pretty till tomorrow," Jan said. She took four paper coffee filters, folded each in half and shredded the center to make a hole big enough for a cat's head.

"Here's the scissors," Helen said. "You can cut a hole."

"Cutting will shear those beautiful ruffs," Jan said.

She pulled a filter over each cat's head. "There," she said. "That keeps off water and food stains. We're done."

"What about Midnight?" Helen asked.

"Damn, I knew I forgot something," Jan said. "Let's go round him up."

The black cat was in a mischievous mood. When he saw Helen, he jumped off the living-room couch and hid in the shadows by the cluster of palms. As she approached, he sprang out. She chased him down the hall, past the cat portraits and trophies and around the kitchen island.

"Herd him down the hall toward the cattery," Jan said.

Helen feinted as the cat tried to pass her by the fridge, and he ran past her down the hall.

Jan popped up, Midnight ducked into the guest bath and Jan slammed the door. Helen and Jan leaned against the wall, breathless.

"That little devil," Jan said, brushing her dark hair out of her eyes. "This is no time for his tricks. I've got to go home and feed my cat before I see Mom tonight."

Her cat? Jan said she didn't have a cat because she didn't have time for one.

"You open the door and I'll stand backup," Jan said.

Helen slowly opened the bathroom door, and Midnight stuck out his head.

"Gotcha!" Helen said, and clamped her hands around his furry black body.

"Mrrrow!" he said. Helen held him tightly, hoping he wouldn't scratch her. Midnight kept his claws sheathed but whipped her arm with his tail. Back in the cattery, Midnight allowed her to comb him without running away.

Jan fed the cats, then rechecked her show list. Helen brooded on Jan's comment about feeding her cat at home. That was the second time she'd mentioned a cat she supposedly didn't own.

Did Jan kidnap Justine after she killed Mort?

According to Amber, Mort's former lover, his fiancée stood to inherit half his substantial fortune. The five hundred thousand Jan got for Justine's ransom would also help her start over in style—and get some cash from Trish, who'd sneered at her as the Other Woman.

I need to get into Jan's home for a look, Helen thought.

When Jan carried the clean litter boxes out to the van, Helen noticed her purse waiting on the counter. Helen removed Jan's wallet and stashed it in her own purse. Just in time. Jan was back in the cattery.

"All our work is done. It's five thirty. I'm ready to go," Jan said.

"Me, too," Helen said. "I'll duck into the bathroom. See you here tomorrow, bright and early."

She waited until Jan left, then got in the Igloo and checked Jan's address on her license. She lived in an apartment on Seventeenth Street, on Helen's way home.

She called Jan's cell phone. "I found your wallet in the driveway," Helen said.

"Oh, lordy, it must have fallen out of my purse," Jan said.

"I'll drop it by on my way home," Helen said.

"No! I mean, that's okay. You can give it to me tomorrow," Jan said.

"And what if you're stopped by the police?" Helen said. "You don't have a license, checkbook or credit cards."

"Well, okay," Jan said. She recited her address. "I'm in unit two, next to the manager's apartment." She sounded reluctant. Helen was doubly suspicious.

Jan lived in a grim beige eight-unit apartment building with a parking lot and a scraggly palm tree. Helen rang the doorbell to her ground-floor unit, and Jan answered quickly. She blocked the entrance, but Helen thought she saw movement behind her. Something gray and catlike.

Justine? Was the search over? Helen had to know.

"Here's your wallet," she said, and pretended to stumble against the door.

A gray-striped tabby came streaking out the front door. Helen captured the cat and it sliced her arm.

"Ow!" she said.

"Get in here," Jan said, and pulled them both inside.

"Now you know my secret," she said, taking the big, green-eyed tabby from Helen. "This is Grover," she said, scratching the cat's thick fur. His eyes were dramatically outlined in black stripes and his nose looked like a red rubber eraser.

She hugged him. "I love him, but my landlady doesn't allow pets. She'll make me give him away."

CHAPTER 16

Friday

"A toast!" Margery said. "A toast to the lucky grass widow! Hey, Helen. Come join us!"

Their landlady slouched in a chaise, her purple caftan hanging crookedly off one shoulder. She waved at Helen with a wide, sloppy swing and the wine sloshed in her glass.

Phil hunched in his chair, his face creased with concern. Margery's cigarette was burning the arm of her chaise. Phil ground it out on the concrete. Their landlady didn't notice, but Helen did.

"Margery, are you okay?" She hurried over to them.

"On topsh the world," Margery said, her words slurred. "My darling ex-husband left me his condo. I'm an heiress of a luxsh—a luxsher—a luxury condo in beautiful Snakehead Bay. Sweets for the sweet! Snakes for the snake! I got the good news from Zachie boy's lawyer this afternoon."

"That's good," Helen said.

"Why?" Margery glared at Helen. "What's good about it? He's behind on the mortgage, the four-flusher."

"Because as soon as the police release the condo, Phil and I can search it for clues and find out who really killed him."

"Be my guest," Margery said. "Maybe you'll have better luck than old Phil here today. He says there are no surveillance cameras inside the restaurant except by the cash register. So nobody saw me not poison the son of a bitch."

"You look tired, Margery," Helen said.

"I'm not tired," she said. "I'm drunk. Say it! You're drunk, Margery."

"Come on, Margery," Helen said. "Let's go inside. Phil will help."

Phil took Margery's liver-spotted hands and pulled her up out of the chaise. Margery flung her arms around him.

"You've got some shoulders on you, boy," she said, as they walked toward her apartment. "Just like Zach. Been a long time since I've felt a young man's arms around me. You gonna carry me over the threshold? That's what Zach did. Carried me over the threshold and then broke my heart. Well, he's dead now and I'm dead drunk. In the morning, he'll still be dead and I'll be . . ."

Margery's voice wobbled, then stopped. Two tears, then four, then a bitter rainstorm ran down her wrinkled face. Helen had never seen their landlady cry. Her heart ached for the pain she must feel.

She opened Margery's door, rushed inside and pulled back the purple bedcovers. Phil gently settled Margery on the lavender sheets. She was asleep by the time Helen tucked the covers around her.

She held Phil's hand all the way back to their apartments. "I'll change into my dancing clothes and meet you out here in twenty minutes," she said. "Don't forget to feed Thumbs."

She was ready in fifteen. Helen felt odd teetering around in three-inch ankle straps after wearing shorts and sneakers, but Phil's reaction made it worthwhile.

"Wow!" he said. "You look dazzling."

Helen liked how her wide-legged silk palazzo pants swirled when she walked and her silver spaghetti-strap top showed off her well-toned arms. Evidently, cat lifting was good exercise. She'd added a black-and-silver belt and long, dangly earrings for her night of dancing.

"You look pretty handsome yourself," she said. "I can't remember the last time you wore a jacket and tie."

"Miss Sherry's Academy of Dance taught me well," he said.

"You took dance lessons?" Helen said.

"Until I was twelve. My mom insisted," Phil said.

"I wish I could dance," Helen said. "My grandma was a lovely dancer. I have two left feet."

"Just follow the beat and your partner's lead," he said, and took her in his arms. He hummed "I Only Have Eyes for You," and they danced along the narrow sidewalk in front of their adjoining apartments.

"I wish we could dance here all night," Helen said. "But we have to go to the Coral Room to find out more about Daisy, Zach's old flame. I'll meet you there."

"We'll learn more if we go separately," Phil reminded her.

Helen wished she were riding with Phil. Driving in those wide pants was difficult. She pulled the floaty fabric up past her knees to keep her pants from tangling in the brake and accelerator pedals.

At least it was a quick trip. The Coral Room was an Art Deco ballroom on Federal Highway. Outside, the old building featured flashing coral neon. Its sign was a landmark—a tuxedoed man dancing with a sophisticated thirties woman in a long ruffled dress.

Outside the vast ballroom, men and women in elegant

dress lined up, many carrying bags with their dancing shoes. Helen remembered her grandmother's dancing shoes. Their suede soles never touched a sidewalk.

As she entered, Helen heard a recording of "This Can't Be Love." Some people in line were tapping their toes, anxious to start. Helen guessed the women outnumbered the men by five to one, and, at forty-one, she was one of the youngest. Dresses ranged from short cocktail frocks with flirty skirts to evening gowns. The men wore anything from Hawaiian shirts to suits.

She paid her ten-dollar fee and got her ticket for a free drink. The ballroom was a step back in time: five thousand square feet of beautifully cared-for hardwood, surrounded by small black tables and chairs. The bandstand was empty, and the walls were decorated with framed autographed photos and posters of Glenn Miller, Benny Goodman, Frank Sinatra, even Fred and Ginger. They'd all headlined at the Coral Room.

Helen saw Phil dancing with Daisy. She envied the two of them gracefully gliding around the floor. Phil winked at her, and when they whirled past he nodded toward the tables by the bar. Helen hoped that was the section claimed by Daisy's fun-loving lady friends. She ordered a club soda from the bar and sat at an empty table at the edge of the section.

The song ended and Des O'Connor sang "Red Roses for a Blue Lady." *That's a slow fox trot, if I remember right,* she thought. *And this is like high school. Once again, I'm a wallflower.*

But then a balding man in his seventies came over. "Care to dance?" he asked.

Saved! Helen thought. "I'd love to. But I'm a little rusty."

"A pretty lady like you?" he said. "I'll have you warmed up in no time." He smelled of bay rum, and his white shirt crackled with starch.

"My name's Helen," she said, as he led her onto the dance floor.

"Bob," he said, and those were the last words they exchanged. Helen stumbled and tried to right herself. Now she was off beat. Her feet couldn't follow his. Bob moved too fast for her, and then too slow. He held up his arm, and she gathered she was supposed to twirl. She tripped in her too-high heels.

That's when Bob dropped her hand like a dead fish and walked away.

Helen was abandoned on the dance floor.

This is worse than high school, Helen thought. Boys didn't dance with me then, but I've never been marooned on the floor before.

She stood like a statue while couples moved effortlessly to the music. Phil floated past with Daisy in rhinestones and ruffled hot pink chiffon. She was chattering and pointing at Helen.

I have to get off the floor, Helen thought.

She made her way back to her table, her face flaming with embarrassment, and sat down. Across from her, a stylish woman in her late sixties sipped a gin and tonic.

"I saw that," she said. "Bob abandoned you. That was rude."

"It's not his fault," Helen said. "I'm a terrible dancer."

"No, you're not," she said. "My name's Susan. Bob can dance, but he's not a good leader. That's the secret of a good ballroom dancer. A good leader will make his partner move in the right way, position his body so your feet naturally follow his. He gives his partner little physical cues so you'll know what to do. At the very least, he talks to you and tells you what he's going to do. Well, I'll talk to him, all right. He won't do that again."

"No, please," Helen said. "Just forget it. I'm fine. Really."

Susan was dressed like an experienced dancer in a

long, full-skirted silver chiffon dress and silver dancing shoes with two-inch heels.

"If I can give you one tip, your heels are too high," Susan said. "For ballroom dancing they should be around two inches. It's easier to stumble in higher heels."

"Do you dance a lot?" Helen asked, hoping to change the subject.

"Every Friday night," she said. "I'm with a group of women who love to dance, and this is the best ballroom in town. It has a 'floating' floor. There's cork or rubber under that wood. People think ballroom dancing is slow, but it's fast. Good exercise. And with the right partner, it's better than sex."

Helen wasn't sure about that.

"Don't let one bad experience spoil dancing for you," Susan said. "Get out there and dance with someone good, a real leader. Like that man with Daisy."

"The tall guy with the long silver-white hair?" Helen asked.

"Yes. Exactly. He's new here, but he's good," Susan said. "Go get him. Don't be shy. The widow Daisy isn't. She's glommed on to him like the last lifeboat on the *Titanic*."

"Daisy," Helen said. "Is she the woman in the ruffled pink dress?"

"You mean the dress two sizes too small?" Susan said. "That's her."

"Hot pink seems an odd color for a widow," Helen said.

"Oh, Daisy's not a real widow. She never married Zach, but they lived together for some thirty years. He just passed away. She called me today crying about how she'd lost the love of her life. Now she's dancing like she hasn't a care."

"Maybe she's trying to forget," Helen said.

"She's doing a good job," Susan said. "I guess I sound

witchy, but she bent my ear for ages, complaining about Zach. She could never get him to tie the knot. I got tired of listening to the same old song. 'Daisy,' I said, 'if he didn't say yes when you were young and pretty, why would he marry you now?'"

Ouch, Helen thought. Susan didn't mince words.

"Daisy lives with her elderly aunt and takes care of her. The old lady has promised Daisy her house when she passes. She even let Zach live there, but she insisted on separate bedrooms. Not many men will put up with that and a crotchety old invalid.

"Daisy finally told Zach, 'Either marry me or move out.' He moved out. But she still chased him. He loved her apple pies, and she baked them for him. I told her to get a backbone and tell him to get lost. But Zach came to her house way up in Delray Beach to pick up his pie. She was convinced she could charm him back into her bed."

That wasn't quite the story Daisy told us, Helen thought, but she'd hardly reveal her failed love life to two private eyes.

Dionne Warwick was singing "Night and Day." "That's a slow fox trot," Susan said. "You really should go tap on that new man's shoulder. Go ahead. Break in on him. Daisy's had him for three dances in a row. You're not supposed to hog a partner. Especially a scarce man."

Helen was still too mortified to go out on the dance floor again. Besides, Daisy might be giving Phil useful information. That's why they were here.

"Oh, too late," Susan said. "Nora got there first. Look at that! She tapped him on the shoulder, and Daisy won't let go. She's going to hang on to that man, no matter what. What nerve!"

Susan shook her head. "Daisy and men. She still acts like she's sixteen. Too bad she doesn't look sixteen. Well, soon we won't have to put up with Daisy for a while."

"Why?" Helen asked.

"She's leaving the country Tuesday."

"For good?" Helen said.

"Just for a month," Susan said. "She has a sister who lives in Sydney, Australia, who's turning sixty. Daisy's going to spend a whole month with her, seeing the sights while they're both well enough to travel. She says she hired someone to watch her aunt while she's gone. Daisy's taking a late-night flight to San Francisco, then heading for Sydney."

The song was over. "Hear that?" Susan said. "That's an international tango. I'm going to dance with the new man, and I'm not taking no for an answer."

Susan got her man. In fact, Phil looked relieved when she cut in and released him. Daisy retreated to the restroom, sulking.

No wonder Susan thought dancing was better than sex, Helen decided. That tango practically was sex, right on the dance floor. She tried not to feel jealous, especially when glamorous Susan whispered into Phil's ear when the dance ended.

She led him by the hand straight to Helen and said, "Phil, this is Helen, and she needs to dance with a good partner."

"My pleasure," Phil said. Buddy Greco was singing "Fly Me to the Moon." "Let's waltz," he said.

"I really am a bad dancer," she said.

"Just follow my lead," he said. "Put your arm here, and your feet like that, and talk to me."

"I saw Daisy staring when I got dumped," Helen said. "What did she say?"

"She said it doesn't make any difference how young and pretty you are; if you aren't a good dancer, no one wants you. I nearly left her right there."

"But you didn't," Helen said.

"A graduate of Miss Sherry's is always a gentleman," Phil said.

"Did Miss Sherry teach you that torrid tango?" Helen said.

"International tangos are easy dances for beginners," he said.

"What did you learn from Daisy?" Helen asked.

"She knows Zach is dead. She says she's going traveling to forget her loss."

"She's visiting her sister in Sydney," Helen said, and repeated her conversation with Susan.

"We didn't learn anything useful tonight," she said.

"I disagree," Phil said. "This is our third time around the floor. You've been dancing. Is it really better than sex?"

"It's romantic," Helen said. "But I'd like to go home for a comparison test."

CHAPTER 17

Saturday

"Look at those beautiful Persians! I like the red one," the woman in the orange Crocs said.

"My favorite is the blue-eyed white," her friend said. "That's one fine pair of queens."

Helen swore Red and Chessie understood what the women were saying. Red adjusted her head to show off her incredible copper eyes. Chessie tilted her head slightly to display her full white ruff.

Pair of queens, indeed. Those two are the biggest hams this side of Smithfield.

When the Gold Cup Southeast Florida All Breed Cat Show opened at nine a.m., some two hundred cat lovers swarmed into Fisher Hall in Plantation, a rich suburb ten miles west of Dee's cattery.

Judging started in half an hour, but the spectators were already delivering their own verdicts—like the two women admiring Chessie and Red.

"She's more orange than red," said her friend. "Like you."

Ms. Orange wore a brilliant orange-flowered top and pants. She was a grandmotherly woman, a bit wide in the hips, who had a difficult time navigating the narrow aisles between the cat show benches. But she was determined to see the cats.

"I like the fluffy white one," said her slender friend, with her own snow-white hair and a pantsuit the color of Chessie's eyes. "How anyone could like that ugly, spidery thing there is beyond me." Ms. White pointed to an elegant, pale brown Sphynx.

Becca, the breeder, moved closer to the show cage, as if to protect her cat.

Helen felt sorry she had to listen to the insults.

"Who wants a hairless cat?" Ms. Orange said. "I wouldn't touch that scrawny thing." She shuddered with disgust.

That was too much for Becca. "Then you're missing a treat," she said softly. "Anubis is a pedigreed Sphynx. He looks hairless, but his muscular body is covered with fine down. You won't find a sweeter cat. He feels like warm suede and smells like potato chips."

"I like a cat that looks like a cat," Ms. Orange said.

To Helen, cats were works of art. There were fashions in felines, and right now, the slender, long-bodied cats with long V-shaped heads, like the Siamese, were in style, as were stylized cats like the Cornish Rex, the Abyssinian and the scorned Sphynx. Helen saw these cats as modern art, difficult for the average person to appreciate.

Fluffy, flat-faced cats like Persians and British shorthairs were popular art. She preferred old-school cats with sturdy bodies and broad faces: Bombays, the American Wirehairs, Tonkinese, even moggies—mutts—like Thumbs.

But she didn't think one type was superior. Just different.

As more people crowded into the hall, the show crackled with frenzied energy. Exhibitors were frantically combing, patting and primping their cats, fluffing up or wiping down coats, depending on the breed's standard. Spectators crowded the vendors' section, checking out cat beds, T-shirts, treats and toys. People roamed the aisles between the benches, passing their own judgments on the pedigreed cats.

The show cages ranged from modest wire ones with homemade curtains to elaborate custom designs. Helen thought one looked like a bordello—okay, a cathouse. Draped with red velvet and topped with swags of spangled red feathers, it displayed two white Angoras lounging on plush, red-tasseled pillows.

Some cages had warnings: PLEASE DO NOT TOUCH. HUGS AND SQUEEZES SPREAD DISEASES! Others sported clever signs: KITTENS FOR SALE: ABLE TO DO LIGHT MOUSE WORK.

No one could resist the kittens, especially the leopard-spotted Ocicats with golden eyes.

Red and Chessie queened it at the end of a bench, silently accepting admiration.

Other cats were not so quiet. One thin, sculpted, seal-point Siamese let the cat world know his displeasure. *"Rorrrrr! Rorrrrr! Yi-rorrrrr!"* His long dark brown ears quivered with rage. His owner, a caramel-haired woman who looked like a large tabby, cradled him, but he would not stop howling.

Cats sniffed, yawned or stretched. A large striped male hissed at his neighbor. Most of the cats slept.

Each show cat was assigned a number, which was called to summon them for judging at one of the four rings. Helen could barely make out the announcements over the hall's noise.

The loudspeaker crackled, "Ring Two, Longhaired Championship: numbers eighty-nine, ninety, ninety-one, ninety-two, ninety-three."

After a blast of feedback, "Ring Three, Longhaired Premiership: numbers one ninety-three, one ninety-four, one ninety-five, one ninety-six . . ."

"Helen!" Jan called.

Helen hurried over to the bench. She felt a slight stab of guilt. She should have been helping the frantic Jan, not looking at kittens. Dee was chatting with a breeder who wanted Midnight for stud service.

"I'm taking Red over to the Premiership judging ring, then I'll come back for Chessie." Jan checked Chessie's cage and her face changed from harried to horrified. "Oh no, Chessie, baby, don't!" she said.

An unmistakable odor rose from Chessie's litter box. "Quick!" Jan said. "Get the box out of the cage so she doesn't step in anything." Helen stashed the box under the bench. "Now powder her backside with cornstarch and use the butt comb." Helen looked at the bewildering array of combs. "That cheap one," Jan said. "It's reserved for the area."

The loudspeaker blared, "Ring Three, Longhaired Premiership. Last call. Number one ninety-five. Number one ninety-five."

"That's Red!" Jan said. "Hurry, Helen, before Chessie's white fur stains. Get her paws, too. I'll be right back." She ran off with Red draped over her arm.

This is the low point of my private-eye career, Helen thought. Phil always asks: What would Bogie do? Well, what would V. I. Warshawski do?

Clean the cat, she decided.

She gently lifted Chessie out of the cage, carefully powdered her behind and combed it. "Listen, cat," she said. "You and your pals better deliver, after all I've gone through."

Chessie rubbed her head affectionately against Helen's hand. She didn't dare hug the cat and flatten her fur.

By the time Helen had cleaned the litter box, Jan was

back. She gave the white Persian a last check. Dee inspected her favorite one more time, fussing over her with Q-tips and cotton balls. Then Chessie draped herself along the length of Dee's forearm. Jan and Helen followed as the star's entourage.

Most exhibitors at least smiled at their friends as they carried their cats to and from the ring. Helen thought people in the cat fancy avoided the sharp-tongued Dee.

Ring Two had sixteen wire cages arranged in a U around the judging stand.

The stand had two poles holding up a fluorescent light; one pole was sisal-wrapped and the other twined with silk flowers. The stand was on a long pink-skirted folding table.

"Nice setup," Jan said. "Some shows don't have the sisal pole or the light."

Next to the judging stand was a pot of pink silk flowers and two bowls of candy. Spectators sat on three rows of folding chairs.

Each wire cage had the cat's number on a card—pink for females, blue for males. The other contenders were two copper-eyed whites, a blue-eyed white male, three blacks, two grays—no, blues, Helen reminded herself; pedigreed cats are blue—plus two big Maine Coons and two Himalayans. One Himi had red-tipped ears and tail; the other looked like hers were dipped in chocolate. In Helen's inexpert opinion, both cats could have been better bathed. They weren't nearly as fluffy as the Chatwood's Champions.

"That tabby Persian needs a good combing," Helen said.

"I think I see a mat in his ruff," Jan said. "We only have to worry about the solid-color Persians. We're looking at tough competition. We're up against a male blue-eyed white, two copper-eyed whites, the three blacks and the two blues."

"No contest," Helen said. "Chessie is the best."

"That's for the judge to decide," Jan said.

A clerk wearing a tiger-striped T-shirt sat next to the judging stand, recording the decisions.

Judge Lexie Deener was as well groomed as Dee's Persians. She wore a dramatic red scarf and a sleek black designer suit with a diamond cat pin. Did Smart Mort's financial advice help buy that pin? Helen wondered.

Dee took a seat up front. "We'll stand in the back row so we can keep an eye on Red in the next ring," Jan said. "The judge is starting with the blue-eyed male."

The white Persian looked at the teaser—and the audience—with disdain and refused to play.

Ms. Orange and Ms. White sat in the front row, hogging the candy bowl. "That cat's too fat," Ms. Orange said when the judge returned him to his cage.

"Humpf!" muttered the woman standing beside Helen. "Fat! Has she looked in the mirror?"

Helen bit back a laugh. Chessie waited in patient silence. The male Maine Coon paced restlessly. Helen tuned in to the spectators' chatter.

"Pretty color," said a thin brunette.

"I like a white cat," the woman said.

"No, I meant your turquoise top."

Judge Lexie lifted Chessie out of her cage next. "Note the beautiful tail, big blue eyes and fluffy coat," she said.

Helen thought Chessie put on quite a show. She played with the teaser and batted the brown feather. Finally, she stood on her short legs and stretched up the sisal pole, clawing it as high as she could reach.

Thwack! Thwack! Thwack! Her claws raked the sisal wrapping.

"Way to go, Chessie," Jan whispered.

The sisal trick was a crowd pleaser. "A pole dancer!" a woman shouted.

"Now, that's cute," a gray-haired woman said. "Persians

are supposed to have short bodies, so stretching up a pole can emphasize a fault, but this cat shows off a well-shaped body."

Jan whispered, "While the other solid Persians have their turns in the ring, let's check on Red."

The judge in Ring Three, a slender brown-haired woman in forest green, was hanging ribbons on the cages.

"Red has a ribbon!" Helen said.

"Don't get too excited," Jan said. "It's for best color, and she's the only red-haired cat in this class. It's kind of like an attendance prize."

"She's got an orange ribbon now," Helen said.

"Rats!" Jan said. "That's second place in Best of Breed."

"Our Red deserves a first," Helen said.

"It's just one judge's opinion," Jan said. "A cat who gets second place in this ring could get a first in another. She's still handing out the other ribbons in this division. Let's go back to Chessie."

Ring Two was quietly tense as Judge Lexie paced from cage to cage. She ran the feather along the cage wire for Chessie and teased both black Persians.

"What's she doing?" Helen asked.

"Deciding who gets the big one, Best of Division," Jan said. "The toy focuses their attention so the judge can see the natural set of their ears. It also makes them open their eyes so she can judge the shape and color."

Judge Lexie started hanging ribbons on the solid-color Persian cages. Chessie got a blue, a black, and a brown ribbon. Helen felt disappointed. "She should have three blue ribbons," she said.

"No, she swept the ring," Jan said. "Chessie got best blue-eyed white female, Best of Color, and Best of Breed. First place all the way for Chessie."

Judge Lexie confirmed Jan's opinion. "The female blue-eyed white has a robust body and an endearing personality," she announced. "She's my Best."

"Yes!" Helen said. She and Jan high-fived while Dee pushed forward to claim her champ.

"Dee's taking Chessie back to her cage," Jan said. "She wants to show her off. I'll return Red."

"Can I stay here and watch the rest of the longhair judging?" Helen said.

"Sure," Jan said. "It's your first show."

The male Maine Coon was next. "You're looking at the only longhaired breed native to the United States," Judge Lexie said. The cat stolidly ignored the feather Lexie lightly brushed across his nose. He turned his back when she waved the teaser at him.

Lexie carried the last cat to the stand. "The Maine Coon is our largest breed," the judge said. "Notice her smooth, shaggy tabby coat, well-tufted ears and toes."

The female Maine Coon was more playful. She batted the teaser with her paw, then chomped the silk flowers. The audience laughed and applauded. She nuzzled the judge. "Suck-up!" someone called, and the audience chuckled.

"She has personality," Ms. Orange said approvingly.

The female Maine Coon won Best of Breed, and the male was second best. Helen agreed with that decision.

Back at the bench, Dee accepted congratulations from spectators for Chessie's performance, while Helen and Jan hand-fed both cats so they wouldn't mess up their coats. "I feel like my girl's at a birthday party, wearing a white dress, and they're serving chocolate ice cream," Helen said.

Jan laughed. "Exactly."

"Is it my imagination, or does Chessie know she's a winner?" Helen said. "Look at the way she fluffs out her fur."

"Oh, she knows," Jan said. "She was born and bred to be admired. Chessie and Red are in the ring again this afternoon. Want to break for lunch and sit outside?"

They bought sodas, limp turkey sandwiches and chocolate chip cookies, and sat on a bench under a tree by the parking lot.

"It feels good to get away from the noise," Helen said. "Here comes the judge. How can she wear black without getting cat hair on it?"

"They teach it at judges' school," Jan said.

Two thirtysomething men strolled out with Lexie, flirting with her. "Are those cat exhibitors?" Helen asked.

"No, they're vendors," Jan said. "The guy in the plaid shirt sells toys. The other man sells organic cat food."

Both men extravagantly admired the judge's car, a shiny black Jaguar with a red leather interior.

"What year is that?" Plaid Shirt asked.

"An 'eighty-six Jaguar," Lexie said. "I'm a cat person. I even drive a cat. These cars are high maintenance but worth it. There's nothing like them on the road. I drove here all the way from North Carolina and loved it."

Helen asked Jan, "What do you know about Lexie?"

"The judge likes fast cars and faster men," Jan said. "She was a breeder for many years. She bred shorthaired Orientals—long, skinny cats with wedge-shaped heads and large ears. Then she switched to Persians. Since she's bred both long- and shorthairs, you could say she's unbiased."

Helen thought she heard some hesitation in Jan's voice. "Would you say that?" she asked.

"She has a good reputation in the fancy," Jan said. "Lexie went to the Gold Cup judges' school and she knows cats. She's judged at cat shows in Canada, France and Britain, as well as the USA."

Britain! Helen wondered if she'd judged at the Gold Cup Coventry cat show. Phil could check. Maybe cleaning up after Chessie had paid off after all.

"But," Helen prompted.

"Here she comes," Jan said. "We'd better get back to work."

CHAPTER 18

Saturday

Helen and Phil weren't dancing Saturday night—they were facing the music. Nancie demanded to see them both in her law office as soon as Helen came home from the cat show.

Phil waited for his PI partner in the Coronado parking lot, and motioned for her to roll down her window. "Quick!" he said. "Nancie wants us now. I'll drive if you're too tired."

"I'm fine, but what's going on?" Helen asked, as he climbed into the Igloo's passenger seat.

"We're not getting results fast enough," he said.

On the drive over, Helen updated him on what Jan told her about Judge Lexie. "She didn't have time to explain what's wrong with the judge," she said. "But something's not right. I'll find out more on Monday, when I go in early to wash the cats."

She slammed on the brakes as a young couple talking and carrying longnecks wandered out into the road.

Helen lightly beeped the horn to bring them back to this planet. The startled pair waved and boozily stepped back on the sidewalk.

Helen's heart was pounding. "That was close," she said. "The Saturday-night celebrating is starting early." She was relieved to park the Igloo at the law office.

"Brace yourself for a chewing-out," Phil said.

"I'm wearing so much cat hair, I may not feel it," Helen said, trying to brush a clump of red fur off her shorts.

"Hurry!" Phil said. "She'll have to take you as is."

Inside, Helen felt like she'd been called into the principal's office. Nancie frowned at them from behind her desk. "So, have you two made any progress?"

"We're working on some promising leads," Phil said.

"I don't want promises," Nancie said. "I want action. I saw our client today in jail. Trish is unraveling. I'm afraid she'll crack under the strain. Jail is wearing her down. We have to get her out of there. Between the kidnapped cat and Mort's funeral, she's ready to snap."

"Has Mort's body been released?" Helen asked.

"Finally," Nancie said. "His mother claimed it. His memorial service is Thursday, and Trish wants to go, preferably not in handcuffs. Their marriage was over, but she still has feelings for the man."

"Who's planning the service and the funeral?" Helen asked.

"His mother," Nancie said. "She believes her daughter-in-law is innocent. Mort will be buried in New York, where he's from, but she wants to have a service for him here in Fort Lauderdale, where he lived.

"Now let's get back to this case. What are those leads, Phil?"

"I'm working on the red medallion found by Mort's body," he said. "We believe it may have been a souvenir from the Coventry cat show in England. The woman who can confirm it should be home late Sunday night. It may be Monday before I reach her, because of the time zones."

"Forget the time differences," Nancie said. "Wake her up. What's she going to do? Fly over here and sue you? Get the information and get it fast."

"I'd also like to talk to someone who worked in Mort's office," Phil said. "Can you give me those names?"

"Mort had a one-person office," Nancie said. "But he had an amazing executive assistant, Carol Berman. She's smart." The lawyer pulled out her cell phone and began tapping on it. "I'm sending you her contact information now and I'll let her know she can talk to you."

"Besides the cat-show judge," Phil said, "I also talked to the pole-dancing girlfriend, Amber Waves. She says Jan Kurtz, Mort's fiancée, inherits half his income."

"She does," Nancie said. "His mother gets the rest."

"Amber has an alibi for the time of the murder," Phil said. "She was teaching a pole-dancing class, so she's out."

"See what you can find out from Mort's assistant," Nancie said. "Carol's peeved because the cops never talked to her. I swear, I've never seen such a shoddy investigation. I can't wait to go after those clowns. Helen, what do you have?"

"Remember the cat-show judge Mort helped with financial advice?" Helen said. "I found out she's an international judge. Phil will check if she judged at that Coventry cat show. There's something off about her. Jan tried to tell me exactly what, but we got distracted at work. I'll find out more when I go back to the cattery early Monday morning. I'm still working there."

"I can see that," Nancie said, and nodded at Helen's cat-hairy T-shirt.

Helen brushed at the hair, but it clung to the fabric. "Let it alone," Nancie said. "You'll just get more on the furniture."

"I also followed Jan, Mort's fiancée, home because I

thought she had a gray cat. She did, but it was an ordinary striped tabby, not Justine."

"She's got a motive," Nancie said. "Helen, see if you can find out what Jan was doing the night of the murder. Amber has a motive, but she's in the clear. The judge is a possibility, if your inquiries pan out, but why would she kill Mort?"

"No reason," Helen said. "Not if Mort was making her money. She sure spends it—lots of it—on her car and clothes. Maybe younger men, too."

"Nothing more on the catnapping?" Nancie asked.

"We would have called you," Phil said. "We're not supposed to hear anything from the kidnapper until Tuesday morning. Do you have the cash?"

"In my safe," Nancie said.

"We should take it with us and stash it in our office safe," Phil said. "The SmartWater CSI kit arrived and we have to mark the money. The catnapper may not give us time to get the money from you and mark it on Tuesday."

"Are you sure SmartWater works?" Nancie asked.

"Oh yeah. Neighborhoods in Fort Lauderdale, Oakland Park and other places are testing it. SmartWater is a clear liquid with a unique chemical signature for each user. You mark your jewelry, computers, TV sets, even cars with a little dab. When the cops catch the thieves or the stolen goods turn up in a pawnshop, your property's chemical signature can be identified with the special black light.

"It works better than the bank's dye packs. The thieves can't see the SmartWater. Even if the catnapper tries to burn this money, the SmartWater signature will show in the ashes."

"Amazing," Nancie said. She hauled a lumpy black nylon duffel out of her safe. "Half a million in used twenties. Two hundred fifty packs, with a hundred bills in each pack. It would have been simpler if the catnapper had asked for fifties."

"He knows South Florida," Phil said. "Counterfeit fifties are rampant down here. Even small stores check each fifty-dollar bill with a special test pen."

Helen and Phil left Nancie's office half a million dollars richer. Phil hid the money in the back of the Igloo.

"Are we going to have to mark each dollar bill?" Helen asked. "That will take us till next Tuesday."

"Nope, I have a plan," Phil said. He stopped at a garden store and bought a plant mister. "We can do this over dinner. How's Chinese sound?"

"Delicious," Helen said.

On the way home, they swung by their favorite take-out Chinese place, Bei Jing, on the corner of Federal Highway and Oakland Park Boulevard. The tiny take-out shop was staffed by a hardworking Asian family, and those in the know said Bei Jing had the best Chinese food this side of Shanghai. Helen ordered her favorite: steamed shrimp with broccoli and garlic sauce. Phil got spicy General Tso's chicken, and the woman behind the counter gave them a large free container of wonton soup.

"Hurry home," Phil said. "I'm so hungry, I'm ready to eat this in the car."

"Me, too," Helen said.

She was practically drooling when she rounded the corner to the Coronado. Helen carried the takeout, and Phil hauled the duffel full of money to their office. "You set out the dinner," he said, "while I mark the money."

Phil opened the navy blue cardboard SmartWater CSI box, took out a bottle of pinkish liquid, and poured it into the plant mister. Then he stacked the money bundles so the edges were standing up and sprayed the edges with a light SmartWater mist. Twice he stopped to wash the mister. "The SmartWater particles can clog it," he said. Once all the money was misted, he carried the table to the window air conditioner and turned it on high. "Should be dry in a minute or two."

"That was easy," Helen said. "Sit down and eat."

But they heard sirens outside and saw uniformed officers and a stout, bristly haired figure striding through the yard.

"What the heck?" Phil said.

"Oh no!" Helen said. "Why are the police here?"

"Quick!" Phil said. "The money's dry. Drop it in the bag and let's go see."

They quickly bundled the bag into their safe, left the food and sprinted downstairs. A uniformed cop stopped them. "Snakehead Bay Police," he said. "We have a warrant to search Margery Flax's apartment." Phil talked his way past the uniform, explaining they had to feed the cat. The officer could hear Thumbs howling.

They gave their cat dinner, then watched a swarm of latex-gloved cops carry boxes out of Margery's house. Two especially unlucky uniforms were rummaging in the spiderwebbed storage area behind her apartment. Their landlady was chain-smoking at the poolside umbrella table under the watchful eye of a young, sandy-haired cop.

"Margery," Phil said. "What's happening?" The sandy-haired cop looked uneasy but didn't interfere. Phil and Helen stayed on the sidewalk.

"That Snakehead Bay detective showed up with a search warrant," she said. "He and his pals are tearing my place apart."

"Whelan? Why?" Helen asked. "What's he looking for?"

"Why? Because Zach not only left me his condo, but also a six-figure insurance policy."

"Oh," Helen said.

"The Snakehead Sherlock said that was enough to cover the work on the Coronado. I didn't know a thing about it."

"Maybe Zach forgot to change your name as a beneficiary after you divorced," Phil said. "It happens."

"No, he changed it back two months ago, the dumb bastard," Margery said.

"And speaking of dumb, Detective Whelan made a big deal out of finding weed killer in my storage area. He knows I had it. Last time he was here, he asked me about it. He saw me killing weeds. So why's he carrying on about it now?"

"The autopsy must have shown that's what killed Zach," Phil said. "Did you talk to this detective?"

"Of course I did," Margery said. "I've got nothing to hide. I told him I cashed in a CD. That's a matter of record."

Phil sighed. "Margery, Snakehead Bay is a small force, if you get what I mean."

"You mean they don't always hire top-notch people," Margery said. "I already figured that out."

The young cop turned bright red to the tips of his ears.

The parade of cops carrying boxes and evidence bags out to the cars had finally stopped.

Detective Whelan swaggered out of Margery's apartment, shutting her door hard enough to rattle the glass slats in the jalousie door. He strutted over to the umbrella table with two uniformed officers.

"Margery Flax," he said. "I'm arresting you for the murder of Zachariah Flax."

"What?" Helen said.

"No!" Margery said.

"Yes!" the detective said. "You have the right to remain silent . . ."

When he finished the well-known warning, Phil said, "Margery, don't say another word. I'll get Nancie Hays."

Margery, stunned into silence, nodded at Phil. The detective took out his handcuffs. "Oh, come on," Phil said. "You've got two burly cops for protection. Do you really think a seventy-six-year-old woman is going to attack you?"

The detective put the cuffs back. "Put out the cigarette, ma'am," he said. "Let's go."

Vital, vigorous Margery seemed to shrivel before Helen's eyes. She shuffled out between the two strapping cops, looking small and old.

As they reached the gate, Elsie appeared in a jaw-dropping outfit—a pink-flowered strapless dress, hot pink mules and cherry-pink hair. The dress revealed mounds of flabby white flesh. Helen wanted to throw a sheet over her.

"Margery, dear, what's wrong?" Elsie said in her fluttery voice. "Why are these policemen here?"

"Because of you," Margery snarled. "Get off my property!"

"But I came to beg your forgiveness—to say I'm sorry."

"Sorry? You pathetic old fool," Margery said, her voice hard. "This sorry mess is what happens when you meddle in people's lives."

Elsie burst into tears, and Phil took her protectively into his arms. She cried on his shoulder, leaving black mascara streaks. "I'm sorry, Phil, I really am."

"Sh," Phil said. "I know you are." He rocked her in his arms.

"We must help her, you know," Elsie said, her eyes shining with tears. "She loved that man to death."

"Let's hope not," Phil said.

CHAPTER 19

Saturday/Sunday

"I'm much more at home with a good, clean murder than a nasty divorce," Nancie said.

Home. Helen wished she were there now, at nine o'clock on a Saturday night. She wished she were sitting by the pool with her landlady, instead of trying to get Margery out of a murder charge.

"Well, now you have two murder cases," Phil said, "Trish's and Margery's. Thank you for taking our landlady's case."

Before the Snakehead Bay detective had slammed the door on his unmarked car, Phil called Nancie. The lawyer promised to meet them at her office in an hour. He and Helen had shared their Bei Jing takeout with Elsie.

Now the PI pair were back at Nancie's office. Even after a twelve-hour day, Nancie was ready for battle.

Helen forced herself to stay awake. Margery, her surrogate mother, was going to be charged with murder one, and Florida was a death-penalty state.

"That means you'll both have to work doubly hard," Nancie said. "And twice as fast. Where are you starting Margery's investigation?"

"At Zach's condo," Phil said. "He left it to her."

"I know," Nancie said. "That's one reason why Detective Whelan thinks she killed him."

"But Zach was two months behind on the mortgage," Phil said.

"Doesn't matter. Property values are really going up in Florida again. If Margery makes those payments and sells his condo, she'll get a nice chunk of change—providing she isn't convicted of killing Zach. Then she can't inherit it."

"Margery gave me the keys to the condo," Phil said, and held them up. "We'll search tomorrow for anything the police missed. She also gave us a box of papers Zach left unclaimed and unopened since 1983."

"The cops didn't take them?" Nancie asked.

"Margery brought them to our office before the search warrant," Helen said. "We expected her to be arrested."

"Smart," Nancie said.

"We're opening that time capsule tomorrow," Helen said.

"Helen, you look tired," Nancie said. "Both of you need to go home now and get an early start Sunday morning."

Helen was relieved to park the Igloo for the last time that night at the Coronado. The old building gleamed in the moonlight. Even the construction scaffolding had a silver sheen. The palm trees whispered invitations to linger in the soft, velvety night.

But the Coronado seemed oddly empty without Margery's overwhelming presence. It looked the same, the way a dead person looks as if she's asleep. But the essence was gone. Helen shivered in the warm evening air.

She escaped with Phil into his apartment, and then to sleep.

Morning came too soon. Helen was awakened by Phil whistling in the shower and the fragrant aroma of hot coffee. Neither private eye was in the mood for love. They chugged their coffee and were at Zach's Snakehead Bay condo by seven o'clock.

Zach had lived on the fifth floor of a soulless steel-and-glass building, all sharp angles and hard, shiny surfaces. Phil unlocked Zach's black-lacquered door, and the PI pair was nearly snow-blinded by the white interior: a vast bone tile floor and hard white leather couches. The icy glass coffee table was angled so people sitting in the deathly pale chairs would bruise their legs when they stood. The air-conditioning was so cold, Helen felt snow-bound.

"Do you think Zach decorated this place himself?" Helen asked.

Phil shrugged. "Do they have a whites-only furniture store for rich people?" he asked.

The only color came from the incredible view of Snakehead Bay out the curtainless windows. The bay was as blue and palm-fringed as a corny postcard.

Helen found a silver-framed photo under a snowy lamp. "Look at this," she said, softly. "A wedding photo of Margery and Zach."

"Handsome couple," Phil said.

They were. Even in the domesticated dreariness of the fifties, Margery had flair. She wore a tea-length white wedding gown, the skirt a graceful bell of chiffon. A short veil covered her lustrous black hair. Zach was leading-man handsome, with broad shoulders and thick, dark curls. Their young smiles hurt Helen's heart. They were glowing with love.

Knowing how their marriage ended made that photo unbearably sad.

Helen set the photo back on the end table as if it burned her hand.

That was the only picture in the room. Helen and Phil searched the couch, looked under the furniture, checked the cushions and baseboards.

"Nothing else," Helen said. "No drawers, shelves or knickknacks. Let's search the bedroom."

More white, an endless Siberian winter. But in a drawer under Zach's socks, Helen found a cache of bills, and spread them on the slick white bedspread.

"The main color here is red," she told Phil. "Zach was deeply in debt. Not only was he behind on his mortgage and monthly condo fees, Zach also had overdue notices for four credit cards. He owed money for a fancy power saw, fine-quality hardwood, suede and sisal."

"Those must be supplies for his Zen Cat Towers," Phil said.

"And this two-inch stack is nothing but doctor bills and lab tests." Helen patted that pile.

"He must have been really sick. Any idea what was wrong?" Phil asked.

Helen shook her head no. "We'll take them with us and check," she said. "I wonder why the police didn't take them."

"I'm guessing Detective Whelan didn't graduate at the top of his police academy class," Phil said. "The detective had a suspect, so why bother with a tedious investigation? His force did a sloppy search."

Zach's closet held only men's clothes. "Look at these polo shirts. Two very different sizes, both fairly new," Helen said, holding up both. "Zach must have lost at least twenty pounds in the last year or so. I wonder if he kept the larger clothes because he expected to get well?"

"Lots of men hang on to their favorite clothes," Phil said. "They don't weed through their closets as much as women do."

Those were the only finds in Zach's bedroom, except for an unopened box of condoms in his bedside table.

His workroom next door smelled pleasantly of wood shavings. The floor was waxed concrete, with a workbench along one side and neat racks and shelves of complicated tools. A partially finished cat tower was clamped onto the bench.

"I wonder how he got by making those towers in his home," Helen said.

"Maybe one of his neighbors tipped off the company that sent him the cease-and-desist order," Phil said.

In the bathroom, the medicine cabinet was empty and the closet held only linens. Even his toothbrush and toothpaste were gone. "The police must have taken everything in here," Phil said.

They searched the narrow kitchen last. Zach was clearly no cook. Helen found the bare-minimum kitchen equipment: four cheap aluminum pots, a coffeemaker, stainless flatware and white china, all selected without thought for style or even function. The pantry held an unopened jar of peanut butter and three cans of beef noodle soup.

"Either he didn't eat much or the police took his other food," Helen said.

"They took everything in the fridge," Phil said, looking inside.

"But left the food on the freezer side," Helen said. "Vanilla ice cream and two homemade apple pies. One pie is cut into six slices, with two pieces missing. Each pie is dated and labeled in a flowery woman's hand. I wonder if that's Daisy's writing and these are the pies she made Zach come back for?"

"Amateur police work," Phil said, shaking his head. He checked the cabinet under the kitchen sink. "Nothing here but dish soap, lemon furniture polish and window cleaner."

"That's not how you look under a sink," Helen said. She kneeled down and began pulling out bottles and boxes. "You missed the scouring pads, the floor cleaner, cleanser and two dried-out sponges. What's behind this plastic scrub bucket? Hello? Something's hiding in the back corner." She pulled out a yellow box. "Rat poison!"

"Hah, I was right," Phil said. "He committed suicide."

"If he did, why would he hide the box?" Helen asked.

"Because Margery couldn't collect on his life insurance policy if he killed himself," Phil said. "She refused to see him anymore, so the miserable old coot committed suicide and left everything to his one true love. It's the one unselfish thing he's done in years."

"Sorry, I'm not buying it," Helen said.

"A new building like this wouldn't have rats," Phil said.

"Rats are everywhere," Helen said. "Especially around waterfront property. Let's go home and look in that box of old papers."

Peggy was reading the newspaper and sipping coffee by the pool when Helen and Phil returned at ten thirty that morning. Pete the parrot sat on her shoulder.

"Can he read the *New York Times*?" Helen asked.

"Yes, but he can't do the crossword puzzle," Peggy said.

"Hello!" Pete said.

"Morning, handsome dude," Helen said.

"Woo-hoo!" Pete said.

"Have you seen Margery?" Peggy asked. "Her car's here, but she's not up yet. Should we check on her?"

"We've got bad news," Helen said. "Margery was arrested for Zach's murder."

"Awk!" Pete said.

"Took the words out of my mouth, Pete," Helen said. She and Phil explained what happened and how they'd taken on Margery's case.

"Do you think the police messed up her apartment when they searched it?" Peggy asked.

"I'm sure they did," Phil said.

"Then that's today's chore," Peggy said. "I'll clean her apartment."

"I'll do the yard work and keep the pool clean," Phil said.

"Right now, we both have to help get her out of jail," Helen said. "Let's open that box, Phil."

Upstairs in the Coronado office, the battered box showed its age. The Florida humidity had softened the brown cardboard and curled the ends of the packing tape.

"Not as heavy as I'd like," Helen said, as she peeled off the tape.

"Look," she said, "an old newspaper. Look at those *Flashdance* fashions! I forgot about leg warmers. Here's a story about Star Wars, but they're talking about missiles, not the movie."

Phil took the paper away from Helen. "While you're strolling down Memory Lane, Margery is rotting in jail."

"Right. Sorry."

"You look through these business papers, and I'll check the photos," Phil said.

Helen riffled through old Coronado leases, receipts for repairs and other apartment business. "I wonder why Margery packed these instead of using them for her taxes," she said.

"She probably wasn't thinking straight," Phil said. "Hey, talk about *Flashdance*, I think this is an old photo of Zach and Daisy."

Zach had a mullet, a shoulder-padded jacket and a guilty smirk. Daisy's gray sweatshirt hung off one shoulder. She had the period's frizzy blond hair, earrings the size of doorknobs, purple jelly shoes and neon orange short-shorts. She was wrapped around Zach like a vine.

"I believe those are called booty shorts in today's

fashion lingo," Helen said. "Even then she was a bit on the plump side."

"Voluptuous," Phil corrected.

Helen glared at him.

"But nowhere near as good-looking as Margery," Phil added quickly.

"Ever notice that? Unless you've got a middle-aged guy on the prowl for a younger model, the other woman isn't as attractive as the wife. It's like the unfaithful husband needs a rest from having to live up to his wife."

He pulled out a yellowing color photo. "Hey, look at this," he said.

"Oh, the eighties," Helen groaned. "That red-haired guy in the neon green Adidas tracksuit looks like a giant leprechaun. The preppie in the black shirt and khakis is okay, but boring."

"The guy with the red headband and wild brown hair is a John McEnroe look-alike," Phil said.

"Who?" Helen asked.

"McEnroe. Tennis star and tantrum thrower. Zach's mullet is outstanding."

"Well, he was a fisherman," Helen said. "That wife-beater shirt sure shows off his muscles."

"If he wasn't dead, I'd be jealous," Phil said.

"You have nothing to worry about," Helen said, and kissed him. He kissed her back hard, then pulled away.

"Look where those four men are standing," he said. "In front of the Fisherman's Tale. I know that bar."

"Of course you do," Helen said, disappointed that he'd stopped when things were getting interesting.

"I mean, it's still in business," Phil said. "It's a hangout for locals. We might be able to track down Zach's old friends."

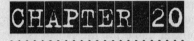

CHAPTER 20

Sunday

"Nancie, we've got a problem," Helen said.

"We've got a lot of problems," the lawyer said. "What can't wait till Monday morning?"

"Phil found an eighties photo of Zach Flax with three men, and we need Margery to identify them. If I visit her at the North Broward jail, I can't take in the photo to show her."

"You wouldn't want to, either," Nancie said. "Citizen jail visits are recorded. Attorney visits are not. I can have a face-to-face visit with her and bring in files and photos. You'll go with me, but I'll have to fax a request. I'll try to speed it up."

"Today?" Helen asked.

"Yes, as soon as you're approved," Nancie said.

They were lucky. Nancie called an hour later. "You're good to go. I'll swing by and pick you up. On the way there, you can tell me what else you found in Zach's condo and that old box."

The trip to the North Broward jail lasted just long

enough for Helen to fill in Nancie on Zach's clothes in two sizes, the stack of medical bills, the overdue bills and the rat poison under the sink.

"Interesting," the lawyer said.

"Why?" Helen asked.

"Not sure yet."

Maddening, Helen thought. The North Broward Bureau, the official name for the North Broward county jail, was run by the sheriff's office. Inside, Helen whispered, "This is grim as an old prison movie."

"Not if you're an inmate," Nancie said. "In the Broward jail system, this is nirvana."

The guard checked their IDs, searched them and their things. The two women were shown to a small room and Margery was brought in.

Helen tried to hide her shock. She barely recognized her landlady. Margery's steel-gray bob was oily and limp. She'd had wrinkles for as long as Helen had known her, but Margery's skin was like elegant origami. Now her face and neck sagged in graceless folds.

Helen had never seen Margery in any color but purple. She looked jaundiced in her prison scrubs. Her nicotine-stained hands, deprived of their ever-present cigarette, moved restlessly.

She reached greedily for the yellowing photo, as if grateful for the distraction, and studied the picture.

"Yeah, I know those bums," Margery said. "They were Zach's shady buddies, one more worthless than the other. Zach was the leader of the pack."

She absently slid a big metal paper clip off a legal document Nancie had left on the table and unbent it.

"We're trying to track them down," Helen said. "Maybe one had a motive to kill Zach or knew someone who did. We need anything you can tell us."

"You're talking thirty years ago," Margery said. "I spent as little time as I could with those barflies."

The paper clip was nearly straight.

"Try. Please? For me?" Helen said, like a mother coaxing a toddler to eat green peas.

Margery frowned at the photo and twiddled the paper clip. "Okay, the red-haired guy in the green tracksuit—the one who looks like the GEICO gecko—went to prison for dealing about the same time that Zach and I split. His name's Mike ... Mike Fernier. Yeah. That's him."

That's one, Helen thought, and wrote down the name. "And the boring preppie in the black shirt and khakis?"

"He was anything but boring," Margery said, twisting the paper clip into a reverse S. "You aren't the first woman to underestimate him. Back when I knew him, he sold burial insurance. Made his living cheating widows and orphans. His name's Xavier Dave Duncan. 'My name is Xavier Dave, like Jesus Saves,' he'd say, and give his smarmy grin. No idea what he's doing now. Hope he's roasting in hell."

Two down. One to go. "What about the brown-haired guy with the red headband?" Helen asked.

"Dick. He's dead, and good riddance," Margery said, and bent the paper clip into a lopsided rectangle. "Shot in a drug bust in the late eighties. No big loss. He probably got Zach into the drug business.

"Look how much Zach has changed," she said, shaking her head. "He used to be such a big, strapping man. When he turned up at my place again, I was surprised he was in such bad shape."

"Bad shape? He was—what?—seventy-six?" Helen asked.

"Yep. Same age as me," Margery said. "But I expected him to age better. He liked his beer, but he worked out and didn't smoke like I did. Damn, I'd sell my soul for a cigarette. Can't smoke in here. Not officially, anyway."

Now the paper clip was twisted around itself.

"When Zach walked through my gate, I could tell he was sick."

"I sure couldn't," Helen said.

"You're too young," Margery said. "All old people still look alike to you. I've lost the ability to tell a twenty-year-old from a thirty-year-old—they all look young. But I can tell a healthy seventy-six from a sick one."

"You're right," Helen said. "We found bills in his condo for lots of different medical tests. The docs were looking for something, but we don't know what. What made you think he was sick?"

"He was popping Tums like candy," Margery said.

"Really? I never noticed," Helen said.

Margery snorted, and for a moment seemed like her old self. "Well, I sure as hell did. He also reeked of garlic."

"I never got close enough to tell," Helen said. "Maybe he had Italian food."

"He hated garlic," Margery said. "Even you could see he'd lost weight. He tried to hide it, but his clothes were hanging off him."

"I did notice the weight loss," Helen said. "We found two separate sets of clothes, one fat and one thin, at his condo. I suspect he lost about twenty pounds."

"More like thirty," Margery said. "Old men get skinny, but they don't lose that much weight unless something's wrong."

"At least he had his own hair," Helen said.

"The hell he did," Margery said. "That's a hairpiece. A good one, but definitely not his hair."

Nancie, who'd been listening carefully, said, "We'll talk with his doctors. Margery, what about the rat poison hidden under his sink? If Zach had a terminal illness, would he commit suicide?"

"He might," Margery said slowly. "His father died of cancer. Thirty years ago, Zach had a real fear of going that way. But he always said he'd take himself out with pills and scotch. He wouldn't slowly poison himself, especially not if he lost his hair. Zach was always proud of his hair. Men hate being bald, you know. Zach would take the easy way out. He always did."

"He was also behind on his mortgage," Nancie said, "heavily in debt, and facing possible legal action for those cat towers he made."

"He told me they were moneymakers," Margery said. "What was wrong with them?"

"A company accused him of being a copycat," Helen said. "Pardon the pun."

Margery rolled her eyes. "Figures," she said.

"Phil thinks he killed himself," Helen said. "I'm not so sure."

"Then you better come up with a good suspect, Helen," Nancie said. "Right now, suicide is our best defense. Now, how are you, Margery?"

"How do you think? I can't smoke." The paper clip was scrunched into a tangled ball.

"You said you can't smoke officially," Helen said. She was used to her landlady's sly ways.

"You can get anything you want in prison," Margery said. "I've scored some tobacco, but the price was high."

"How high?" Helen asked.

"The jail has these things called Care Packs that family and friends can send. You buy them online through a Web site. I need you to send ten weeks of the thirty-dollar protein-pack Care Packs for this inmate here." She handed Helen a scrap of paper. "This has her prisoner ID number, name and the Care Pack Web site. Don't lose the ID number. That's more important than her name.

"She gets one protein pack a week. You can't order more, and it has to start right away."

"You paid three hundred dollars for tobacco?" Helen asked.

"I've been smoking for sixty years and I had to go

cold turkey," Margery said. "I would have signed away the Coronado for a smoke."

"Of course I'll do it," Helen said. "What's in this protein pack?"

"A festival of junk food," Margery said. "Beef and cheddar sticks, salami sticks, chili cheese corn chips, cashews, peanuts, a hot fudge sundae Pop-Tart, two kinds of cookies. There's more, but you get the idea. It's the death penalty by coronary."

"You've got the contraband tobacco," Helen said. "Where are you getting the rolling papers?"

Margery looked piously at the ceiling and said, "My pocket Bible is a great comfort to me."

"Huh?" Helen said. Margery had never used that particular B-word. But Nancie knew what she meant.

"Margery, if you're caught using Bible pages for rolling paper—if you're caught with any contraband—you understand the penalties are severe."

"Worth the risk," Margery said. "Besides, I'm a harmless old lady." She tried to look sweet, and failed.

"How's the food in here?" Helen asked.

Margery shrugged. "Bland. You know what BSO stands for?"

"Broward Sheriff's Office?"

"Baloney Sandwiches Only."

"Would you like a Care Pack?" Helen asked.

"Would I! I'll pay you. I'm starving. I've got the munchies since I quit smoking."

"Quit?" Helen said.

"Cut back," Margery said.

"I'll send you one a day," Helen said.

"Can't," Margery said. "Like I said, prisoners are limited to one Care Pack a week."

"How are the other prisoners treating you, besides smuggling you contraband?" Helen asked.

"Okay. Some are mean, some are crazy and some are

mad-dog dangerous. Most like me because I killed my old man. They'll be disappointed when they find out I'm innocent."

Nancie looked alarmed. "You aren't talking to them about Zach's murder, are you?"

"I've watched enough TV to know about jailhouse snitches," Margery said. "Right now, it helps if they think I'm a stone-cold killer." She grinned like the old Margery.

"Is there anything else I can get you?" Helen asked.

"Yeah," Margery said. "Out of here."

CHAPTER 21

Sunday

Sweat dripped into Phil's eyes, but he couldn't wipe it away. He was using both his hands to clean the clogged Coronado pool filter.

Helen felt a mean stab of satisfaction when she found her man up to his elbows in rotting leaves and unidentifiable debris. She'd had to clean countless litter boxes for Trish's case.

"I'm nearly finished," he said. "How did the jail visit go?"

"Margery looks awful," Helen said. "But she ID'ed all three men in the photo. Here's the list."

"Good. I'll shower and look them up on my computer," Phil said.

They heard the vacuum cleaner whining in Margery's apartment.

"Peggy's still cleaning?" Helen asked.

"She'll be there awhile. The cops really trashed the place."

Helen tracked down Peggy in the living room, a dust

rag slung over her shoulder. Her dark red hair seemed to glow as she vigorously vacuumed the purple rug. She shut off the howling machine when she saw Helen.

"The living room looks good," Helen said. "Smells like lemon furniture polish instead of smoke."

"Took me all morning to clean this room and the kitchen," Peggy said. "You won't believe the mess. The cops even dumped the coffee, sugar and flour canisters on the kitchen counter. How's Margery?"

"So-so," Helen said. "She's busy breaking laws in jail." She told Peggy about the visit, then asked, "How can I help?"

"Put the bedroom back together while I work on the bathroom."

Margery's bedroom has been ransacked. The mattress was stripped, its covers heaped on the carpet. The contents of the dresser drawers and closet were dumped on the floor. Helen put away everything as best she could, washed the bedding and dusted. She was making the bed with clean lilac sheets when Phil knocked on the apartment door, fresh from his shower.

"Looks good," he said. "Smells nice, too."

He hugged Helen and she rubbed his strong back. "So do you," she said, playfully yanking his slightly damp ponytail. She liked the contrast between his young face and silver hair. She also liked sultry love on a sweltering summer afternoon.

"You don't suppose we could go to your place—or mine?" she asked, her voice husky. She kissed him. He kissed her back, but didn't linger.

"Not yet," he said. "We have work to do. I made an appointment for us at seven this evening. We're talking to Carol Berman."

"Who?"

"Carol is Mort's assistant, remember?" Phil said. "Nancie says she's smart and itching to tell someone what she knows. The Peerless Point detective never bothered talking to her."

"Are we meeting Carol at Mort's office?"

"No, at her town house, by the pool. I thought she'd be more forthcoming at her place and feel safer outside. A woman alone feels more comfortable talking if another woman is there."

"Good move," Helen said. "Maybe we'll finally have something useful for Nancie."

"I also found Mike Fernier, Zach's scrawny friend who went to prison for dealing. He was released six months ago. He's staying at a halfway house in Broward County. The other man in the photo, Xavier Dave, has switched from swindling widows to selling used cars. He rents a one-bedroom apartment two blocks from the Fisherman's Tale."

"He hasn't gone far since 1983," Helen said. "Think he walked over to the bar for a Sunday-afternoon beer? We have time to go there before we meet Carol."

"It's better if I go alone," Phil said. He looked up and said, "Hey, Peggy. Good work on Margery's apartment, but your shoulder looks bare without Pete."

"He's not a fan of vacuums," Peggy said.

"I was just telling Helen why she shouldn't go with me to the Fisherman's Tale. It's a dive," Phil said. "If our subject is there, he won't talk if I walk in with Helen."

"Then I'll go there alone," Helen said.

"You could take your good friend—me," Peggy said. "A cold beer would taste good now. We'll drive over in Helen's car, as soon as I change."

"Don't dress up," Phil said.

The Fisherman's Tale, decorated in early beer sign, was a cinder-block building on an industrial stretch of Powerline Road. It had the hallmarks of a dive: duct tape on the red vinyl bar stools, restrooms marked POINTERS and SETTERS, and a sign over the cash register that said,

OUR CREDIT MANAGER IS HELEN WAITE. IF YOU WANT CREDIT, GO TO HELEN WAITE.

Phil was at the bar, drinking a longneck Pabst and chatting with the bartender, a flabby, tattooed man whose stained apron protected a dingy T-shirt. Phil wore his redneck disguise: a dark ball cap with its own built-in curly brown mullet, dirty jeans, and a saggy T-shirt that read SILENCE IS GOLDEN, DUCT TAPE IS SILVER. Helen was amused that he blended in with the men at the bar. The only woman was a worn blonde whose tube top threatened to roll off her substantial chest. The gap-toothed man next to her never took his eyes off that trembling top.

When Helen and Peggy walked in, the other men watched them with avid eyes. Helen was glad she couldn't read minds, or she'd have to wallop the lot of them. She and Peggy quickly sat at a table near the bar.

"Atmospheric," Peggy said nervously.

"If you like the scent of Pine-Sol," Helen said, equally uneasy. "I don't think they have table service. What can I get you?"

"I still want that cold beer," Peggy said.

Helen ordered two cold ones at the bar. "Wanna glass?" the bartender asked, as he pulled two from the overhead rack. One had lipstick on the rim.

"We'll drink from the bottle, thanks," she said.

"You know how many men find that sexy, little lady?" he asked.

"Heh-heh," Helen said inanely, and hurried back to the table.

After ten long minutes, Phil swaggered over with his beer and said, "Can I sit down, ladies?"

"Sure, dude," Peggy said, giggling and batting her eyelashes.

"Our friend will be in Monday night," he said, his voice low. "Ready to go?"

"I was ready when I walked in here," Helen said.

They left the bar together. "I'll drop you off at home, Peggy," Helen said, "then Phil and I will drive over to see Mort's assistant."

"Hurry. We're cutting it close for a seven o'clock appointment," Phil said. "It's six-thirty now."

"Give me the keys to your Jeep and I'll drive it home," Peggy said.

They waved good-bye and Phil climbed into the Igloo's passenger seat. "Head east toward Ocean Drive," he said. "When we get near Carol's town house, I'll give you directions. I'm going to call Mrs. Gender, director of the Gold Cup Coventry All Breed Cat Show."

"You can do that on your cell phone?" Helen asked.

"Our plan isn't restricted to the US," he said. "It's eleven thirty in the UK. I hope Mrs. Gender is still awake." He put the phone on speaker so Helen could hear.

Jinny Gender was home and grumpy. "I've just returned from holiday," she said. "You do know what time it is?"

"I do and I'm sorry," Phil said. "I'm calling from Fort Lauderdale, Florida, on the East Coast of the United States."

"I know where Florida is," Jinny said sharply.

"I'm sorry to disturb you at this hour, but it's a matter of murder. I'm Phil Sagemont, a private investigator. Did the Coventry cat show fly in a Gold Cup judge from the United States, a Ms. Lexie Deener?"

"No."

"Did your show give away a red souvenir medallion with a wild cat on it—a cougar or panther, some kind of big cat?"

"Certainly not! Why would we do that?"

"Some cat shows have wild cats on exhibit."

"In the States, maybe," Jinny Gender said. "We believe it's barbaric to keep a wild animal caged for the amusement of others. Good night, Mr. Sagemont." She hung up.

"That kills my theory on the medallion," Phil said.

They were in Lauderdale-by-the-Sea, a seaside community with a broad beach, sidewalk cafés, and midcentury modern apartments and houses.

"Turn left here on Bougainvillea and you're on Carol's street," Phil said. "Her town house is about halfway down."

Carol's home, in a cluster of two-story pink stucco town houses, was as pretty as her street's name. It was hidden behind a high wooden fence. Phil pressed the gate buzzer, and Carol met them. A cool beach blonde about Helen's age, Carol had money and taste. She wore a classic aquamarine tunic and skinny white jeans. Helen had spent enough time in retail to recognize designer Tory Burch. Helen felt definitely down-market in her jeans and T-shirt.

A fluffy white dog trotted at Carol's white sandaled feet. "This is Tory," she said, and led Helen and Phil back to a turquoise pool, where three glasses of iced tea waited at an umbrella table. Tory settled at her feet.

"I miss Mort," Carol said. "I worked for him for fifteen years and he was a wonderful employer. He even let me bring Tory to work. Not many employers will do that."

"You're not a cat person?" Helen asked.

Carol shrugged. "They're nice, but they're not my life. That's how Mort felt about Justine."

"Who do you think killed him?" Helen asked.

"I wish I knew," Carol said. "He was such a good guy."

"Trish?" Phil suggested.

"Their divorce was bitter, but Trish loved him in her fashion. Mort had a heart of gold, and Trish—I like her, but she's a teeny bit of a gold digger."

"I heard Mort gave good financial advice," Phil said.

"Very good. That's how I got the nest egg to make the down payment on this town house."

"Did he ever give bad advice?" Phil asked.

"Nobody in this business is infallible," Carol said. "Mort had a better record than most. He had to be good. He gave Trish a free hand on remodeling and redecorating those two huge houses. She was fond of antiques and two-hundred-dollar-a-yard fabric.

"Some of his customers said they wanted high-yield, high-risk investments, but when those tanked, they were furious."

"Anyone in particular?" Phil asked.

"I'd rather not say," Carol said. "Mort kept his clients' information confidential."

"But it's not confidential, not really," Helen said. "Not like something you'd say to a doctor or a lawyer. You don't want to protect Mort's killer, do you?"

Carol shook her head no.

"Did anyone threaten Mort when his advice went haywire?" Helen asked.

"Two clients were very emotional. Both made scenes at the office. One was a man, Logan Lovechenko. He was a Russian, or maybe Ukrainian, businessman who wanted Mort to invest his considerable fortune. Mort wanted to diversify, but Logan insisted on high-risk Chinese investments, even after Mort warned him that the Asian markets are volatile. Logan didn't lose everything, but he lost a lot.

"He showed up here one day and said he expected Mort to make good on his losses. Mort couldn't do that. Logan told Mort to drive carefully and left the office."

"Drive carefully?" Phil asked.

"His exact words," Carol said. "If Mort had been killed in a car crash, I would have insisted the police listen to me. But he wasn't."

"Was Logan with the Russian mob?" Phil asked.

"Mort didn't stereotype people of Russian or Italian descent," Carol said. "I do know that Logan used to live in Brighton Beach when he first came to America."

"Who was the other man?" Helen asked.

"Woman," Carol said. "She was in sales. Medical equipment. Lives in North Carolina but comes down here often. She's also a cat-show judge, of all things."

"Really?" Helen said. She and Phil were now hyper-alert.

"Her name was Dexie? Dixie? No, Lexie," Carol said. "That's it. Lexie Deener. She stormed into Mort's office, mad as, well, a wet cat."

Helen, who knew about wet cats, didn't correct her.

"Lexie said his so-called insider advice had lost her entire pension. 'I was planning to retire next year,' she told Mort. 'Now I'll have to work until I drop. I'll do everything in my power to ruin you. I'll make sure that damn cat of yours never wins a ribbon. Not in my ring.'"

"You heard all that listening at Mort's door?" Helen asked. Carol didn't seem the type.

"Oh no," she said. "He recorded it and asked me to make a transcript. Mort did that when he was worried his clients would be trouble. He kept a tiny recorder in the pen cup on his desk."

"I thought single-party recordings were illegal in Florida," Helen said.

"They are," Phil said. "But so is accepting investment tips in exchange for favorable judgments at a cat show."

"When was Mort threatened by Lexie?" Helen asked.

"The Friday before he died," Carol said.

"And the Russian?"

"That took place about two weeks before he was killed," Carol said.

They talked a little longer, then thanked Carol, and she walked them to her gate.

Inside the Igloo, Phil said, "Mort liked beautiful

women. Do you think he was having an affair with Carol Berman?"

"No," Helen said. "Mort's beauties are all cat crazy, and Carol could take them or leave them."

"Sounds like Mort didn't mind investing mob money," Phil said. "He was playing a dangerous game."

"What's our next step?" Helen asked.

"I'll look into Logan tomorrow and check his alibis and Lexie's for the night Mort was killed," Phil said. "I'll check if any of Mort's neighbors saw any strange cars in Mort's drive."

"Good luck with that," Helen said. "Peerless Point estates are so big you can't even see the house next door. Judge Lexie will be at the pet-day assembly tomorrow. I'll snag her water bottle or soda can and see if we can get her prints off it. Maybe she's the unknown print on the medallion."

"So what?" Phil said. "The medallion wasn't given out at the Coventry cat show. We don't know where it's from. That unknown fingerprint could belong to a jeweler, a parking valet, even a bumbling Peerless Point cop."

"So we're back where we started," Helen said.

"Worse," Phil said. "We're behind."

CHAPTER 22

. . . .

Monday

Monday morning started with a sting. Helen was at Dee's cattery at six a.m., under-coffeed, covered in cat hair and choking on vinegar fumes.

"Monday morning was wash day for my grandma," Helen said. "But she never washed cats." She wondered what her small, practical St. Louis grandmother would make of these coddled cats.

"Red and Chessie have to look pretty at the Hasher School Pet Appreciation Day this morning," Jan said.

The vinegar fumes from the rinse stung Helen's eyes. Worse than the vinegar sting was the bitter knowledge that she and Phil had failed—twice. His theory about the cat medallion found near Mort's body was dead wrong. Judge Lexie had never been to the Coventry cat show. And Helen's suspicion that Jan was hiding Justine was equally off base.

Where did that bloodred medallion come from? Who dropped it? Was the unknown print on it from Mort's killer? If the private eyes knew that, they'd be closer to solving the case.

They had no leads for Margery's case, either. Phil wasn't even sure Zach had been murdered.

All Helen could do this morning was wash cats, talk to Jan and hope she could save two innocent women trapped in jail.

Helen was rinsing the last of the vinegar while Red watched her with those hypnotic copper eyes. "So, how did our two beauties do at the show Sunday?" she asked.

"Not bad," Jan said as she shouted over the dryer. Chessie's flat fur looked comical, but Helen would never laugh at the proud beauty.

"Chessie did better than Red," Jan said. "She got six bests and two seconds."

"What's that mean?" Helen asked.

"Chessie was Best Cat in six judges' rings, and Second-Best Cat in two rings. That's at an eight-ring show," she said. "Dee is campaigning her for a national win, and Chessie came close to sweeping the show.

"Red ended in the top ten with three bests, two thirds, a fifth and two sevenths."

"You lost me again," Helen said.

"Red won Best Cat in three Premiership Class rings, Third-Best Cat in two rings, one Fifth Best and two Seventh Bests."

"Oh," Helen said. "Red deserves better."

She gently lifted the Persian out of the sink and wrapped her in a warm towel.

Helen dried the cat's feathery ears with a cotton ball and hoped she wouldn't hear the next sentence. "I think Red's prettier than Chessie," she said. "She looks like a bonfire, with her copper eyes and flaming fur."

Jan turned on the hair dryer and started drying Chessie's coat. "Chessie has a good shot at a national win this year," she said. "Partly it's her color. Whites require extraobsessive upkeep and they look dazzling when they're well cared for. Plus Chessie puts on more of a show with her pole-dancing routine."

Red nuzzled Helen's hand with her broad head, and Helen gently washed her face with a warm cloth.

"It's sort of like having two beautiful daughters," Jan said. "You tell yourself you love them equally, but your heart still plays favorites. I want them both to win, but realistically, I know Chessie has a better chance."

"What if Red doesn't get a national win this year?" Helen asked.

"Dee will probably retire her. She's planning to breed Chocolate and Mystery again, and she'll see if they produce any show-quality kittens."

"What will happen to Red after she retires?"

"We should be so lucky," Jan said. "She'll hang out here in the cattery with her pals. Dee, for all her faults, loves her cats, and Red will have a good life."

"Tell me about this Pet Appreciation Day at Hasher elementary," Helen said. "Why is Dee doing this?"

"We do a couple of educational assemblies every year," Jan said. "Gold Cup believes in community outreach. It's good for the fancy, and it's good for Dee. The school is in Plantation, a rich community, and the kids' parents are potential kitten customers. Pet Day really is educational. You'd be surprised how many kids are afraid of cats or dogs. The assembly teaches them how to act around animals.

"The school has a vet talk about proper pet care, an American Kennel Club breeder brings some show dogs, Dee will have her cats and there's a service dog to teach the children pet safety, including the best way to approach strange animals. Lexie, the show judge, is there as a bonus. The kids love to hear how cats are judged. They like to know that even animals get grades."

Both cats were combed and sleepy from the warm

dryers. Helen and Jan fitted them with their coffee-filter collars to protect their clean ruffs, and carried them to their sunny, carpeted window shelves for a snooze.

Soft gray Mystery patted Helen's leg as she passed and said, *"Merp?"*

"You're right, little cutie," she said, picking her up. "You've been neglected all weekend. How about a good combing and some playtime?"

"Same for you, Chocolate," Jan said.

The two cats sat on adjoining grooming tables while Helen and Jan petted, combed and scratched them. Mystery was in a playful mood and batted the comb. Chocolate closed her eyes and smiled, a contented woman luxuriating at a spa.

"They really need exercise," Jan said.

Helen and Jan set both cats on the tile floor and brought out the teaser wands. Chocolate and Mystery jumped and batted at the wands, then chased each other around the pet carriers. Midnight heard the thumps and giggles and padded in to join the two cats. Now all three were romping.

Like nannies in a park, Jan and Helen watched the cats play. Helen wanted an answer for the question Jan had left hanging on Saturday.

"At the show, you started to tell me why you don't like Lexie, but then lunch was over and we were overwhelmed with work."

"I can hardly look at that woman," Jan said, her blue eyes narrowing. "She has no business being a judge. She was charged with animal cruelty."

"What? What did she do?" Helen asked.

"She had a fat cat."

"That's cruel?" Helen asked, and felt a flash of guilt. Her vet had warned her that Thumbs was two pounds overweight.

"I guess the term is 'morbidly obese,'" Jan said.

"Nobody in the fancy knows, or Lexie would never be a judge. I only know because I heard about it from my grandparents. They live in Dobbsville, North Carolina, in the Research Triangle. This happened in the mid-eighties, before I was born, and before that part of North Carolina was flooded with newcomers.

"Dobbsville is a pretty little town not too far from Raleigh, though back then, it was out in the country. Lexie's cat, King Tut, was the talk of the town. Tut was a sweet gray shorthair who was supposed to weigh maybe fifteen to eighteen pounds. But Lexie had a sales job then and her territory included a huge chunk of the Southeast coast, from North Carolina all the way down to the tip of Florida, so she was on the road for days at a time.

"Rather than pay someone to feed Tut, hire a sitter or even get a pet feeder on a timer, Lexie used to open a twenty-pound bag of cat food and leave the lid up on the toilet for the three or four days she traveled.

"She joked that the toilet was her cat's emergency water supply."

"Yuck," Helen said. "We have to keep the lid down to keep Thumbs out of the commode."

"That's what any responsible pet person does," Jan said. "Lexie had plenty of money to spend on that fancy car of hers, but she neglected her cat. And now she's a judge! It just makes me sick.

"Cats get lonely, too, and poor Tut sat around and ate and ate," Jan said. "He could barely move. He'd crawl over to sun himself by the sliding glass door. The neighbors saw he was eating himself to death and complained to the local humane society.

"Tut was taken into custody and the vet examined him. He said Tut was morbidly obese—he weighed twenty-six pounds. The poor cat couldn't clean himself properly and he had bedsores because he could hardly walk.

"Lexie was charged with animal cruelty, but the charges

were dropped when Tut died of a heart attack. The story made the paper, too, the *Dobbsville Guardian*."

"That's awful," Helen said.

"That's what everyone in Dobbsville said. A couple of years later, Lexie got herself promoted to a desk job and became active in the fancy. First she bred cats and then, nearly fifteen years later, she retired as a breeder and became a Gold Cup show judge. Most of the Dobbsville people who were around when she was charged with cruelty had either moved or died, like my grandparents. But Lexie's neighbor, Mrs. Pickett, was horrified.

"She told Lexie she was going to write to the Gold Cup association," Jan said, "and they wouldn't let her be a show judge with her history. Lexie hired a lawyer and threatened to sue Mrs. Pickett if she sent that letter, and she backed off. The poor lady was eighty-two years old. A lawsuit would have ruined her."

"But doesn't Gold Cup do background checks on its judges?" Helen asked.

"They do," Jan said. "But this was ten years ago, and the Dobbsville paper's archives weren't online yet." Ten years was an eternity in a fluid society.

"They're available now," Jan said. "I think the paper just put its archives online in the last year."

"Did Mort know that Lexie was charged with animal cruelty?" Helen asked.

"Oh yes," Jan said. "I told him. But Mort never used it against her and made me promise I wouldn't tell, either. He was a more-flies-with-honey type. He hated blackmailers.

"Instead, Mort gave her financial advice. He was determined to help his Justine win, but he'd never stoop to blackmail."

And that kind gesture failed when Mort lost the judge's money, Helen thought. Now Justine's missing and may never be shown unless we find her.

"Mort was so good and generous. That's why I love—loved—him. Well, I guess I still love him. I miss him so much. We had a wonderful life planned. I was going to devote myself to the care and showing of Justine and my Persians. We were going to travel the circuit and go to all the major shows. All those dreams are gone now."

Midnight raced by, chased by Mystery. Jan scooped up the black cat. "Time for your combing, sir," she said, "or you'll get mats." Midnight glowered at her with his copper eyes, but Jan carried him to a grooming table.

"Helen, will you clean the litter boxes? Then we have to go to Hasher School."

"Sure," Helen said.

She took her purse, ducked into the bathroom and called up the *Dobbsville Guardian* archives. She found a story from August 31, 1986, that Lexie Deener was charged with multiple counts of animal cruelty involving a cat named King Tut. Three weeks later, a follow-up story said that the charges were dropped against Ms. Deener.

The paper didn't mention that the cat had died.

Helen called Phil, excited by her find. "We've got a break at last," she said, and told him about Lexie.

"It's a start," he said.

"A start!" Helen said. "It's more than that."

"How?" Phil said. "How do we prove the judge killed Mort? And what's that got to do with the cat medallion?"

"Nothing," Helen said, as her excitement died.

That's what they had once again. Nothing.

CHAPTER 23

Monday

"Valerie Cannata!" Helen said. "What's an investigative reporter doing at a grade-school pet-appreciation day?"

The Channel 77 star was professionally glamorous in a black sheath dress and tailored beige blazer. Her makeup and dark red hair were perfect.

Helen felt like a frump after a morning of washing cats. She picked a bit of Chessie's fur off her T-shirt. "Pardon the pun, but you don't usually do fluff."

"My new producer is an animal lover," Valerie said, her smile too bright. "His daughter, Paige, is in the sixth grade here at Hasher School."

"Oh," Helen said, and hoped that syllable sounded sympathetic. Valerie was a hard-hitting reporter whose stylish clothes and flawless makeup tempted the unwary to underestimate her. Her exposés had helped launch Coronado Investigations.

"Why are you here?" Valerie asked.

"I'm cat wrangling for Chatwood's Champions," Helen said. "This is my associate, Jan Kurtz."

"I need your help," Valerie said. Helen was surprised that the tough reporter sounded so desperate. "I don't know anything about pets. I'm—I'm scared of dogs, ever since one bit me when I was eight. I'd rather face a lawyer than a Labrador. My producer expects me to get at least three features here."

"Stick with us," Helen said. "We'll show you the stories."

Valerie spoke quickly to her photographer, a big, ponytailed man built like a bowl of melting ice cream. He nodded, and they followed Helen and Jan into the school cafeteria.

"If you want an easy interview, start with the cats," Helen said. "Our employer, Deidre Chatwood, breeds prize Persians. Once you get Dee talking about her cats, your biggest problem will be shutting her up."

"Good," Valerie said. "We can always edit her. Who else?"

"The AKC dog breeder is supposed to be here shortly," Jan said. "He'll be good."

"Okay," Valerie said, drawing out the word.

"Unless you want to skip him," Jan said. "The other participants are at the tables along the window. How about the hot guy with the brown hair? Dr. Bob is a local vet."

"Very telegenic," Valerie said.

"Especially the muscles," Jan said, and winked. "Dr. Bob loves to talk about pet care."

She nodded toward a sweet-faced brunette with a brown pug. "I know you'll get cute video at Jill's pet safety session with the service dog, Barney. He's the tiny pug wearing the little red vest. He may even help you conquer your fear of dogs."

"Those are good starts," Valerie said, but she eyed the pocket-sized pug doubtfully.

Helen saw Lexie's black Jaguar glide into the parking lot. "Oh, wait," she said. "I almost forgot. Lexie Deener, the cat-show judge. Show judges are natural teachers. She'll tell you all about the Gold Cup Cat Fanciers' Association."

"Perfect," Valerie said.

Why is Jan glaring at me? Helen wondered, then remembered Jan hated Judge Lexie—for good reason.

Get over it, she thought. My friend needs a story.

"I'll introduce you to Dee now," Helen said. "She goes on first, about ten o'clock. That's her up front."

Dee and her cats made a theatrical picture on the cafeteria's little stage. Dee wore a crisp white pantsuit with a flame-red scarf, the same colors as her cats. Helen and Jan had set up Red's and Chessie's show cages with the fancy curtains and showy rosettes on a table next to her.

"What beautiful cats," Valerie said. As if she'd pressed a button, Dee launched into a talk about Red's and Chessie's awards, their bloodlines and their future.

Helen and Jan leaned against the wall, enjoying the bottled water and chocolate-chip cookies the school gave the participants, while colorfully dressed students filled the cafeteria.

"These are the older kids, grades four through six," Jan said.

Some sixty students pushed, shoved and noisily settled themselves on the floor while their teachers vainly tried to keep order.

Rich kids really are different, Helen thought. They have confidence I didn't get until after college. Maybe it's the knowledge that nothing bad has ever happened to them. They have their parents, their family money and their lawyers to protect them.

"Why aren't the students sitting on the cafeteria chairs?" she asked.

"They like the floor better," Jan said. "It's a kid thing. They're more bendable than we are."

Valerie was still interviewing Dee, but now the reporter had a slightly glazed look. "I'm campaigning Chessie for a national win this year," Dee told her.

"And if she wins?" Valerie asked.

"She'll win," Dee said, "and then she'll give me the most beautiful kittens."

Valerie noticed a teacher, barely older than her students, hovering nearby. "Looks like you're about to go on," Valerie said to Dee.

The teacher was slender but determined. "Good morning and welcome to Pet Appreciation Day," she said.

The students continued talking, and she shouted over them. "Before we start, we have a celebrity with us today: Channel Seventy-seven investigative reporter Valerie Cannata. Anything you'd like to ask Miss Cannata?"

The noise quieted as a tiny blonde in a GIRLS ROCK T-shirt raised her hand.

"Ashley?" the teacher said.

"Valerie, are those Chanel T-straps you're wearing?" Ashley asked.

"Yes, and they're very comfortable," Valerie said.

"I *meant*," the teacher said, "does anyone have any questions about reporting?"

An uncomfortable silence settled on the audience. "Okay, then," the teacher said. "We're very grateful to our guests for taking their time to attend our Pet Appreciation Day. Let's start with Mrs. Deidre Chatwood and her two gorgeous pedigreed Persians." She smiled at Dee.

"This is going to be fun," Jan whispered to Helen. "Dee is terrified of public speaking."

"I've read that some people are more afraid of giving a speech than dying," Helen said.

"Dee's one of them," Jan said. "Remember how she chewed you out in her office?"

Helen rubbed her derriere. "How could I forget that—or the day's docked pay?"

"You're about to get your revenge," Jan said. "She'll start off strong, then, about halfway through, she'll panic."

Helen heard some of the girls talking about the pretty kitties. Dee's voice rose above them, clear and confident. She introduced each cat, then discussed their accomplishments, grooming, and awards. The two Persians seemed to feed on the attention. Both cats fluffed their fur and gazed at the audience with their amazing eyes.

"How many of you have cats?" Dee asked, and about twenty-five students raised their hands.

"My brother's allergic," someone said.

"Lots of famous people owned cats," Dee said. "Queen Victoria had an Angora cat, which is longhaired like a Persian but has a different face. So did Queen Marie Antoinette. She used to let her cats roam the table."

The class stared at her, and Dee faltered. She looked out at her audience and Helen saw her fright. The students seemed to sense it, too. Dee started talking faster, almost tripping over her words.

"John Lennon, the Beatle, loved cats," she said.

"My mom listens to him, but he's dead," a boy in a blue polo shirt said.

Helen could sense Dee's growing panic. She was on a tightrope and she'd looked down.

"Yes, well, Freddie Mercury, the founder of Queen, liked cats."

"He's dead, too," another boy said.

"Martha Stewart has calico Persians and blue-point Himalayans. You know Martha Stewart, the businesswoman famous for elegant living. She's rich and famous and alive."

The class watched her with hard, silent faces.

"And Vanna White," she said. "Vanna White on *Wheel of Fortune*. The TV show." Someone snickered. "Any questions?" Dee asked brightly.

Jan whispered, "Betcha a nickel they ask how much money she makes."

"Thank you, Mrs. Chatwood," the teacher said. "Who has questions?"

A boy with buzzed hair and a green-striped shirt raised his hand.

"Yes, Austin?" the teacher said.

"How much money do you make breeding cats?" he asked.

"You win," Helen said to Jan.

"The little darlings ask it at every assembly," Jan said.

Helen could pick out the boy's teacher. She rolled her eyes, then looked mortified. The other teachers smiled knowingly.

"How much do I make? Nothing!" Dee said. "Not one cent. You don't go into the fancy for money. I do this because I love cats and want to better the breed."

Another hand went up. "Yes, Paige?" the teacher said.

The producer's daughter, a blonde in skinny jeans, a coral shirt and a long yellow scarf, asked, "How much does that white cat cost?"

Paige's teacher stifled a groan.

"Chessie's not for sale," Dee said. Now her fear was gone. "But she will be having kittens later this year, and those will be for sale. I don't sell my kittens to just anyone. I have to meet you and your parents. I want to know if you have other pets and if you take care of them. Most important, I have to see you with my kittens. If you and my kitten are not a good match—if you don't hit it off—you don't get to adopt one."

This news created another buzz.

"Adopting a cat is a big responsibility," Dee said. "Not everyone wants to care for a longhair cat. Persians have to be combed every day and bathed once a week."

"Every day!" The phrase ping-ponged through the cafeteria.

"That's right," Dee said. "Their fur mats. If you don't comb them, it mats when they sit. Longhairs are beautiful, but if you don't want the work, you can adopt a shorthair from the Humane Society."

"More questions?" the teacher asked. "No? Thank you, Mrs. Chatwood." The teachers applauded as Dee fled the stage. Helen and Jan carried the cat cages to a side table as Judge Lexie Deener strutted onstage.

The older girls studied her hair and her outrageously expensive outfit. Is her suit this season's style? Helen wondered. Carol Berman, Mort's assistant, said Lexie was furious when the moneyman's bad advice ruined her financially. The cat-show judge had screamed she'd have to work till she dropped.

Was Lexie angry enough to kill Mort? Helen flashed on Mort's blood-soaked body and the red medallion with the unknown fingerprint. Phil said that print could belong to "a jeweler, a parking valet, even a bumbling Peerless Point cop." How about a cat-show judge? The police wouldn't have Lexie's fingerprints.

As she passed Helen, Lexie tossed her water bottle in the trash. Helen picked it out with a pen through the mouth and slid it into a plastic bag in her purse.

Lexie was not afraid of the students. She held their attention with a short, concise talk about a judge's duties, schooling and cat shows.

At question time, a tall boy in a gray hoodie raised his hand.

"Derek?" the teacher said.

"Do you own that awesome black Jaguar?"

"I do," the judge said, basking in the praise and forgetting about four-legged felines.

"Can we, like, go out and look at it?"

"Can they?" the judge asked.

"It's like a history lesson," Derek said. "We'll never see a car like that up close. Even at a car show, it would be behind a velvet rope or something. Please? It's right outside the door."

Some sixty pairs of eyes turned toward the teacher. Even the judge seemed to be begging permission to show off her car.

The teacher caved. "Okay, but make it quick."

Outside, Judge Lexie's car was surrounded by admirers. Like the Persian cats, Judge Lexie seemed to expand and glow in the students' praise.

"It's perfect," Derek said. "This is, like, the most beautiful Jaguar ever made, except for the E-Type."

"The E-Type was certainly handsome," Judge Lexie said. "But it wasn't a good road car. That long nose had a tendency to spin out at high speeds. I still drive my Jaguar. I brought it here all the way from North Carolina."

Judge Lexie opened the car's doors so the students could see the shining red leather interior, burled oak dashboard and leather steering wheel.

She shut the doors and the students went back to praising the exterior. "I like the silver cat on the hood," Paige said.

"The cat is a Jaguar," Lexie said. "That's Blackie's hood ornament. It's called a leaper."

Blackie? Helen wondered. Why was that name familiar?

"Is Blackie your car's name?" Derek asked. "My mom calls her beater the Blue Bomber."

"Blackie is short for Black Beauty," Judge Lexie said.

Helen felt suddenly alert, energized. Her mind was sparking, making connections. She remembered the conversation Jan had overheard between Mort and Lexie at the pet store. *"It's serious," Lexie said. "I need at least five thousand dollars to save Blackie."*

"I can make you a lot more than that," Mort said. "You'll be able to keep him in style."

"You'd better be right," Lexie said. *"I love him. He's part of my image."*

Jan had thought the judge was talking about a sick cat. But Jan cared about cats. Lexie wanted a major repair for her Jaguar, Blackie.

The Hasher School students were still admiring Blackie while Lexie drank in their praise like a life-giving fluid.

"Look at the snarling cats on the hubcaps," Austin said.

Ping! Another connection. That phrase—"snarling cats"—set off a sunburst in Helen's brain. She bent closer for a look at the cat face in the center of the closest hubcap. She'd seen that cat before.

"That's why this car is so awesome," Derek said. "Everything works. What year is it? A 'ninety-five?"

"Absolutely not," the judge said. Her smile vanished. "Jaguars were made by Ford in the nineties. I wouldn't own a Ford. My Jaguar is the real thing, made in Coventry when Jaguar was British owned."

Coventry! Helen thought. She stared at the snarling cat face on the hubcap. The same cat was on the bloodred medallion by Mort. She remembered the brass loop at the top. Was the medallion part of a key chain or key ring celebrating a genuine British Jaguar?

Only a true car snob would know or care if she had a Coventry Jaguar. Helen's brain made rapid-fire connections about cats, blood, medallions and murder.

"It was Lexie! She killed Mort!" Helen said softly.

"What?" Jan said. A few minutes ago, she'd been giggling with Helen. Now the blood drained from her face. She was deadly serious. "Helen, what are you talking about?"

"Lexie Deener killed Mort," Helen whispered. "He lost her money and she killed him out of revenge. She dropped her Jaguar medallion by his body. I saw it."

"No!" Jan screamed, as if she'd been stabbed in the heart. "Not my Mort."

As soon as she heard Jan's scream, Helen knew she'd made a mistake. She was supposed to be undercover, but she'd gone too deep. She forgot that Jan was not a trusted colleague but part of the case.

"I beg your pardon!" The judge's voice was frosty but equally loud. "If you ladies have something to say, share it with everyone."

Jan collapsed against the pillar, sobbing as if she'd just heard Mort was dead.

Dee abandoned her cats and ran over to her assistants. "Helen Hawthorne," she said, "why are you making a scene? Jan, what did she say?"

"Tell us what you said," Judge Lexie commanded. "What did you do to that woman? Why is she crying? You've interrupted my presentation and I demand to know why."

"So do I," Dee said.

"Uh." Helen stalled for time, trying to find a way past her blunder. The Hasher School students were silent. The only sound was Jan's heartbroken weeping. Helen could see Valerie and her photographer edging closer to video the scene.

"Tell me or you're fired," Dee said.

Helen saw Jan's desolate figure and took a deep breath. She'd wounded a good woman with her careless words. She was going to be fired anyway. Might as well go public. Maybe she could get justice for Mort and Jan.

"You killed Mort Barrymore," Helen said, her voice faltering. The crowd strained to hear. Several people said, "What?" and "Louder."

Helen raised her voice and said, "Lexie Deener, you killed Mort Barrymore, your financial adviser. I found him. That was your key chain medallion with the roaring Jaguar on the floor by his body."

"I have no idea what you're talking about," the judge said.

"Yes, you do," Helen said. "You killed Mort because he gave you a bad tip and lost all your money. You can't retire because his advice wiped out your account."

"You're crazy! I'll sue you for slander!" Judge Lexie said.

"Go ahead," Helen said. "You lost your key-chain medallion when you killed Mort at his house. You bashed in his head with a mahogany cat tower. That's your fingerprint on the medallion! I have your prints from your water bottle in my purse. I can prove you did it."

"Call the police," someone yelled.

"Shut up, Helen," Dee snarled.

Jan had stopped crying and stared at Lexie. Helen saw Valerie and the photographer shooting this heated exchange. Lexie stayed rooted to the parking lot.

"Valerie, here's your third story," Helen said. "Lexie Deener killed Mortimer Barrymore."

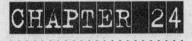

CHAPTER 24

Monday

It was a dog fight. A cat-tastrophe. The Hasher School Pet Appreciation Day was chaos and Helen caused it.

After Lexie Deener demanded a lawyer, she didn't say another word. But everyone else was shouting.

Several people called the police and the Broward Sheriff's Office. Or maybe the BSO heard the chatter on the radio about a ruckus at the school.

The school parking lot was flooded with dancing light bars and sirens, which made poor Barney the pug howl. Red and Chessie prowled restlessly in their cages, mewing unhappily.

In the confusion, Helen slipped out and called Phil and Nancie. She met Phil a block from the school and handed off Lexie's water bottle in a plastic bag. He promised to check it for prints. Nancie said she'd wait in her office until Phil confirmed the fingerprint was Lexie's before she acted.

The lawyer congratulated and chewed out Helen at the

same time. "You'd better pray that's Lexie Deener's print on the medallion," she said. "Otherwise you've slandered her in front of witnesses. If Valerie runs with that story, it's libel. Either way, Deener can sue for defamation."

"Valerie won't run the story until it's confirmed," Helen said.

"Good," Nancie said. "Warn her anyway."

When Helen snuck back into the cafeteria, the school was on lockdown. The teachers had quickly herded the students into the closest room. The little darlings texted Mom or called Daddy, and panicked parents materialized to carry away their children. Law enforcement determined that Lexie was not an immediate danger to the students and the lockdown order was lifted. The parents pushed their way into the building, ignoring the principal's protests that no murder or violent act had occurred. The parents wanted their children and they wanted them immediately.

None of the Pet Day presenters were allowed to leave until the police figured out what was going on. They waited glumly, tantalized by the smell of pizza and cheeseburger sliders. Helen tried to tamp down her hunger with memories of her school's mystery meat.

Everyone glared at Helen, and she wished she could disappear. She was relieved when Jan, her eyes red from crying, pulled her behind a pillar near the stage. "I am so sorry," Helen said. "I shouldn't have surprised you with that information." She felt like something scraped out of a litter box.

"Who are you?" Jan asked. "How could you spring this information about Mort's murder like this? It's so cruel."

"It is. I'm so sorry," Helen said. "I realized what Lexie did while she was talking to the students. I was wrong to blurt it out, but it may be the only way to catch Mort's killer."

Jan looked at Helen, her blue eyes filling with tears again. "Did that cat-show judge really kill my Mort?"

"Yes," Helen said. "You might as well know I'm a private detective investigating Mort's death. I went to work at Dee's to find out more about you. I also talked to Mort's office assistant, Carol Berman. She said Mort gave Lexie bad financial advice and she lost her retirement money."

Jan's smooth, pretty face was twisted with hate. "I hope Lexie fries," she said. "I hope she spends the rest of her life in prison. I hope—I hope she loses her damn Jaguar."

"That will probably hurt worse than prison," Helen said. "Lexie's nuts about that car."

"Dee's furious at you," Jan said. "If this cafeteria wasn't wall-to-wall cops, she'd strangle you. The cats are going crazy with the noise and we need to take them home."

"I'll help pack," Helen said.

"No, Dee's going to fire you."

"I expected that," Helen said, hoping she hid her glee. She'd miss Jan and the cats, but not the work.

"One more thing," Jan said. "A BSO deputy is looking for you. He wants to know why you caused this. That's him."

A lanky man about thirty-five approached them. His dark blond hair was threaded with silver, but he had cop's eyes, shrewd and alert.

"Are you Helen Hawthorne?" he asked.

She nodded.

"I'm Deputy Webster Maddow. You care to explain why you caused this circus? Your stupid remarks endangered those children. I should arrest you."

"I'm sorry," Helen said. "But I'm a private eye with Coronado Investigations, working on the Mort Barrymore murder." She brought out her credentials.

"The big-deal financial guy?" he asked.

"Right. He was bludgeoned in his home. A Peerless Point detective arrested the wrong person. I have proof."

Helen told the deputy what she had: the soda bottle with Lexie's prints, the medallion, the executive assistant who heard Lexie's angry words with Mort the Friday before he died.

"That's all?" Deputy Maddow asked. "Sounds weak to me. You may not even have a usable print. It's tricky comparing a latent print from a plastic bottle to a latent from that medallion."

"Can't you take Lexie's prints?" Helen asked.

"Not without her consent," he said. "You think she's in a mood to cooperate?"

Lexie sat near the steam table, silent and scowling like a cornered cat.

"But what about the shouting match at Mort's office?" she asked. "Carol Berman, his assistant, heard it."

"So they yelled at each other," the deputy said, and shrugged. "His assistant told you Ms. Deener was angry. She swore his cat would never win a ribbon. That's hardly a death threat."

"But she was furious," Helen said. "My partner and I discovered Mort's body. Someone who was really angry beat him to death. The killer would have blood on her—probably on her shoes or clothes. You could spray her car with luminol and get it off the car seat, the gas pedal or the carpet."

"Luminol isn't like what you see on TV, Ms. Hawthorne," the deputy said. "It doesn't light up like Times Square. The glow isn't much more than a watch dial. We'd have to tow her car to a garage, and a search warrant would be in order. Even if we did that, all we'd know was there's blood in the car. We'd need a DNA test to prove it was the victim's."

Helen's heart was thudding with fear. She was in

trouble. Big trouble. She'd shot off her mouth in front of dozens of witnesses. Angry witnesses trapped in a school cafeteria. They'd happily testify that she'd defamed Lexie Deener. She glimpsed a grim future of disgrace and bankruptcy.

While she was contemplating her ruined future, Deputy Maddow said, "Wait a minute. Peerless Point. They just got police cameras."

"You mean the red-light cameras that give you tickets?"

"No, more than that," he said. "Police cameras are a couple dozen cams throughout their little belt that capture tag numbers and instantly check the tag against wanted vehicles. The town keeps a record of the tags. This kind of camera shows the date and time of travel to and from.

"Peerless Point is real proud of that new technology. They've made four arrests with their new cameras."

"Do they even have crime?" Helen said.

"In a rich area like that? You bet. Break-ins, especially after the economy tanked. Somebody comes back from vacation and says their home was robbed. The police-cam database can help. The cam system also caught a stolen car driving through their town."

Helen felt a slight flutter of hope. "It would help if we could prove Lexie Deener was at Mort's," she said.

"The system cost more than a quarter of a million dollars, and the vendor charges another nine or ten thousand a year to maintain it," the deputy said. "Right now, the DEA is picking up the tab, but eventually the force is going to have to pay for its new toy with city money."

"I really want this to work," Helen said. "But Peerless Point has already arrested Mort's estranged wife for his murder. If you say you're looking for another suspect in a cleared case, will the police help you reopen that investigation?"

"No, but they don't need to know," Maddow said. "The little towns often don't do their own investigations. They have to ask the sheriff for help, but for whatever reason this time Peerless didn't. We have powers county-wide so we can start a parallel investigation. This would be a perfect gateway."

"I don't think the Peerless Point detective ever looked at anyone but Mort's wife, Trish," Helen said. "She really ticked them off."

"What did she do?" the deputy asked.

"Wanted them to put out an Amber Alert on her cat," Helen said. "When the officer refused, she did the 'Do you know who I am?' routine."

"That'll do it," he said. "I know someone there I can ask to have that license plate traced for me. Do you remember the date and approximate time of the crime?"

"Sure," Helen said. "It was Sunday night. Mort held up his arm to defend himself, and his watch took a direct hit at six p.m. I don't know Lexie's tag number, though."

"It's sitting right outside," he said.

"Oh. Right," Helen said. "Thanks. I don't know why you're helping me after all the trouble I caused."

"Because Ms. Deener's not acting like an innocent woman. You accuse her of murder in front of witnesses. She threatens to sue, which makes sense. But then she refuses to talk to anyone and wants a lawyer."

"That is her right," Helen said.

"Maybe so, but it's not how an innocent person acts," the deputy said. "Now she's got me curious."

"Mort's house is at Forty-two Peerless Point. Big white house with all the arches."

"I know it. Wrought-iron gate, buncha statues and red bougainvillea. Good. That stretch is where most of the cameras are. I'll see if her car was anywhere near his house around six Sunday night."

"Could be she was visiting him," Helen said.

"After he lost all her money and she made a scene at his office, she stops by for a friendly Sunday-night chat? I don't think so. If her car was nowhere near his house, I'll forget about it, and you, lady, are in big trouble."

Helen's cell phone buzzed. "May I get that?" she asked.

He nodded. It was Phil. "No luck on the print," he told Helen. "It was too smudged. We'll have to get her prints."

"Working on that now," Helen said. "I'll fill you in as soon as I have something."

The police were letting the Pet Day presenters leave, except for Helen and Lexie Deener. Helen tried to help pack up the cats, but Dee turned on her. "Get away from here," she hissed. "You're fired. Without references. And I'm docking you a day's pay." She stalked away.

Jan came over to say good-bye. "Thank you," she said. "You gave me a terrible shock, but now that I'm calmer, I understand why you did it. I hope you get Lexie. Are you coming to Mort's funeral Thursday?"

"I'll try," Helen said. "What about your job?"

"Let Dee fire me," Jan said. "I'm going."

"I enjoyed working with you," Helen said. "I wish I could tell the cats good-bye."

"I'll give them extra scratches," Jan said. "They're all too used to people leaving suddenly."

Dr. Bob, the veterinarian, saw her hauling the carriers and offered to help. Jan smiled at him, and he took Chessie's show cage and curtains. They made a handsome couple, the black-haired, blue-eyed Jan and the boyish vet. Maybe it was his profession, but Helen thought he followed her with puppylike devotion.

Helen paced the cafeteria, keeping far away from Lexie, glowering in her corner. The leopard-spotted insets on her suit rippled, and Helen thought the show judge's blood-tipped nails twitched whenever she looked Helen's way. She could almost feel the waves of hate rolling off Lexie.

"Helen!" Valerie breezed in, hair perfect, smile glowing, trailed by the tubby, grumpy photographer. "I had no idea Pet Appreciation Day would be so exciting. I have to head back to the station now, but I can't thank you enough."

Helen saw a tow truck pulling into the lot and Deputy Maddow loping into the cafeteria. "You might want to watch Lexie Deener," Helen said.

The deputy showed Lexie a warrant and said, "Ms. Deener, your car was photographed in the vicinity of Mortimer Barrymore's Peerless Point home between five forty-seven and six-oh-six the night he was murdered. I have a warrant to examine your car, and I'm going to take you into custody for questioning. You have the right to remain silent . . ."

"No!" Lexie screamed, as if she'd been knifed through the heart. "No, you can't."

"The hell I can't," the deputy said.

"You can't tow my beautiful car with a hook-and-chain truck. You'll damage the paint. You'll ruin the transmission! You have to use a flatbed truck. Don't hurt my beautiful Blackie!"

Deputy Maddow finished cautioning Lexie Deener, but it took four deputies to take her into custody. She fought like a wildcat.

CHAPTER 25

Monday

If Lexie Deener was distraught when the sheriff's office towed her car, she would have screamed bloody murder at what happened next.

The classic black '86 Jaguar was sprayed with luminol inside and out. The lab found bloody handprints on the driver's door, inside and out, and the red leather center console. A partial footprint smeared the carpet.

When the technicians photographed and then dismantled the door, they chipped Blackie's seven coats of black paint and clear lacquer and scratched the red hand-painted pinstripe. The pristine Connolly Leather panel was scarred when they processed the print on it. The hinges on the red leather center console were damaged when the compartment door was removed. The original Wilton wool carpet was cruelly sliced with a scalpel. The BSO needed the best evidence available.

The footprint was inconclusive, but the handprints

matched Lexie's. The blood was A negative, Mort's type. It occurred in about seven percent of the population.

Lexie Deener was arrested for the murder of Mortimer Barrymore. She still refused to talk without a lawyer.

Deputy Maddow told Helen that DNA tests were ordered. That's when Nancie Hays stepped in.

She didn't threaten. She didn't need to. Nancie's fierce reputation was threat enough. She simply said that an innocent woman was still in jail and she needed to be freed as soon as possible. Her client's husband was being buried Thursday morning, and Mrs. Barrymore had to attend his funeral for her health and mental well-being.

Repeated calls by reporter Valerie Cannata asking for a statement about Lexie Deener's arrest also probably helped speed the process.

DNA tests normally took three to four weeks because of the huge case backlog. But a DNA test for a murder—especially a high-profile killing that had attracted an insistent lawyer and an investigative reporter—got a rush order.

Back at the Coronado, Helen paced restlessly, waiting to hear the test results. If that wasn't Mort's blood in Lexie's car, she'd be sued sideways. True, A negative was fairly rare. And while only seven percent had it, that was still a staggering number—more than sixty-two thousand men in Broward County alone.

"Go take a shower," Phil told her. "Your pacing is driving me crazy, and you've got cat hair on your clothes."

Helen showered and washed and dried her long brown hair, but the dryer failed to blow away her worries. Phil poured her a glass of wine, but she left it untouched. At four o'clock, Valerie called and said, "Helen, I can't thank you enough. You're the lead story on the five-o'clock news."

"So, it's confirmed Lexie Deener killed Mort?" Helen asked hopefully.

"Not quite, but I have enough for a story," Valerie said.

Helen nearly wore a groove in the terrazzo floor, waiting for the news at five. At four fifty, Phil popped his delicious, made-from-scratch popcorn, then forced her to sit on his black leather couch. He handed her the wineglass and said, "Drink." He didn't have to tell her to eat the popcorn. She absently munched handfuls until the news came on.

When Valerie was on the trail of a hot story, she practically sizzled on-screen. She'd freshened her makeup and changed into an eye-catching lilac sheath for this story.

Her story began with video of Lexie lecturing the Hasher School children. "Lexie Deener, a senior supervisor for a North Carolina medical equipment company and a Gold Cup Cat Fanciers' Association show judge," Valerie said, "was accused of murdering Peerless Point financier Mortimer Barrymore today by a partner in Coronado Investigations, the successful South Florida private-eye firm."

Helen groaned and took a gulp of wine while she watched herself on video calling Lexie a killer.

"The incident occurred at the Hasher School Pet Appreciation Day. Mr. Barrymore's estranged wife, socialite Trish Barrymore, has been charged with murdering her husband by the Peerless Point police.

"Ms. Deener denied the allegations made by private investigator Helen Hawthorne, then refused to talk to anyone, including the police and this reporter."

More video of Lexie frowning and shaking her head.

"BSO Deputy Webster Maddow checked the Peerless Point camera system and confirmed that a car fitting the description of Ms. Deener's"—the camera panned the glossy black Jaguar—"was videoed in the vicinity of Mr. Barrymore's home at the time police say he was bludgeoned to death.

"Deputy Maddow obtained a warrant to tow Ms. Deener's car to the lab." The dramatic video of Lexie screaming that her car had to be towed on a flatbed truck followed.

"As you can see, Ms. Deener was cautioned and taken into custody," Valerie said. "Neither Deputy Maddow nor the BSO would comment further on the case, but two sources have confirmed that bloody handprints were found in Ms. Deener's vintage Jaguar. The prints match Ms. Deener's, and the blood type matches Mr. Barrymore's.

"Channel Seventy-seven is the only station with this story, and we will continue to keep you updated as it develops."

A commercial for laundry soap followed. Helen realized she was sitting with her mouth open, holding a handful of popcorn.

Phil was all smiles. "Valerie played the story straight, but still gave the impression that Lexie is guilty," he said. "Nice plug for our business, too."

"I just hope we have a business," Helen said. "We're dead if that's not Mort's blood."

"Of course it's Mort's," Phil said. "Who else would it belong to? You worry too much."

And you don't worry enough, Helen wanted to say.

She glanced at her watch. "It's five thirty," she said. "Aren't you supposed to go to the Fisherman's Tale tonight and meet Zach's dodgy friend, Xavier Dave?"

"You're right, darlin'," Phil said in his annoying fake-redneck drawl. "Got me a new T-shirt at a thrift shop for my disguise, too."

Five minutes later, he was wearing his ball cap with the built-in mullet, seat-sprung pants and a stretched-out T-shirt sporting a Lab holding a six-pack and this legend: REDNECK RETRIEVER—CUZ I'M FIXIN TO HAVE ME A COLD ONE.

"How much did you pay for that shirt?" Helen asked.

"Twenty-five whole cents," he said.

"You wuz robbed," she said, grinning and gathering her keys and her purse.

"Whoa, whoa, where are you going?" he asked.

"To the Fisherman's Tale, so I can eavesdrop. I'll meet you there."

"But that's no place for a woman alone. Sleazy guys will try to pick you up," Phil said.

"That's their problem," Helen said. "I'm in no mood to play wifey and wait for you at home."

She unlocked her car, waved good-bye and drove to the Fisherman's Tale.

Phil was already seated at the bar when Helen entered. She was slapped in the face by Pine-Sol and stale air. The same lowlifes seemed to be at the bar, except this time the lone woman had carrot-red hair and no front teeth.

Helen's skin crawled when she felt the bar-goers eyeing her. She swung by the bar to buy a beer, and saw Phil slide two twenties across the water-ringed surface, way too much for a beer in this joint.

"That's him at the table behind you," the bartender said.

Phil slapped down another twenty and said, "Gimme a couple bags of peanuts, two packs of beef jerky and a beer for my friend at that table."

He took both beers and the snacks and invited himself to sit down. Helen ignored the bartender's ham-fisted efforts at flirting and sat at the sticky table behind Phil, where she could listen.

If Xavier Dave was a car salesman, he wasn't a successful one. He wore the only sports jacket in the bar, navy with shiny elbows. His shirt was dingy white, and the cuffs of his khakis were frayed. His red tie hung limp around his neck, as if it had surrendered.

Helen looked up and saw a scrawny man with a Guns N' Roses T-shirt and stringy hair that could be called dirty blond for its color and condition. "Why's a pretty little thing like you all alone?" he asked.

"Because I like it that way," Helen snarled, and he backed away.

"Okay, okay," he said. "If I wanted to be yelled at, I'd be home with my old lady."

Phil and his offerings of beer and snacks had sparked a conversation with Xavier Dave. Helen tuned in.

"You can call me XD," he said.

"You had it right, Phil. Ol' Zach really did a number on poor Mike."

Mike, Helen thought. That would be Mike Fernier, the skinny red-haired guy who went to prison for dealing years ago.

"Zach owed Mike twenty grand, and when the feds started nosing around, Zach disappeared with the money. Now Mike's out of jail and wants his money. He coulda rolled on Zach, like you said, but he didn't. Mike asked him nicely for the money. Said Zach could pay him back in installments.

"Zach taunted him, telling him, 'I ain't got it. So sue me.' Mike needs that money. The only job he can get is with a lawn service, and it's hot, sweaty work, killing weeds and cutting grass. Cuttin' grass. How do you like that? Some friend Zach was."

"Mike deserves to get his money back," Phil said, nodding sympathetically.

"Damn right he does," XD said.

"Like I said, I'm working for Zach's estate," Phil said.

Technically true, Helen thought. Margery did inherit Zach's condo and life insurance.

"I might be able to help out you and your friend," Phil said.

"You think?" XD said.

He sounded absurdly hopeful. Nobody's as gullible as a con artist, Helen thought.

"Do you think Mike was mad enough to poison Zach?" Phil asked. "Not that I care. I never knew the man personally, but he didn't seem to be any great loss."

"That twenty thou would have made Mike's life much easier," XD said. "I was here when he asked Zach for it. He was real polite about it, but Zach refused to give him a nickel. Next time Mike came in and talked to Zach, trying to reason with him, they ended up fighting. Mike swung at Zach and they broke a chair, and Mike got himself eighty-sixed.

"Now Mike's barred from this place permanently. It ain't fair. But I think Mike would hesitate before killing someone. He's afraid of going back to jail again.

"You ask me, Zach did himself in. He started losing his health about six or eight months ago and felt life wasn't worth living. I'm not surprised Zach committed suicide."

Another one for the suicide theory, Helen thought.

"Maybe. But rat poison is a nasty way to go," Phil said.

"He was tired of doctors running tests on him," Mike said. "Kept saying they didn't find anything, but Zach always felt kind of unwell."

"What was wrong?" Phil asked. "Can I get you another beer?"

"You sure can, and more of that beef jerky."

Helen waited for Phil to return, mentally circling her table with barbed wire to keep the barflies away. They were still watching her, and she was uneasy.

Phil was back with two cold ones and another round of snacks. "You were telling me Zach hadn't been feeling well for six months or so."

"Yeah. He had a rash he couldn't get rid of on his stomach and numb, tingly fingers—which didn't help in his line of work. He lost all his hair. You'd never guess it, he had such a good wig, but he hated being bald, and he had the trots all the time. It was wearing him down.

"He told me he was ready to end it all. He didn't like

guns, so I don't think he'd shoot himself. I could see him pouring rat poison in his beer, though.

"Zach felt even lower because he tried to hook up with his ex-wife, Margery, and she wouldn't give him the time of day. He actually got on his knees and begged her, and she kicked him in the nuts. She's a real piece of work.

"When Margery told him to get lost, he just gave up. You might think it's silly for someone our age to die of love, but that's what finished him. You ask me, Margery killed Zach."

CHAPTER 26
· ·

Monday/Tuesday

Zach didn't commit suicide. Helen knew it. Phil's conversation with XD convinced her she was right: A man as vain as Zach wouldn't deliberately lose his hair. Someone poisoned him.

She was so excited by this insight, she could hardly wait to get back to the Coronado. She muttered and growled at the traffic on her way home from the Fisherman's Tale. Each red light, every snarled intersection kept her from looking up the symptoms for arsenic poisoning on her computer.

At home in Phil's apartment, she breezed past her husband on her way to the computer. "Good work at the bar," she said, kissing him lightly. "Inspiring, too. I'm checking a theory."

"What theory?" Phil asked.

"Let me get the facts first," she said.

She got the information—almost too much. She read it and then read it again. It confirmed her suspicions.

"Phil, Margery couldn't have poisoned Zach with weed killer," she said. "Listen to the symptoms if he'd swallowed a big slug of arsenic-based weed killer: He'd have had nausea, vomiting, massive diarrhea and more, ending in heart failure.

"I don't see anything about instant hair loss, and we know he wore a wig. Margery saw him popping Tums, so he must have had nausea, but the other symptoms sound so severe he couldn't have walked into Beachie's restaurant."

"He barely walked out, remember?" Phil said. "He had to be helped out."

"Okay, he was sick," Helen said. "Definitely. But what he had sounds more like a low-dose poisoning over a long time. That's where he'd get the rash on his gut, the hair loss, numb fingers and generally lousy feeling."

"So, you're saying the cops, his doctors and the medical examiner made a mistake?" Phil asked. Thumbs jumped into his lap, and he idly scratched the cat's ears.

"Highly likely," Helen said. "The detective saw Margery using weed killer, knew she inherited Zach's estate and hated his guts. He jumped to the conclusion that she killed her ex."

"And everyone else was wrong, too?" Phil asked.

"You'd be surprised," Helen said. "I found a slew of studies that show the official cause of death is wrong about one-third of the time."

"A slew?" Phil said. Thumbs was kneading his leg with his big paws.

"Highly technical detective term meaning 'a whole bunch,' " Helen said.

"Nice work," Phil said. "Except, who did kill Zach?"

"His former good buddy Mike," Helen said. "With his job, he has access to weed killer and the time to slowly poison him. XD, who still saw Zach after Mike was eighty-sixed from the bar, could have kept slipping small doses in his beer."

"Possible," Phil said. "But how do we prove it?"

"We're back to nothing again, aren't we?" Helen said, and sighed.

At least she'd quit pacing. A phone call from Valerie at eleven thirty that night confirmed the news Helen had been waiting for: That was Mort's DNA in the Jaguar. Lexie Deener literally had Mort's blood on her hands. She'd left her prints in the car and on the cat medallion. She was formally charged with the murder of Mort Barrymore.

Helen had escaped a libel suit.

Helen and Phil celebrated in bed, then fell asleep, but this time they left the phone on.

Nancie's call woke up the pair of PIs at two fifteen in the morning. "I'm leaving the North Broward jail," she said. "Trish has been released."

"Huh? What?" Phil said.

"Trish has been released from jail," Nancie said.

"So quick?" Phil said.

"Impossibly quick. The Peerless Point cops were falling all over themselves to get her out of jail," Nancie said. She couldn't resist a touch of bluster. "They know I'm coming after them. Meet me in my office at three o'clock."

"Three a.m. today? Right now?" Phil asked, still sleep stupid.

"If I wanted to talk to you in the afternoon, I would have waited till morning to call," Nancie said, her voice crisp as starched cotton. She hung up before he could say anything else.

Helen threw on a clean shirt and jeans and slipped into her sandals. She didn't bother with makeup. Phil put on the same shirt and pants he'd tossed on a chair the night before, and they stumbled outside. The night air wrapped around them like a warm, moist blanket. The Coronado looked eerie and abandoned in the moonless night.

"The place feels so dark and empty without Margery,"

Helen said, and yawned. "At least I'm free to help you work on her case now that I've been fired. I won't have to wash cats in the morning. You drive. I'm afraid I'll fall asleep on Federal Highway."

"The Jeep doesn't have air-conditioning," Phil said.

"I'm too tired to care," she said.

Helen snoozed for most of the drive. She was awakened by a police siren at a no-tell motel near Port Everglades and stayed awake until Phil parked at Nancie's law office.

Inside, the office smelled of freshly brewed coffee. Helen and Phil poured themselves cups and sat across from Trish.

Jail and the strain since her husband's murder had taken its toll on Trish. Helen caught a glimpse of how their client would look in old age. At this hour, her pale, papery skin was crisscrossed with fine lines and her blond hair was frizzed and straggly. She'd lost so much weight, her wrist bones looked like knobs. Trish's navy pantsuit emphasized the dark circles under her eyes.

Nancie, who had superhuman powers, was alert and ready for battle, but even she showed signs of wear. Her suit was wrinkled and her dark hair was limp and flat.

Helen and Phil sat like a pair of pups expecting to be congratulated for their good work. Instead, Nancie swatted them both.

"Helen, you had a narrow escape today," the lawyer said.

Helen kept her head bowed, but Phil jumped to her defense. "Helen took a risk, but she was right," he said. "She jump-started the process. There's no way Trish would be free so fast if Helen hadn't accused the killer in front of witnesses. We're lucky the press was there. Valerie was a big help."

"What good is being free if I don't have my baby?" Trish wailed. "She's my reason for living."

The cat! Helen and Phil had forgotten about Justine.

Helen tried not to look at Phil. How could they have forgotten that blasted cat?

"We could ask the prosecutor to make a deal so Lexie tells us where she stashed the cat," Phil said.

"You're supposed to find her," Trish sobbed. "That's why I'm paying you."

Nancie interrupted Trish's tears with a harsh dose of reality. "Not a chance, Phil," she said. "Justine may be Trish's baby, but to the law, she's a cat."

Trish's howls ascended the scale and made the hair stand up on Helen's neck. She's crying as if she really did lose a child, she thought. Helen tried to be sympathetic, but Trish didn't cry that much over Mort.

"The prosecutor is not going to make a deal on a murder case to find a missing cat," Nancie said. "Animals and humans are still not equal under the law."

"And that's the problem," Trish wept. She reached for the tissues beside her chair with shaking hands and blotted her tear-reddened eyes.

"Did you ask Lexie where Justine is?" Phil said.

"Me?" Nancie said. "Why would she talk to me? She's not my client."

"Her lawyer, then," Phil said. "You could make sure she's not charged with animal abuse."

Trish's crying rose to a frantic, hysterical shriek. "My baby's out there all alone, with no food or water. Locked away someplace, frightened and hungry."

"Sh, Trish," Nancie said. "You have to concentrate if we're going to help Justine.

"I talked with Ms. Deener's lawyer, Phil. He assures me that his client does not have your cat. She swore up and down that she didn't kidnap Justine."

"And you believe that?" Helen asked. "A half-million dollars' ransom would restore her lost fortune."

"I could give her a reward if she helped find Justine," Trish said, sniffling into a tissue.

"I don't think she can," Nancie said. "Her lawyer told me he mentioned the catnapping to her and she seemed surprised. Ms. Deener told him there's no way she'd kidnap a cat when she was on a road trip—it would be too difficult to keep. As a criminal lawyer, he says he's used to dealing with liars. He believes his client is telling the truth about the cat."

Helen heard that lawyerly quibble "about the cat." Did Lexie tell her lawyer she'd murdered Mort—or was she lying about that, too?

"I was sure when we found the killer we'd have the catnapper," Nancie said, "but now I think the killer and the kidnapper are two different people. We'll know for sure tomorrow. Isn't that when the kidnapper is supposed to call you?"

Helen and Phil nodded like a pair of bobble-head dolls. Helen tried to hide another yawn.

"Today, actually," Phil said. "The special phone number's all set up and we're monitoring it. We have the kidnapper's cash in our office safe, marked with SmartWater and ready to go. The kidnapper will probably call right before the exchange, so we won't have time to check out the setup or bring in additional operatives."

"Are you sure the kidnapper can't see that the money is marked?" Trish asked. "I want my Justine and I won't take any risks with her life. I don't care about the money. My baby comes first."

What's it like to be so rich you don't care about half a million bucks? Helen wondered. If someone kidnapped Thumbs, would I pony up that much cash? She felt uneasy that she even had to ask herself that question.

"It's safe, I promise," Phil said.

"You'll call as soon as you hear from the kidnapper, won't you?" Trish asked.

"We'll call as soon as we can," Phil said. "If we have to

be someplace in a hurry, we may call you after it's over and we have your cat safe and sound."

That provoked a fresh round of tears.

"Trish!" Nancie said sharply. "I know you're tired and emotional, but this isn't helping you or Justine."

"You're right," Trish said. "I have to pull myself together. Now that Mort's gone, she only has me."

"What if we brought in the police for backup?" Phil asked.

"The police! After the way they treated me? Those bunglers?" Trish spat out the words. "The kidnapper will see them and kill my baby. They couldn't even find the right killer. You did that. I'd still be in jail if it wasn't for you. I don't trust anyone in Peerless Point."

"After the way they treated Trish, can you blame her?" Nancie asked.

"Trish, are you able to drive home now? I need to discuss another case with Helen and Phil."

"Arthur, my fiancé, will take me home," Trish said. "I called him from your car, remember? He's probably waiting in your parking lot now."

Nancie walked Trish outside to Arthur's waiting arms. Helen dozed off during the short time the lawyer was gone.

"Helen!" Nancie said, and she snapped to attention. "What have you and Phil found out about Margery?"

"I met with Zach's buddy, XD, at a bar," Phil said. "He believes Zach killed himself because he was in love with Margery and she gave him the boot."

"Do you think XD would sign a statement and testify to Zach's state of mind if Margery's case goes to trial?" Nancie asked.

"Another beer or two and maybe a burger and I think he'll say yes," Phil said.

"I still don't think Zach killed himself," Helen said. "I did some research about arsenic, and Zach's symptoms—his feeling off, the skin rashes, weakness and hair loss—point to slow, long-term arsenic poisoning. Someone was feeding him small doses and slowly killing him. If he'd taken one large shot of rat poison, like Phil said, he'd have had a much more violent end."

"Right now, we need XD's information about Zach's possible suicide," Nancie said. "It will muddy the water nicely if we have to go to trial. Helen, you keep working on the murder theory.

"Phil, I want you to investigate Mike the ex-con and this XD character and see if you can get a statement from XD about his belief that Zach committed suicide. Skip the burger. Spring for a steak.

"And, whatever you do, don't screw up the cat ransom tomorrow."

"Today," Phil corrected.

CHAPTER 27

* * * * * * * * * * * * * * * * * * *

Tuesday

C ats are magical creatures, Helen thought, as she
sipped her coffee on the couch in Phil's apartment.
Her own cat, Thumbs, was curled up next to her,
purring. Cats can't talk or walk through walls, though they
seem to have those powers. But they are calming.

Since nine o'clock this morning, I've downed four cups
of coffee, waiting for the catnapper's call. Phil's worked
himself into a sweaty, twitching mess of caffeine nerves.

We both know we have to recover that kidnapped kitten. Our reputation—the future of our agency—is wrapped
up in Justine's small gray paws.

I'm scared, too. Phil may be the only man in the world
for me, but he can't help me wait out this crisis. All we
can do is worry together. Thumbs and his rumbly purr
ward off the gnawing anxiety.

Thumbs weighs only fifteen pounds. He has no pedi-
gree. By any breed standard, his soft, six-toed paws are
deformed. Yet he rules our household through the force

of his personality. Phil and I run on his schedule: his breakfast is served at seven a.m., his dinner is at seven p.m., his litter box is cleaned, his ears are scratched and he scores an occasional shrimp treat.

He's smart enough to be content with that. Thumbs knows the secret of serenity. He gives it, too. He has an uncanny knack for coolly sidestepping mayhem. His first owner was murdered. I swiped him from his second owner and used the cat's DNA to send that person to prison. Thumbs has stayed with me ever since. He adopted Phil, and now he's sitting with me during this crisis, watching me with those shrewd golden-green eyes outlined with dark feline mascara. His sturdy body is a patchwork of stripes and pure white fur. He's a creature of many parts.

Helen was scratching the thick fur along the cat's shoulders when she heard the special ring tone for the kidnapper's line. She checked the clock: ten forty-five. Helen jumped.

Phil pounced on the phone and hit the Speaker and Record buttons.

"Mrs. Barrymore." The voice was cold, mechanical, computer generated.

"This is Mrs. Barrymore's assistant," Phil said. He and Helen had rehearsed this opening a dozen times.

"Where. Is. Mrs. Barrymore?" the inhuman voice demanded, flat and uninflected.

"If you really have Justine, you know where Mrs. Barrymore is," Phil said. Nancie and the BSO had agreed to withhold the news of her release for twenty-four hours, and Valerie was cooperating, with the promise of another hot scoop.

"If. This. Is. A. Trick. Justine. Will. Go. To. A. Kill. Shelter," the eerie voice said. "We. Know. What. Will. Happen. Next."

"Mrs. Barrymore wants her cat back," Phil said. Helen saw sweat beading on his forehead. "I'll follow your instructions. I have five hundred thousand dollars in twenties in a duffel bag ready for the transfer." The cash-stuffed bag was waiting by his front door.

Helen held her breath. So far, so good. She reached for her keys and purse, ready to go.

"Do you know the Dive Bar?" the voice asked, each word a separate sentence.

"The one on A1A near Oakland Park Boulevard?" Phil asked.

"That's the one. On the Northeast Thirty-third Street side of the building there is a mural."

"The seascape?" Phil said.

"Yes. There's a planter under the mural. Leave the bag under the naked lady."

Naked lady? Helen wondered, but Phil simply nodded. "I know the spot," he said.

"The cat will be returned in the same spot at noon in its carrier. Someone will be watching you. If you try to follow, you'll never see the cat again."

Helen's heart was thumping so loudly, she could hardly track the slow, mechanical voice.

"How about proof of life?" Phil said. "Can you e-mail me a photo of Justine?"

"You want proof of life?" the voice intoned. "How about this?"

Helen heard a small, indignant *"Yerp!"* The cat sounded more annoyed than injured. They'd have to take it on faith that was Justine.

"You think I'm a fool?" the voice said, each word slow and pronounced the same. "E-mails can be traced. For your stupidity, I've cut five minutes off your time. Drop off the money at exactly eleven o'clock. And hope the draw-bridge doesn't go up, or the cat goes to the kill shelter."

The phone disconnected, and Helen and Phil were out the door and running for their cars. He had the duffel bag of marked money in his hand.

"I'll make the drop-off," he said. "You go ahead and

park in one of the spots across from the mural. Wait for the kidnapper to pick up the money. I'll drive away, park in the next block and jog back. We'll follow the catnapper's car in your Igloo. Whoever picks up the money will have a hard time making a left onto A1A, so they'll probably go right. Hurry!"

They started their cars and raced through midmorning traffic, recklessly passing slower cars. Helen prayed they didn't hit any pedestrians crossing at the lights. They both shot through yellow lights and crossed their fingers they weren't caught by the dreaded traffic cameras. The Dive Bar was on A1A near the edge of the concrete condo canyon known as Galt Ocean Mile.

At precisely ten fifty-nine, tense and breathless, Helen turned left into Northeast Thirty-third Street and slid into an angled spot with a clear view of the Dive Bar's seascape mural.

Phil's Jeep slammed onto the side street shortly after her. He drove past the Igloo, while Helen watched the area. Northeast Thirty-third was a sliver of Old Florida, a stretch of sidewalk cafés, wine bars and upscale shops shaded by spreading trees and manicured hedges.

The Dive Bar was no dive, but a sea-themed saloon with sidewalk tables. Chalk signs advertised local bands and daily specials. Helen's stomach growled when she caught the perfume of broiling burgers. The outside mural was a bold blue design with swirling waves, colorful fish and bright coral, but she didn't see any naked woman on the wall.

Phil parked the Jeep next to the mural, jumped out with the bag and left it in the planter. Now she saw the lady—what looked like waves were actually the discreet outlines of a nude woman. Phil drove away.

Helen held her breath. Once Phil's Jeep was gone, she waited, hoping no casual pedestrian noticed the dark nylon bag in the planter. How could she tell a passing shopper from the real catnapper? Would the kidnapper's bag person be a man or a woman? She didn't know.

Two women, chatting and carrying shopping bags, passed the spot, oblivious. Helen relaxed a little, until she saw a sixtyish woman with spiky black hair, gold lamé shorts and matching tennis shoes walking a Chihuahua with a gold bow. The little dog stopped at every bush and tree, each time inching closer to the money bag.

The spindly four-pound dog must be all kidneys, Helen thought. She held her breath as they neared the planter.

Would this woman pick up the kidnapper's money? Was she the catnapper?

The pair trotted past the planter without a second glance.

Eleven-oh-four. Where is the kidnapper? Helen was uneasy. A half-million dollars was sitting in a planter. Shoppers, diners and tourists were strolling along the crowded sidewalk. Someone could spot the bulging bag at any moment. The wrong person could walk off with Justine's ransom money. They'd lose that poor cat and their agency.

Where was Phil? If the kidnapper grabbed the money, Helen would have to take off and follow the car. She glanced in the rearview mirror and thought she might have seen her PI partner loping along the sidewalk across the way, but she didn't dare turn around and lose sight of the money bag.

A man in brown work khakis stopped beside the planter, directly in front of the spot where the bag nestled, and lit a cigarette. He blew out long dragon streams of smoke and surveyed the busy street scene.

Come on, Helen thought. Pick up the bag and go. Let's get this over.

Then Khaki Man made his move. He stubbed out his cigarette and sauntered into the bar.

That's when a slender brunette in a red Dodge Charger squealed up in front of the planter, hopped out, grabbed the bag, tossed it in the front seat and jumped in after it. A Toyota behind her beeped its horn. The Charger was blocking traffic. The brunette hit the gas, roared out of Thirty-third Street and turned right on A1A, going much too fast.

Helen saw Phil jogging toward her. She opened the Igloo's door and said, "Hurry! The catnapper just grabbed the bag. It's a woman, a fit-looking brunette, heading south on A1A. We caught a break. She's driving a bright red Charger, so she'll be easier to track. Buckle up and let's go."

Phil had barely snapped on his seat belt when Helen swung out of the space and turned onto A1A.

"There it is," she said. "The red car waiting at the stoplight."

"Middle lane," Phil said. "She's not turning onto Oakland Park. We're about six cars behind. Let's try to keep it that way."

Highway A1A ran along the ocean, but this morning they weren't there to look at the water. Helen followed the red Charger for about a mile, until they came to a section with impressive towers on the west side and about four blocks of small apartments on the beach side.

"Her signal's on," Phil said. "She's turning left at the next street."

"Good," Helen said. "The security won't be as good in these small buildings."

They followed the Charger for a block, then it turned left again onto a street lined with midcentury-modern apartments painted white, pink and turquoise.

"Funky little area close to the beach," Phil said. "We'll have to explore it sometime."

"Later," Helen said, then realized she sounded abrupt. "Sorry. I didn't mean to snap at you."

"Keep driving," Phil said, his voice soft. "Don't slow down and don't stop. She's turning into that pink apartment lot. Keep on going."

CHAPTER 28

Tuesday

Helen ditched the car in a parking spot around the corner and tossed a couple of quarters into the meter. She and Phil ran the half block to the street with the pink apartment. Once they were in sight of the building, they strolled along, hand in hand, another couple going for a walk near the sea.

"What department's jurisdiction is this?" Helen asked.

"Ireland Beach PD," Phil said.

"Look," Helen said. "She's lugging the money bag inside the pink apartment."

The midcentury-modern building, pale pink with black accents, was starkly framed by straight, tall palms. The deceptively simple building had been beautiful once, but after sixty-some years of storms and salty ocean air, the paint was faded and peeling, the gutters were rusted and the aluminum window frames were pitted and tarnished.

A thirtysomething brunette in black booty shorts, ankle-strap heels and a turquoise tank top teetered along the building's cracked sidewalk. Helen saw the ropy muscles bulging in her right arm as she hung on to the duffel bag. She seemed strong, but hauling that bulging bag of marked money slowed her down.

"Does she look familiar to you?" Helen asked.

Phil shook his head no.

"I think I've seen her before," Helen said. But the only brunettes she could remember from this case were Jan Kurtz and Gabby Garcia, Dee's maid. Both would be working now.

The private eyes slowed their walk as the brunette opened the outer glass door. They hustled up the walkway as she elbowed her way through the inner door.

"No doorman and no security," Helen said. "Bless these old buildings with cheap landlords."

By the time they were inside, the steel elevator doors had swallowed the mystery woman. The lobby, a dirty pale pink, was littered with take-out menus and free newspapers. A dusty silk ficus molted in the corner.

They watched the fourth-floor number light up over the elevator. "She's on the top floor," Phil said. "You take the stairs on the right and I'll take the fire stairs on this side. Meet you at the top."

Helen ran up the grimy black-painted stairs splotched with old chewing gum and sticky with spilled drinks. The pink walls were decorated with a haphazard collage of handprints and missing patches of plaster.

When she finally reached the fourth floor, Helen was puffing slightly. She paused to catch her breath and read the hall sign. Apartments 40 through 44 were on the left, 45 through 49 on the right.

Helen heard the rattle of a door handle around the corner to her left and sprinted toward it. The industrial gray carpet was stained and dirty, but it silenced her footsteps. She hoped Phil was doing the same thing on the other side.

The mystery woman was unlocking the apartment at

the end of the hall—number 44. Helen saw the fire-stairs door was open about an inch on the other side. Phil.

The catnapper had the bag of cash tucked between her feet as she twisted the doorknob. It didn't open. Stuck. She slammed her shoulder against the door. Helen saw the fire-stairs door slowly open, and she raced down toward the woman.

As the mystery woman grabbed the money bag, Phil and Helen shoved her through her own door. The three of them tumbled inside the apartment and Phil shut the door.

The woman's brown wig slid loose. Helen pulled it off and recognized the flattened honey blond locks of Amber Waves, Mort's pole-dancing girlfriend.

"Amber!" she said. "You're the catnapper!"

Amber gave a little scream and tried to escape, but Phil blocked the door and shot the bolt.

"Mrs. Raines is right next door," Amber said, her voice shaking with fear. "When she hears me shout, she'll call the police."

"Good," Phil said. "We're calling the police anyway."

"Why?" Amber said, looking at Phil with wide, not-so-innocent brown eyes.

"You stole Mort's cat, Justine, and held her for ransom," Phil said.

"What cat?" Amber said. "I don't see any cat."

Helen saw a dingy living room with a sagging, yellow-flowered couch, a floral riot gone wrong. One lampshade was dented, and the oak coffee table was scratched.

"Mew!" A tiny noise. A smoky blue-gray fur ball slid out from under the couch and patted Phil's shoe with one dainty paw. *"Mew!"*

Helen was transfixed. The gray kitten seemed to dominate the grungy room. Helen had seen enough champions to recognize the proud chest, haughty carriage and glossy fur of a natural winner.

"Well, hello, Justine," Phil said, scooping up the fluffy

kitten. She was so small, she nearly fit in the palm of his hand. Her copper eyes glowed like new pennies.

"That's my kitten," Amber said.

"Really?" Phil said. "You can afford a pedigreed Chartreux? Amazing. A kitten like this must cost a month's rent at this dump."

"I got her at the pound," Amber said.

"Well, that's easy to prove," Phil said. "Justine was microchipped. We'll have a vet scan her."

Helen pointed to the bejeweled bus-shaped carrier. "And that's Justine's Baby Coach sitting near the TV," she said. "She never travels in anything else."

"That's right," Amber said, quickly changing her story. "I'm cat-sitting for Mort, and you can't prove otherwise." She shifted effortlessly from fear to defiance.

"You're an extremely well-paid cat sitter," Phil said. "That's half a million dollars in that bag."

"So?" Amber said, her voice insolent. "It's mine."

"Can you prove it?" Phil said. "Because we can prove it doesn't belong to you. Where did you get it?"

Helen stepped in front of Amber and grabbed the bag. Amber lunged for her, slashing at Helen with her pink-painted claws. "I said it's mine!"

Phil caught her arm and twisted it behind her back, still cupping the kitten in one hand. "Easy, there. That's a question for the police," he said. "You've kidnapped this cat and tried to get half a million for her from Mort's wife, Trish."

"Prove it!" Amber was brazen, but then, she'd had time to master that skill pole dancing in the clubs.

"We recorded you," Phil said. He held up his cell phone. "Right here."

"Play it," Amber challenged him.

"Mrs. Barrymore," the computer-generated voice said.

"Sounds just like me," she said with a sneer.

Helen saw a black speaker box, a snake coil of cords and a headset piled on the coffee table. "And what's this?"

she said, picking it up. "Looks like a voice changer to me." She examined the connectors. "For an iPhone. Amber, Amber, you used your own cell phone to make the catnapping calls. Very foolish and very traceable."

Helen unzipped the Baby Coach and gently lifted the little cat into her traveling home. Justine gave a loud, contented purr as she settled in.

"Kitchen," Phil mouthed, and Helen and the cat retreated around the corner into that dreary, cluttered room.

Phil kneeled in front of Amber, took her long, smooth hands in his, and looked into her eyes. Helen knew how persuasive he could be when he talked to someone that way. She couldn't help admiring his chiseled jaw, strong shoulders and silky silver-white hair.

Neither could Amber.

"Amber," he said, his voice soft and sympathetic. Helen almost expected him to put his collar on backward to hear her confession. His absolute attention and intensity made susceptible people want to unload ugly truths. "You're in a lot of trouble. Mort's dead, his cat is missing and your DNA was found at the murder scene." That last part wasn't true, but Amber didn't know that.

"We know the time of the murder, because Mort put up his arm to defend himself when he was beaten, and his watch stopped at exactly six o'clock Sunday night. The Peerless Point police have a camera system that tracks license plates along the main road where Mort's house is, and your car was videoed going to the house. There's about a ten-minute break, and then your car leaves his home. Don't you see, Amber? You're at the scene at the time of his death. You have a motive. You thought Mort would marry you, and he chose another woman. You're on the hook for his murder."

"I didn't do it," Amber wailed. "I didn't kill him. I went to his house because he promised to give me a parting gift—a check for six months' rent on my pole-specialist studio. When I got there, his front door was open and there was blood on the doorstep. I knew something was wrong, so I used my scarf to open the door and stepped around the blood. I didn't want to leave prints."

"Clever," Phil said.

Conniving, Helen thought.

"Mort was lying on the floor"—she paused dramatically—"dead. There was no doubt. I looked everywhere for my check, but I didn't see it.

"Instead, I saw Justine, hiding in the bottom of her cat tower. So I packed her in her carrier and took her."

Helen was shocked and disgusted. Amber had left Mort, the man she wanted to marry, dead on the floor while she looked for her money, then stole his cat.

"You didn't call the police?" Phil asked gently.

"I was too upset," Amber said. "I wasn't thinking straight."

But you weren't too upset to run off with the one valuable you could turn into quick cash, Helen thought.

"Mort's death was the end of my dreams," Amber said. "I didn't think his relationship with that Jan Kurtz would last." She said Kurtz like "curse."

"I thought he'd come to his senses and marry me. But when I saw him lying there, I knew that would never happen. He owed me! He promised me money to start my own studio.

"I was only trying to get what was rightfully mine," she said, "but I didn't kill him. You understand, don't you, Phil?"

Amber smiled at him and fluttered her eyelashes.

"Perfectly," he said.

"And you won't call the police?"

"Absolutely not."

She smiled wider. The sun was coming out after her tears.

"Helen will make the call," Phil said. "We're only witnesses. Our client Trish Barrymore will decide if she wants to press charges for theft and extortion."

CHAPTER 29
· · · · · · · · · · · · · · · · · · · ·

Tuesday

"Hell, yes, Trish will press charges," Nancie shouted into her office phone. The lawyer quickly lowered her voice. "Is this conversation safe?"

"Of course I'm safe," Phil said. "I'm surrounded by Ireland Beach's finest." They couldn't put Phil's cell phone on speaker, but Helen stood close enough to hear the conversation. They'd been banished to Amber's hallway.

"No jokes, Phil," Nancie said. "I'm not in the mood. After what that Amber Waves woman put my client through, I want the cops to throw the book at her—robbery, extortion, failure to report a death and anything else they can think of. She's looking at maybe fifteen years in prison.

"I'd really like to hang her from a pole by her dyed blond hair. No, I want her head on top of the pole." And separated from her neck, Helen thought. If Nancie had the power, she would have sent Amber to the chopping block.

Helen couldn't tell if the lawyer was revved up by the prospect of clearing Trish's case or getting rid of a demanding, difficult client. Either way, she'd never heard her so elated.

"Whoa! Calm down, Nancie," Phil said. "It's going to take time to sort things out."

"Calm down? Where the hell have you been?" Nancie said. "It's almost noon. Trish started calling me at six this morning. She called every twenty minutes until ten o'clock, when I told her to get a drink, pop a Valium or have a friend sit with her, but I wouldn't take any calls from her for one full hour."

"How'd she take that?" Phil asked. "Trish is used to getting her way."

"She wasn't happy. I don't mind babysitting clients, but I can't take the weeping, shrieking and hand wringing hour after hour. It wears me down."

Helen couldn't imagine anyone wearing down Nancie. The woman was rock solid, but even granite could crack.

"Where is she now?" Phil asked.

"With Mort's mother, Cynthia," Nancie said. "They've stayed friends through the divorce. Cynthia's pretty sensible. She realized the marriage was over, but didn't want to antagonize Trish for the sake of what she calls her grandcat. She also believed Trish didn't murder her son. Cynthia's in town preparing for Mort's memorial service, and Trish invited her over to choose photos of Mort. That should keep her occupied. But she's going to be calling me in about seven minutes. This time, I'll have good news for her. Where do we go to start the party?"

"The Ireland Beach police station, near Oakland Park Boulevard," Phil said.

"I know where that's at," Nancie said.

"Meet us there in about three hours, at three o'clock,"

Phil said. "They're still processing the crime scene. The CSI techs are photographing Justine for evidence. Then she'll go to the closest animal shelter to have her microchip scanned and prove that she's really Trish's cat."

"I don't want Trish there for that," Nancie said. "She's too emotional."

"Especially when she hears they need the photos in case the cat dies or is otherwise unavailable for trial," Phil said.

"Don't even say the D-word out loud," Nancie said.

"Technically, the cat's evidence," Phil said. "But they'll let Trish keep the cat before the trial."

Helen heard Nancie give a loud sigh of relief.

"Although there's a uniform here who seems quite captivated by her," Phil said. "He's made Justine a cute toy mouse out of string and a crumpled piece of paper."

"For heaven's sake, don't tell Trish," Nancie said. "She'll want the string to be woven by Swiss virgins, the paper handmade and everything certified organic."

"I don't know," Phil said, teasing her. "Justine seems mighty attached to her new toy."

"I'll forget to deduct the cost of that blotter you owe me if you lose it," Nancie said.

"You should see Justine," Phil said. "She's sitting on her back legs, batting it with her little paws. She's having such a good time. It would be a shame to deprive her of so much fun."

"All right, Phil, what do you want?" she asked.

"Permission to bill our client for any red-light-camera tickets we got while delivering the ransom money and following the catnapper to her apartment. We each ran at least two red lights and the tickets are a hundred fifty-eight dollars each."

"Done!" she said. "Trish can afford it. Submit copies of the tickets with your expenses and make sure to circle the ticket times, so I can prove you were working. Just don't let that cat out of your sight."

"Helen will stay with her," Phil said. "I'm going with the money. I've already hit it with my special flashlight and it lit up like a Christmas tree. The cops are taking the cash to the Fort Lauderdale police to confirm the results before they charge Amber. They're familiar with Smart-Water because of all the test programs the company has with local law enforcement.

"The bad news is Trish won't get the money back until after the trial."

"She won't care," Nancie said. "She'll get her cat, and that's what counts. The cash is an unexpected bonus. Just make sure the cops understand *all* the money is marked with SmartWater. We don't want any disappearing from the evidence room."

"Will do. SmartWater will provide the expert witness to testify at Amber's trial," Phil said.

"That kit was a bargain for us," Nancie said. "Nice work, both of you. I'll tell Trish the good news. Meet you at the Ireland Beach police station at three."

From the outside, the IBPD looked like a vacation cottage, painted pink and surrounded by palms and red impatiens. Inside, it turned into a cheap motel lobby decorated with yellowing Wanted posters and a database of dirty fingerprints on the walls and plastic chairs.

Helen and Phil arrived about ten minutes early, but Nancie and Trish were waiting on the orange plastic chairs, along with a third woman Trish introduced as Cynthia Donnelly Draco, Mort's mother.

Nancie looked triumphant, and Trish was tense but hopeful. Cynthia was harder to read. Helen guessed she was sixtysomething and met her age fearlessly. She saw no signs of collagen, Botox or surgical nips and tucks. Cynthia was as tall as Trish, and her blond hair was expensively shaded with platinum. Artful makeup couldn't hide the sadness in her eyes or the shadows under them. She shook Helen's and Phil's hands and said in a soft, warm voice, "Thank you for finding my son's killer and helping Trish. She's the daughter I never had."

"It's time to press charges," Nancie said.

It took more than two hours for the police to get written statements from Trish Barrymore and witness statements from Helen and Phil. Nancie was present when her client and each detective were questioned.

The evidence had already been collected. "You can check the traffic cameras and video on Northeast Thirty-third to verify our story," Phil said. "I have a recording of the extortion call, but if that's illegal, you can check Ms. Waves's cell-phone number for the time of the calls. I believe your CSI techs found the voice changer in her apartment."

Amber claimed she'd been attacked by Helen and Phil, and her public defender had her scratches and bruises photographed. She insisted on medical treatment for her injuries.

Amber said she was carrying a bag of money that was a gift from her boyfriend, Mort Barrymore, when she was attacked in broad daylight by Helen and Phil.

She could not explain why her gift was marked with SmartWater. After that, her public defender would not let her say anything else. She was arrested for extortion and a satisfyingly long list of charges. She had two previous arrests for prostitution and possession of a Class B drug.

It was after five o'clock when the five—Helen, Phil, Trish, Cynthia and Nancie—were free to go. Phil was anxious to leave. He wanted to get to the Fisherman's Tale and bribe XD with a steak dinner. The preppie barfly's signed statement about Zach's state of mind would be a powerful weapon in their campaign to free Margery. At the very least, in Nancie's capable hands it would give the jury a good reason to believe that Margery didn't kill her ex-husband.

Helen promised to take Phil to his car, parked near the Dive Bar and surely decorated with tickets by now. But first she wanted to see Trish reunited with her kitten. She deserved that payoff.

Justine looked like a copper-eyed powder puff when the burly uniformed officer carried her out. He was obviously smitten, if the loopy grin on his face was any indication. Justine licked his huge hands with her scratchy pink tongue. Then she looked up and saw Trish waiting on the other side of the counter.

Justine gave a little squeak.

"My baby!" Trish said, tears streaming down her pale cheeks. "My baby's home!"

She gathered the gray fluff ball into her arms, covering Justine with lipstick kisses. "You're safe," Trish said. "You're free. I'm going to devote the rest of my life to taking care of you and raising you the way your daddy wanted."

And I am not going to cry because a rich woman got her cat back, Helen thought.

Those tears in my eyes are from allergies, that's all.

CHAPTER 30

Tuesday

Helen and Peggy held a sad sunset salute under a sky painted bloodred with veins of molten gold. The pink glow highlighted Peggy's dark red hair.

"Do you know what causes that incredible sunset?" Peggy asked. "Dust. Red African dust. I heard about it on the news. Sahara Desert dust travels five thousand miles so we can enjoy this spectacular evening sky."

"We have enough dust of our own," Helen said. She could see her sandal prints in the powdery layer covering the pool concrete.

"But construction dust is gray and gritty," Peggy said. "I see Phil hosing down the pool deck every morning before the work crew creates more dust."

"It builds up if he doesn't," Helen said. "He's doing a good job of supervising the repairs without Margery. The foreman thinks the work should be finished by late September."

Neither woman dared consider the next question: Would their landlady be out of jail by then? Unless

Margery was restored, the place wouldn't be the same. Margery was the Coronado's life force. Rather than answer, they both drank their wine.

Helen and Peggy were trying—and failing—to cheer each other up.

In the setting sun's crimson glow, the Coronado courtyard looked like an abandoned battlefield, strewn with debris.

The fight to save their home had been a bloody battle. Their landlady, Margery, was in jail for murder one because Millard Whelan, the Snakehead Bay detective with the permanent bad-hair day, believed she'd poisoned her ex-husband, Zach.

Now the old apartment's crumbling facade was drilled out, covered with metal scaffolding, and patched with scabrous gray stucco. Piles of rebar, a generator and paint-spattered canvas drop cloths littered the yard. A thin, ashy film drifted on the pool.

Helen and Peggy had carved out a small oasis by the pool. Before they could kick back and enjoy their wine, they had to scrub the dust off the umbrella table with vinegar and water, or it smeared into sludge.

Peggy was dressed for a date with Daniel, her lawyer lover. She carried out her slim black clutch and ankle-strap heels and draped her chair with a dark beach towel to protect her black sheath. Helen had changed into jeans and a gauzy shirt after a long day of dealing with the catnapper and the cops.

Both drank white wine and dragged pita chips through a bowl of hummus.

"Nice dress," Helen said, "but it doesn't look right without Pete the parrot patrolling your shoulder."

"He's confined to quarters tonight," Peggy said. "As soon as Daniel arrives, I want to leave for dinner. Now that the case of the kidnapped cat is closed, you can concentrate on catching Zach's killer."

"Phil's working on that now," Helen said. "He went to the Fisherman's Tale to persuade XD to give him a statement about Zach's state of mind."

Peggy looked puzzled, then said, "Oh, right. Xavier Dave, Zach's con-man friend who hangs out at that disgusting bar."

"Frenemy, if you ask me," Helen said. "I think he helped Mike Fernier, the drug dealer, poison Zach."

"Why?" Peggy asked.

"Zach refused to give Mike the twenty thou in drug money he owed him after Mike got out of prison. Instead, Zach taunted Mike, telling him, 'Sue me.' But Phil and I can't prove those two killed him, and Nancie, Margery's lawyer, says a statement from XD that Zach was sick and suicidal will help Margery's case. So Phil is taking him out to dinner to try to get him to make that statement."

"I don't know how hungry XD is," Peggy said, "but dinner at that dive wouldn't be much of an inducement for me."

Helen sipped her wine and scooped up more hummus. She'd missed lunch.

"Phil's just meeting him there. He's taking him to a steakhouse, J. Alexander's."

"The place on Federal Highway? Daniel loves eating there. He calls it the Man Cave because it has big booths, open fires and slabs of grilled meat. But didn't you say XD looks kind of scruffy? Can he get in a place like that?"

"It's Florida," Helen said, and shrugged. "We're not known for formal dress here. Where are you and Daniel dining?"

"He wants to try a new restaurant downtown," Peggy said. "It's a surprise. He said to dress up and we'd make a night of it. Lately, he's been working such long hours at his firm, the real surprise is spending a whole evening with him.

"Tonight's the first time I've seen Daniel in three

weeks," she said. "I'm tired of watching old DVDs of *Once Upon a Time.* I've seen the first two seasons twice."

"You like that series, too?" Helen said. "*Once Upon a Time* is good enough to make me believe that fairy-tale characters can be cursed by an Evil Queen, lose their memories and be transported to a small Maine town called Storybrooke."

"Hey, if Jack Bauer can go twenty-four hours without sleep," Peggy said, "then fairy-tale characters can be real. Live in Florida long enough, and you'll believe anything can happen."

"My favorite actor is Robert Carlyle," Helen said. "He plays Rumpelstiltskin in the fairy tale and Mr. Gold in Storybrooke. He has an interesting face."

"I like the brunette, Lana Parrilla," Peggy said.

"She's the fairy-tale Evil Queen who's also the mayor of Storybrooke?" Helen asked.

"That's her," Peggy said. "Robert Carlyle is a good actor, but the Evil Queen/mayor has a harder job. She has to be evil without overplaying. I've never looked at apples the same way since I saw that show."

Apples? Was it the wine or the long day? Helen felt something stir in her brain.

"There are lots of apples in that show," Peggy said, "especially in the Storybrooke scenes. The mayor usually has a big bowl of shiny red apples on her office desk and in her kitchen."

Apples, Helen thought, feeling more alert. Who else had apples in their kitchen? Think. "Doesn't the Evil Queen bake something with the apples?" she asked.

"Snow White eats a poisoned apple given to her by the Queen," Peggy said. "And the mayor bakes something. A pie?"

Pies. Where had Helen heard about apple pies? It was important. She could feel it. She tried to make the connection.

"Not a pie," Peggy said. "A turnover. The mayor makes a poisoned apple turnover in one episode. She wants to kill Emma, the woman who's supposed to save Storybrooke from its evil spell. Instead, Emma's boy, Henry, eats the poisoned pastry, winds up in a coma and she waits for him to wake up."

Wake up! That's when Helen had the answer to the nagging puzzle.

"Apples!" she said. She felt sparks flying from her head. "That's it. That's what killed Zach. Poisoned apples! His buddies Mike and XD didn't poison him.

"I think it was Daisy who was slowly poisoning him. And she did it with apples—by baking them into pies! Zach had two of Daisy's apple pies in his freezer. Phil and I found them when we searched his condo. One pie had two slices missing.

"Oh, this is perfect. Perfect. Susan—she's part of Daisy's weekly dancing group—said Daisy gave Zach an ultimatum. He walked out on her and then he begged Margery to take him back. But Zach still wanted his apple pies, and Daisy still baked them for him. Susan said she told Daisy to get a backbone and tell him to get lost. But Zach came to Daisy's house to pick up his pies. She was convinced she could charm him back into her bed.

"But that's not what Daisy was up to," Helen said. "She was slowly killing him. Making him drive all the way to Delray Beach to get his dose of poison. Her plan turned out better than she imagined. Zach died in his Snakehead Bay condo. The police did a halfhearted search of Zach's condo and cleaned out the fridge, but left the pies in the freezer. The detective saw Margery killing weeds in this yard and pinned Zach's murder on her."

"So Margery was blamed for Zach's death," Peggy said. "She's going on trial for murder."

"Not if we can stop Daisy. Her homemade apple pies

are still in Zach's freezer," Helen said. "We have the evidence to free Margery. Nancie can get an independent lab to test them for poison."

"Then the police can arrest Daisy," Peggy said.

Helen set down her wineglass, her face pale as plaster. "Oh no! She's leaving tonight for Australia. What time are the flights? Can you get a direct flight to Down Under from here?"

Peggy took her iPhone out of her purse. "My boss went to Australia last year. He flew to San Francisco, and from there to Australia."

She checked her screen. "Let's see. There's a flight to San Fran leaving Fort Lauderdale at ten twenty-nine tonight. Or Daisy could fly out of the West Palm Beach airport at midnight."

"It's almost six-thirty," Helen said. "It will take me forty minutes to an hour to get to her house in Delray, if I don't get snarled in traffic. I have to stop her from leaving. If she finds out we're onto her, she'll never come back to the US."

"Helen, stop!" Peggy said. "You can't confront a killer alone. I'll go with you."

"I'll be okay," Helen said. "I won't eat anything at Daisy's house. You go out with Daniel. I have to get there before she leaves the country."

"No!" Peggy stood up and blocked her way. "Call Phil. Now." Helen had never seen her friend so determined. "He can meet you at Daisy's house. Don't be stupid. Here." She found Phil's number and handed Helen her cell phone.

"Helen!" Phil said. She could hear what sounded like soft chatter in the background. He sounded relaxed and expansive. "We're finishing dinner in the bar at J. Alexander's. The steaks were good and everything is signed and sealed."

"Glad to hear it," Helen said. "But I think I know

what really happened to Zach. He didn't kill himself. He was murdered, but not by his drug-smuggling buddies. Daisy did it."

"His old girlfriend?" Phil said. He was alert now.

"I'm almost sure of it. You've got XD's suicide statement as backup if I'm wrong, but I'm betting Daisy poisoned him with those pies we found in his freezer. I'm heading to Delray to stop her before she skips the country."

"I'm signaling for the check now," Phil said. "I'll drop XD at home and then hit the highway for Daisy's house in Delray. Promise me you won't do anything till I get there."

He hung up before Helen could say yes.

CHAPTER 31

Tuesday

"Helen, even if you drive to Daisy's house, how are you going to keep her from leaving the country?" Peggy asked. "Tie her to a chair?"

Peggy's plea was as intense as her red hair. She followed Helen to her apartment, begging her to wait for Phil, offering to go with her to Delray Beach, volunteering Daniel's services as a bodyguard.

Helen refused all her offers.

"Phil is on his way there," she said.

"Call him and ask him to pick you up," Peggy said. "Don't go alone."

"Phil has to drop XD at his apartment. If he swings by here, it will slow him down."

Helen gently shut her bedroom door in Peggy's face so she could change. She slipped out of her sandals into sensible tennis shoes, then traded her gauzy top for a practical plaid shirt.

"Once you dash up to Delray Beach, then what will you do?" Peggy asked.

"Make Daisy confess," Helen said.

"Right," Peggy said, her voice syrupy with sarcasm. "I'm sure when you confront Daisy, she'll break down and say, 'I did it! I poisoned Zach and now I'm leaving the country.'"

Helen opened the bedroom door and showed her a mini digital recorder. "I have this," she said, and buttoned it into her pocket. "I'll trick her into talking."

"So? It's not admissible in court," Peggy said.

"You're only dating a lawyer. You're not one."

"Listen to me, Helen," Peggy said. "I'm begging you."

"I'm listening," Helen said. "But I know what I'm doing. When I record Daisy admitting she murdered Zach, that will be enough for Nancie to jump-start a new murder investigation. She'll get the poisoned pies in Zach's freezer tested at a lab."

"You don't know they're poisoned," Peggy said. "They haven't been tested yet. You're risking everything on a hunch. If you're wrong, that's the end of Coronado Investigations. Daisy will sue you sideways."

"It's a risk I'll take," Helen said, picking up her purse. "How much longer do you think Margery will last in jail? She saved me more than once. I have to save her now. Isn't that Daniel's car in the parking lot?"

Peggy looked out Helen's front window. "It is!"

"Put on your shoes and have a good time," Helen said, shooing her out the door. "Don't worry about me."

"Hah!" Peggy said.

But she ran to the umbrella table, slipped on her black stiletto heels and gracefully glided to Daniel's waiting car, moving over the cracked concrete sidewalk like a model on a runway. Peggy and Daniel were gone by the time Helen fed Thumbs and unlocked the Igloo.

She didn't start the car and roar off. Helen sat in the Igloo, mentally mapping the fastest route to Daisy's house in Delray Beach at the end of the rush hour.

I have less than an hour to save Margery, Helen thought. After Daisy leaves the country, Zach's murder will become an international legal wrangle. I can't even stop her flight to San Francisco. Once Daisy goes through airport security, she's untouchable.

If Daisy's the killer—and I know she is—she won't wait for the midnight flight from West Palm Beach. She'll fly out of Fort Lauderdale at ten thirty tonight. That means Daisy has to leave her home by seven thirty, maybe earlier if she's taking an airport shuttle.

She'll be at the airport two hours ahead of time. Smart travelers don't arrive at Florida airports at the last minute. Too many unpredictable TSA tangles and clueless tourists slow down the lines.

Think! she told herself. Margery's case has been dogged by bad luck and dumb decisions. You have one chance to get this right. Her freedom, even her life, depends on your decision.

So, what's the fastest way to Delray Beach at six forty on a weeknight?

US 1—Federal Highway—is safe but slow. A major artery from Maine down to the tip of Florida, Federal Highway is clogged with stoplights.

The interstate—I-95—is quicker but riskier, she thought. I could be delayed by a late rush-hour traffic jam, an overturned tractor-trailer, even cops chasing drug mules with flashing lights and blazing guns. All those happen on I-95. The nightly TV news is a chronicle of highway disasters.

If the interstate is blocked, I can always get off and take old, slow Federal Highway, Helen decided, and got on I-95.

She breezed past the first few exits at top speed, artfully dodging a dented pickup loaded with mattresses at Cypress Creek Road in northern Fort Lauderdale.

I'm making good time through Broward County, she thought.

Then she crossed into Palm Beach County, and the traffic picked up. The graceful curve near Glades Road was a string of red brake lights, sparkling like jewels on a trophy wife's necklace.

Helen checked her watch. Seven o'clock. Her stomach knotted. Thirty minutes to save Margery.

The Igloo crawled forward. Helen changed lanes twice, hoping each one would move faster. Instead, she found herself stuck behind a white box truck that blocked her view. Finally, she saw the Delray Beach exit: Atlantic Avenue was one mile ahead.

Helen threaded her way through the heavy traffic. She was off the highway and waiting impatiently at the red light at the end of the exit, drumming her fingers on the steering wheel. Seven twenty-one. Finally, the light turned green and Helen headed east toward the beach, where the traffic was thickest.

Daisy's bungalow was on the edge of downtown Delray. Helen prayed there wasn't a special event that night. She ran a red light, made a left turn and found herself in front of Daisy's periwinkle picket fence.

Daisy lived on a street of pricey Caribbean cottages painted like dollhouses and exquisitely landscaped. No one was outside in the humid evening.

Helen saw a light on in a side room, but no sign of Daisy. She parked at a real estate agent's office a block away, switched on the recorder in her shirt pocket, and hurried to Daisy's turquoise and hot pink home. It looked the same, except for the For Rent sign planted in the garden with a rental agent's phone number.

Was Daisy leaving for a month or for good? Helen wondered.

Floridians who lived near the beach often rented their homes to travelers for fat fees. Even if she was gone a month, Daisy could make enough to cover a big chunk of her trip to Australia. If she wasn't planning to return, her pretty cottage would provide a steady income. Daisy's front gate was unlatched. Helen slipped through it, then angled off toward the small landscaped jungle on the left. She crept through a thick hibiscus hedge, snagging her shirt. Now she was under the lighted side window, framed in hot pink. Helen carefully raised her head to eye level and peeked inside.

Daisy sparkled in a cobalt blue pantsuit trimmed with rhinestones. Her fluffy blond hair seemed electric. She was struggling to zip a pink flowered suitcase the size of a cedar chest. She must have packed everything she owned.

Helen moved her head an inch higher. Yep, the closet was open and empty, except for a few hangers. The open dresser drawers looked empty, too.

Helen saw Daisy's plump finger poke at something pink in the path of the zipper. Once the obstruction was out of the way, she dragged the zipper around the final corner. Daisy sighed with relief when the bulging case was zipped, and sat down beside it on the red-flowered spread.

Daisy definitely liked color, Helen decided. And flowers.

A mosquito stabbed Helen's neck. She swatted it and Daisy looked over her shoulder at the window. Did she hear the slap? Helen wondered. Time to move on.

Helen edged around the side of the house. Most of the backyard was taken up by an enormous turquoise wooden garage, trimmed in cheerful pink. The rest of the space was more gaudy flowers—all real—a birdbath with a silver gazing ball and a gravel path. Helen's legs were long enough that she could step over the crunchy gravel path. She wanted to see the turquoise garage.

Ouch! Helen tripped on a concrete cherub treacherously covered with moss. She limped over to the garage and opened the side door. It creaked. She froze.

Helen counted to ten, holding her breath. No sound from inside the house. The back door, only ten feet away, stayed closed.

Inside, the garage was neatly organized and smelled pleasantly of potting soil and sawdust. A red Ford Fiesta subcompact took up almost half the space closest to the door. It was crammed with dark shapes. Helen peered in the car window and saw boxes on the seats marked KITCHEN, LIVING ROOM, BEDROOM.

Florida houses rarely had basements. Was Daisy storing her personal possessions in the car while she was gone? Was she planning to come back? Where was she going? Australia, or some country without extradition? Sweat trickled down Helen's forehead and her shirt stuck to her chest. The garage was hot and airless.

Helen tiptoed around the car and saw a workbench neatly lined with well-used gardening tools: trowels, sharp-pointed weeders, pruners and cruel, curved instruments. A jug of weed killer, the same brand Margery used, squatted on the bench.

Progress! Helen thought. Not proof, but progress. She found a few grains of sawdust behind the bench and wondered if this was where Zach made his cat towers before he moved out.

More long-handled gardening tools hung on the walls—a leaf rake, a pitchfork, a hoe, three steel shovels. Daisy or her aunt Tillie must do a lot of yard work. No, not Aunt Tillie. Daisy said her aunt was old and sick and she had to care for her.

In the far corner, an old-fashioned white chest freezer hummed beside the workbench. It was nearly as big as the Ford. Maybe Daisy had more poisoned pies in the freezer, Helen thought. Then she'd have proof to link her to Zach's murder.

The longer Helen stayed in the sweltering garage, the more her dash to Daisy's house seemed foolish. She had nothing to link her to Zach's murder. Worse, if Daisy caught Helen, she could accuse Helen of trespassing, breaking and entering, even theft. She felt sick and dizzy in the smothering heat.

The freezer had to have the answer.

She lifted the heavy, yellow-white lid of the old freezer and got a blast of frosty air. No pies, just neatly stacked pizzas and bags of peas. Damn. Helen was sure she'd find Daisy's pies in here.

Wait! What was that under the frozen peas? Something wrapped in white. A pie? No, too big for a pie. Wrapped in white plastic trash bags, it took up the whole length of the freezer. It felt like . . . meat? That couldn't be right.

Helen tossed three bags of frozen peas, then grabbed the sharp-pointed weeder to rip open the white plastic trash bag.

She peeled back the edges for a look inside.

The old woman's blue face was frozen in a peaceful expression.

Helen screamed.

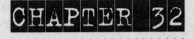

CHAPTER 32

. . . .

Tuesday

"Y ou!"

Daisy filled the garage doorway, rhinestone top sparkling in the dying light, baseball bat aching to batter Helen. Helen slammed the freezer lid on the poor, permanently cold woman and looked for a way to escape.

Did Daisy kill her sick old aunt? Helen wondered. Is she going to kill me now?

She was trapped.

Daisy was fast and light for a large woman. She swiftly rounded the red Fiesta and swung the bat at Helen.

Strike one! Helen ducked, then lashed back with the sharp-pointed weeder, digging a long scratch into Daisy's arm, ripping her cobalt blue sleeve.

"My blouse!" Daisy cried. "You tore my blouse." She clung to the bat as blood ran down her arm.

"You killed Zach," Helen said.

Stuck between the workbench and the freezer coffin,

Helen tore the long-handled pitchfork off the wall and held it in front of her. Daisy swung at her again. Helen parried the swing, but felt the bat strike into the sturdy wooden handle and rattle her bones.

Where the heck is Phil? she wondered.

"Prove it!" Daisy said, and slammed the bat at Helen again. She missed. Helen ducked and staggered back against the bench.

"Easy," Helen said, hoping her talk would distract Daisy. "I've got the poisoned apple pies you made for Zach, each pie dated and labeled in your handwriting. They're still in his condo freezer. Margery inherited his condo."

Helen enjoyed delivering that little dig. Daisy stepped back as if Helen had knifed her, then laughed and swung the bat again, so close Helen heard it whistle past her ear.

"Missed again!" Helen said.

"Margery!" Daisy said, and sneered. "Zach's true love is in jail. The Keystone Cops think she killed him. I hope there's life after death, because I want Zach to roast in hell while his darling rots in jail."

Daisy swung again, and the bat sent the garden tools on the bench clattering to the floor. Helen dropped with them. She tried to catch her breath in the hot, airless garage. Sweat ran down her forehead and soaked her shirt.

Come on, Phil, she thought. Get here before Daisy shatters my skull.

"I can see why you're mad at Zach," Helen said. "He refused to marry you." She hoped that opened another wound.

From her shelter under the bench, Helen reached for a wicked three-pronged cultivator, closed her eyes, gritted her teeth and aimed for Daisy's blue-sandaled foot, right in front of her. She swung it like a hatchet.

Helen winced. She could feel the prongs stab Daisy's

meaty instep. The killer's pink-painted toes curled in pain.

Daisy howled and whacked the sturdy front legs of the heavy workbench so hard it shuddered.

"I gave him thirty years," Daisy said. Helen heard the tears in her voice and saw them drip on the concrete floor. "I cooked. I cleaned. I loved that man, and I was still no match for Margery."

Helen was crouched under the bench. She retreated into the corner closest to the humming freezer, where Aunt Tillie was in cold storage.

Daisy's got me boxed in, Helen thought. I'm thirty-five years younger, but she's fifty pounds heavier, strong from gardening and supple from dancing.

Where are you, Phil? You should be here by now.

Helen heard the bat whipping overhead and Daisy snarling about her injured foot. Thick red blood pooled on the clean concrete floor from the new wound Helen had inflicted.

I have to run for it, she thought, and there's no way I can pass Daisy without getting pounded by the bat. My only chance is to slide under the car, then make a break for the door. I'll make my move in midsentence, and keep her talking until I do.

Helen grasped the long handle of the pitchfork, the devil's weapon. She'd need it to fight thirty years of Daisy's demons.

"I can understand killing Zach," Helen said, launching herself under the red Ford, pitchfork in her left hand. Her upper body went under first, and she hit her head on the driveshaft running down the center of the car. Her shoulder scraped the rusty undercarriage. Her hips were safe, but Helen's long legs still stuck out.

Helen slid her left leg under the car, but she wasn't fast enough with the right. Daisy swung the bat and thwacked Helen's ankle. Shock waves of pain undulated up her leg.

Helen bit her lip to keep from crying out and used her free hand to drag her wounded leg underneath the car.

In its shelter, she wiggled her toes. Her ankle wasn't broken. She hoped she could walk—no, run—when she made her break for the side door.

Keep talking, Daisy, she prayed. Phil, where are you?

"But why did you kill Aunt Tillie?" Helen said.

"I didn't kill her," Daisy said. "She died of a heart attack. The doctor warned her she was digging her grave with her teeth, but Aunt Tillie didn't like health food. I helped her along by fixing her favorite fattening food, but I was just making an old lady happy. Her last meal was roast pork with mashed potatoes and gravy, lima beans in cheese sauce, and apple pie with ice cream and real whipped cream. She ate nearly half an apple pie, then said she felt tired and went to bed. When I brought her bacon and eggs in the morning, she was dead."

Daisy seemed to need this break as much as Helen did. She also needed to tell her story. The words poured out, like pus from a lanced boil.

"Dear Aunt Tillie was getting old all alone, so she invited me, her only niece, to live with her. Said she'd give me the house if I'd take care of her. She even let Zach stay here, though she insisted on separate rooms. Didn't believe in us living in sin—her words."

Keep talking, Helen thought. She gripped the pitchfork for her upcoming dash to the door and cursed whatever kept Phil from showing up.

"But Aunt Tillie broke her promise?" Helen prompted.

"Oh no," Daisy said. "She made sure I saw the will. Made a big deal of summoning her lawyer to the house to change it in my favor. Got Zach to witness it, since he didn't benefit from the will. She also gave me power of attorney in case she got sick. Then she introduced me around town as her dear niece. Told everyone I'd moved into her home to help her.

"Help her! Hah! I was a live-in maid. A slave! Spent my days fetching and carrying and cleaning for the old bat. 'Get this!' 'Do that!' 'Go to the store and buy me Welch's Grape Jelly, Daisy. It's on sale. I want the eighteen-ounce jar.' So I did. But she wasn't happy. They were out of the eighteen-ounce size, so I brought her the twenty-two-ounce jar. She made me go back to the store and return that size, then drive to another store five miles away to get the size she wanted. Spent twenty dollars on gas to save a nickel.

"I was at her beck and call, day and night. I couldn't do anything right. If I bought peanut butter, it wasn't the right brand. If I got the right brand, it was creamy instead of chunky. She'd make me return it until I got exactly what she wanted.

"The house was never clean enough for her. 'You've got to get in the corners with a knife, Daisy,' she'd say. 'That's where the wax builds up.' 'There's soap scum on the shower tile, Daisy. Clean it off.' And the garden! I'd get up at six in the morning to weed, before the day got too hot. When I finished, her majesty would go out and inspect her estate. No matter how hard I worked, she'd still find something in the garden that needed pruning or edging or deadheading. Grubbing in the garden was ruining my hands. Scrubbing floors was killing my knees.

"And Zach, she had him painting the house, then the trim, then the stupid picket fence. Whenever he finished one house project, Aunt Tillie would find another."

Sweat trickled down Helen's face, and she licked it away. Phil, she thought, hurry! I have to get out of here and I'm wounded. I can't move fast.

But Helen saw the dark blood pooling by Daisy's sandaled foot and realized her attacker was hurt, too.

Daisy was still telling her story. If she hadn't tried to kill me, Helen thought, I might feel sorry for her. Might.

"But dear Aunt Tillie did me a favor when she had me

drive all over town," Daisy said. "People got used to seeing me in her car and at her house. I discovered most of the neighbors didn't know who she was, and if they did, they tried to avoid her. The rest of the people around here were newcomers who didn't know she existed—or didn't care. Aunt Tillie never went out. She had no friends.

"She sent me to the bank all the time. All the bank tellers knew me and thought I was so sweet to take care of my poor, sick aunt. That's how I discovered her Social Security checks were direct deposit. Between Tillie's money from Uncle Sam and mine, well, we had a nice little income—for one."

"So when Tillie died suddenly," Helen said, "you didn't want to spend that money on an expensive funeral."

"And I didn't want to lose her Social Security check," Daisy said. "So I put her in cold storage and collected her money. It wasn't like I hurt her or anything. She was resting in peas. Get it?"

Helen shivered. She could almost touch Tillie's resting place.

"Tillie taught me one thing. I could keep posing as her dutiful niece, and no one realized she was gone."

"Not even Zach?" Helen asked.

"He'd moved out by then. Her constant demands finally drove Zach away. She wanted him to shingle the roof next. A man his age, crawling around on a roof in the heat! Zach bought his own condo in Snakehead Bay. He wanted me to move in with him. I was tempted, but he wouldn't give me the only thing I'd wanted for three decades: marriage. So I told him to beat it.

"But he couldn't stay away. He liked my pies, especially my apple pies." Helen could sense that Daisy's story was running down. She'd have to make a run for it soon.

"So you poisoned his pies," Helen said.

"Just a little," Daisy said, and laughed. "A little arsenic

goes a long way. He was a health nut. He wasn't going to drop dead of a heart attack, like my aunt. Zach lost that fine hair he was so proud of. He went to doctor after doctor, but not one was smart enough to figure out what was wrong."

Helen could tell by the light on the floor that Daisy had left the side door open. The killer's voice was stronger. It was time for Helen to leave.

"You must have loved how he drove up here to get his own death," she said.

"I relished every . . ."

Helen inched forward until her head was free of the car on the other side.

". . . second," Daisy said.

Helen quickly crab-crawled to the door while Daisy said, "Knowing Zach couldn't live without my apple pies—and wouldn't live when he ate them—"

Helen slammed the door shut and stood up slowly, gasping for breath. The yard spun and she held on to the garage wall to steady herself. Her ankle was swelling. She could hear Daisy running around the car, then rattling the doorknob.

Helen limped across the yard toward the side of the house, when she saw Phil rounding the corner.

"Helen!" he said. "Sorry it took me so long. You won't believe the traffic on I-95. What's going on? You're hurt!"

A blood-soaked Daisy burst out of the garage, brandishing the baseball bat. She tripped over the mossy cherub and hit the mirrored gazing ball. It shattered.

"Oops," Helen said. "Seven years' bad luck."

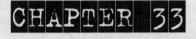

CHAPTER 33

Saturday

M argery was waiting outside the county jail four days later, dressed in her familiar purple and puffing on a Marlboro. Her steel gray hair stuck out like an angry cactus and she'd lost weight.

But she was Margery again, proud, angry and commanding.

Helen cried when she climbed out of the Igloo at high noon to greet her landlady. She limped over to her, wearing a blue surgical boot.

"Stop that crying," Margery said. "I'm free and it's over. Now we're going to sue the Snakehead Bay Police Department."

"Just what I wanted to hear," Nancie said, shaking Margery's hand. "I've brought the paperwork. We can go over it while Helen drives us home, and I'll file suit first thing Monday morning. What do you want now?"

"To go home," Margery said.

The lawyer held the car door open for Margery, who

thoughtfully ground out her cigarette before she sat down. Helen nodded her thanks. Once Nancie and her client were in the backseat, Helen started the Igloo.

"Nice footwear, Helen," Margery said. "What happened?"

"She was wounded in the line of duty," Nancie said.

"It's not that bad," Helen said. "Daisy cracked my ankle with a baseball bat. I'm stuck with the boot for six weeks. She needed seven stitches when I sliced her arm with a three-pronged cultivator and she's wearing her own surgical boot."

"I hope you broke her foot," Margery said.

"No such luck. I stabbed her foot, but she broke it when she tripped over a concrete cherub while she was chasing me."

"I love the symbolism. Tripped by an angel," Margery said. "I don't mean to sound ungrateful, but what took you so long? Daisy was arrested Tuesday night."

"She was taken into custody when the police found the body of her Aunt Tillie in the garage freezer," Helen said.

"Daisy killed a sweet old lady?" Margery said.

"Old, definitely," Helen said. "But nobody called Aunt Tillie sweet. She'd promised Daisy her house in Delray after she died and let Daisy and Zach move in with her. Then the old tyrant turned Daisy into a drudge and cracked the whip on Zach."

Margery snorted. "How long did that last?"

"Not sure," Helen said. "I do know Zach bailed and bought his Snakehead Bay condo six months ago. After Zach moved out, the aunt died peacefully of a heart attack. Daisy stashed her body in the freezer and kept collecting Tillie's Social Security.

"Zach asked Daisy to move in with him, but she refused unless he married her. It was the one thing she'd wanted since they met."

"And Zach wouldn't marry her," Margery said.

"He was still in love with you," Helen said.

Margery smiled, savoring her triumph over an old rival. Helen watched her landlady in the rearview mirror.

"Tillie's death taught Daisy how easy it was to get rid of someone. Everyone thought she was taking care of her beloved aunt. Nobody missed Tillie. Daisy knew Zach was too healthy to die of a heart attack like her aunt. But Zach was crazy about her apple pies, so she slowly poisoned him."

"Good old Daisy," Margery said. "She believed the way to a man's heart was through his stomach, when she got old, anyway. Before that, she took the shortcut through his zipper."

Nancie laughed.

"Be glad he loved her pies," Helen said. "They were the cold, hard evidence of Zach's murder, neatly stacked in his freezer and labeled in Daisy's handwriting."

"The Snakehead Bay police never examined the pies?" Margery said.

"Nope. They took the food from the fridge, but not the freezer," Helen said.

"Bozos," Margery said.

"I'll make sure they pay for their incompetence," Nancie said. "I'm grateful Phil and Helen were smart enough not to touch those pies. Once Helen caught Daisy, I made sure they were taken as evidence and tested at a police lab. I also got a piece for my own private lab test."

"The Delray Beach police found arsenic-based weed killer in Daisy's garage," Helen said. "Also in her kitchen, with the baking supplies. Right next to the brown sugar."

"I love it," Margery said.

"Finding Aunt Tillie's body in the freezer was enough to keep Daisy in custody Tuesday night," Helen said. "But the ME had to wait for the poor woman to thaw before she could be autopsied. It takes a while to defrost one hundred pounds of tough meat."

"Helen!" Nancie said.

"It's true," Helen said. "The autopsy showed Aunt Tillie had been fed a hearty last meal and died of a massive coronary. Even if Daisy had called 911, she wouldn't have been able to save her aunt."

"Helen recorded Daisy's confession," Nancie said. "It's not admissible in court, but it confirmed her aunt's autopsy findings."

"A second autopsy of Zach showed he died more slowly," Helen said. "Daisy put small doses of arsenic in her pies, giving him dozens of unpleasant symptoms. You noticed some of them, Margery, including the Tums he took for his upset stomach. And you were right. Zach lost his hair."

"Of course I was right," Margery said. "I know a wig when I see one."

"Daisy gloated that he was bald."

"Zach always was vain about his hair," Margery said.

"She tormented that man, killing him one piece at a time," Helen said.

"Was that a pun?" Margery asked.

"You were stuck in jail until today because the lab tests took time," Nancie said. "Once they established that Daisy had murdered Zach, she was charged with first-degree murder. She didn't kill her aunt, but Daisy was charged with failure to report a death and improper disposal of a body. The police also found evidence of identity theft, fraud and misuse of a Social Security number. Daisy kept cashing Aunt Tillie's Social Security checks after she was dead.

"Florida is a death-penalty state, and messing with Social Security is a federal crime. Daisy will probably plead guilty rather than risk a trial."

"Now, that news is worth waiting for," Margery said.

"I've got other news you may not find so welcome," Nancie said, quietly. "Zach doesn't have any family to claim his body. You are his sole heir. He asked to be cremated. Will you handle his funeral?"

"I owe him that much," Margery said.

"On a brighter note, Phil's planning a welcome home barbecue tonight," Helen said. "Are you up to it?"

"Am I!" Margery said. "I can't wait to eat something besides baloney sandwiches. Who's coming?"

"Peggy and Pete," Helen said. "Her lawyer, Daniel, has to work late."

"So do I," Nancie said.

"Phil and I will be there," Helen said.

"What about Elsie?" Margery said.

Helen fought to find the right words. "Uh, do you want her there?" she asked. "You said some harsh things the last time you saw her."

Margery sighed. "Elsie can be dumber than a post about people, but she's still my oldest friend. She has a good heart. Neither one of us is getting any younger. I should forgive and forget. I'll call her and invite her."

"The party starts at five," Helen said. "She can bring a covered dish if she wants."

"All that's left is the pleasant business of going over your lawsuit against Detective Whelan and the Snakehead Bay police," Nancie said.

"Can we get him fired?" Margery asked.

"He certainly deserves it," Nancie said. "Let's discuss your options."

"Consider the chauffeur's privacy window up," Helen said. "I'll concentrate on driving us home. Nancie's car is at the Coronado."

Margery was initialing and signing the last page of some legal papers when the Igloo rounded the corner.

Helen parked in front of the Coronado. Margery climbed out, lit a cigarette, and surveyed the construction work with satisfaction. The metal scaffolding looked like a teenager's braces, and the smooth white stucco had a temporary case of gray acne. But they could see the building would soon be beautiful.

"Will you look at that," Margery said, blowing out a long trail of smoke. "I was gone at the right time. I missed the worst of the dust and the noise."

"Phil handled it for you," Helen said.

Phil, Peggy and Pete were waiting for Margery in the backyard.

"Hello!" Pete said from his perch on Peggy's shoulder.

Peggy, in a summery white pantsuit, presented Margery with a graceful purple orchid plant.

Phil gave her a kiss and a bottle of champagne.

"Let's put that on ice for this evening," Margery said, parading across her property in a triumphant cloud of tobacco smoke, a goddess surrounded by nicotine incense. "I want a shower and a nap. I'll meet you outside by the pool later."

She unlocked her jalousie door and was greeted by the scent of lemon polish. The furniture sparkled and the windows shone. "You've cleaned my home," she said. "The place hasn't looked so good since I moved in. Thank you."

"Welcome back," they said.

"It's good to be home," Margery said, and carefully shut the door.

At four thirty, Margery emerged from her home, a queen returning to her court. She wore her purple caftan like a royal robe, her hair was a silver crown, and a dramatic amethyst necklace caught the late-afternoon sun. Her wrinkles were once more elegant folds.

She handed Helen a plate with six raw shrimp. "I thawed these for the fur bag," she said. "He might as well celebrate, too."

Margery settled onto her chaise and lit a cigarette. Phil poured her a glass of wine, and went back to tending the barbecue.

Helen fed Thumbs his treat, then brought out a platter of antipasto and a garlicky green salad for dinner. At Phil's request, Peggy made his favorite casserole: green beans in mushroom soup topped with canned onion rings. Pete was given a cashew to celebrate Margery's return.

A little after five o'clock, Elsie tottered in on red platform shoes, wearing a sleeveless plaid jumpsuit. Red and blue streaks carried the colorful theme to her spiky hair.

"Elsie!" they shouted. Helen took the platter of deviled eggs, and Phil carried off the bowl of mayonnaise potato salad she'd brought.

"That's all the food I could put together on short notice," she said, in her soft, high voice.

"It's wonderful," Helen said, hugging her. "And you're here. We're so glad."

Elsie went over to visit her old friend. Helen and Peggy kept busy with the antipasto to give the women privacy, but they caught a few phrases: "so sorry . . . overstepped . . . still friends." Margery patted Elsie's pale, veined hand and Phil poured another round of drinks.

Soon after the reconciliation, Phil served a feast of meat—barbecued chicken, burgers, pork steaks and slabs of ribs—as well as butter-drenched roasted ears of corn. They filled their plates and sat at a folding table covered in purple. The graceful arc of the orchid served as the centerpiece.

"Tell us about the cat case, Helen," Margery commanded, and she did.

"Justine stirred up a powerful lot of emotions for a tiny kitten," Helen said. "Greed, envy, hatred—and love."

"Too much love, if you ask me," Margery said. "Trish Barrymore paid half a million dollars to ransom that cat? Is Justine really worth that much?"

"She is to Trish," Helen said. "She loves that kitten and plans to show her at the next Gold Cup cat show in

Fort Lauderdale. She has full custody now that Mort's dead. She'll get her ransom money back after the catnapper's trial, but I don't think she's worried about it."

"Imagine being so rich you don't care if you get a half million dollars back," Peggy said. "Is the cat case over now?"

"Yes," Helen said. "I've been fired—again—from my undercover job. But it really ended when Phil and I went to Mort's funeral Wednesday. His fiancée, Jan Kurtz, was there. So were Trish; Carol Berman, Mort's executive assistant; and so many friends and colleagues there was barely room to move. Mortimer Barrymore was much loved."

"A good send-off for a good man," Phil said. "He'll be missed."

"We're so glad to have you here, Margery," Peggy said.

"This has been a splendid day," their landlady said. "I want to thank you all."

They saluted the setting sun with pale, dry champagne.

"The Coronado is just another building without you," Helen said. "You make it our home, Margery."

"You're born with your family, but you choose your friends," Margery said. "I chose well."

"Hear, hear!" they said, and raised their champagne glasses to the blazing pink and gold summer sky. "To friendship."

CHAPTER 34

Six weeks later

Margery threw a double coming-out party on a Saturday night. There were two reasons to celebrate: Helen was finally freed from her awkward, ugly boot. And the Coronado Tropic Apartments' stunning restoration was finished.

Helen and Phil, Elsie, Peggy and Pete the parrot, Peggy's mystery lover, Daniel, and Nancie were at the dual celebration. The two lawyers seemed uneasy without their customary suits. They both showed up in navy polo shirts and khakis and joked about their weekend uniform.

Peggy, looking young and hip in her cool green sundress, presented Daniel as shyly as a daughter bringing home a date. Helen liked him instantly. Daniel was a muscular, thick-bodied man with short brownish hair. Helen wondered if his ancestors had carried pikestaffs on British battlefields. Now he fought a war of words in courtrooms. Daniel had a merry glint in his eye. Peggy was clearly crazy about him, and Pete liked him, too. The Quaker parrot deserted his perpetual perch on Peggy's shoulder to hop onto Daniel's meaty finger. Daniel looked pleased with that honor.

Helen showed the Coronado colors: white shorts, turquoise top and strappy white sandals. Her toes reveled in their freedom after their confinement in the heavy boot.

Daniel's eyes bugged when Elsie tottered in wearing a black faux-leather cage dress that bared most of her shoulders and chest. Squares of fish belly–white flesh strained against the cage bars.

"That's a spectacular dress," Peggy said, hugging Elsie.

"Cutting-edge," Helen said, kissing her powdery cheek. Elsie's blond hair was tipped with black spikes.

"I got it on sale," Elsie said, smiling happily. Red lipstick crept into the lines of her lips.

"I can tell," Margery said. "It's half off." Her smile took the sting out of her words.

Margery looked like a fairy godmother in a fluttering lavender butterfly caftan. She waved her cigarette wand toward a purple-draped table and said, "Grab a drink and some appetizers, and then we'll take the tour."

"Caviar!" Elsie said, admiring an immense glass bowl of the fishy delicacy nestled in shaved ice.

"Beluga," Phil said. "Served right, with capers, chopped hard-boiled egg and toast triangles."

"There's also smoked salmon and three different cheeses," Margery said. "Phil has the grill going and he'll start your steaks after the tour. Help yourself to wine, beer and champagne."

Peggy took Pete to her apartment so he wouldn't be tempted by the delicious, fattening food.

After cocktails and appetizers, Margery led the group on a renovation appreciation tour, pointing out the improvements with a smoky wave of her Marlboro.

The Coronado rose above the palm trees, cool and

white as ice cream, its turquoise trim now fresh and summery. "You can't see it," the landlady said. "But the rusty rebar has been removed, the cracked stucco has been patched, and the rust trails from the old window air conditioners are gone."

"We can hear that last improvement," Helen said. "The new air conditioners are much quieter."

"And energy efficient," Peggy said. "I'll see that improvement on my electric bill."

"You're walking on another improvement," Margery said. "All the cracked concrete has been replaced, the sidewalks and the pool deck."

"I like your retro sidewalk with the turquoise diamonds," Daniel said.

"And last but not least, fresh sod and more flowers," Margery said, and pointed toward the waterfall of purple bougainvillea surrounding the pool. The walkway was lined with gentle lavender impatiens and spiky salvia.

"Purple, of course," Helen said.

"The new palms aren't purple," Margery said. "And these elephant ears are lime green."

"Dramatic," Nancie said. The lawyer was nearly dwarfed by the plant's fan-shaped giant leaves, and seemed overwhelmed by the colorful company.

"There's something that should bring you more green," Helen said, pointing to the For Rent sign in the window of Cal the Canadian's former apartment. "Any prospective renters yet?"

"Just started looking," Margery said. "But I'm open to suggestions."

"We'll work on it," Helen said.

They would, too. They knew you didn't rent at the Coronado. You were adopted.

"It's time for dinner," Margery said. "Tell Phil how you'd like your filet cooked. Let's eat!"

The evening was cool and pleasant, the dinner was

simple and sumptuous—grilled steaks, twice-baked potatoes, crispy garlic bread and buttery asparagus—served at a round table by the pool.

Helen and Phil regaled them with stories about their investigations, the tales they could tell in public, anyway.

"How's your foot feel now that you're out of that boot?" Peggy said.

"Ten pounds lighter," Helen said.

"I heard Daisy the killer broke her foot," Daniel said. "Is she still wearing her boot?"

"I lost contact with her after she was arrested," Helen said.

"Last I heard," Nancie said, "Daisy pleaded guilty and got ten years in prison."

"At her age, that's a life sentence," Margery said.

"What if Daisy hadn't tripped over that concrete cherub?" Peggy said. "I don't like to think what would have happened to Helen."

"It was close. Fools rush in and tread on angels," Helen said, and the group groaned.

"Phil and I want to ask a favor, Margery," she said. "We're going to Key Largo for a week. Would you watch Thumbs? Our cat can't stay with Peggy. He thinks Pete is fast food."

"Do I have to have that fur bag in my apartment?" Margery asked.

"He'll be fine at Phil's," Helen said.

"Then the answer's yes," Margery said.

Helen, Daniel and Peggy helped clear the table while Margery served two desserts: champagne and strawberries, and warm brownies with whipped cream.

Elsie asked the one question the others didn't dare: "How did you afford this awesome renovation, Margery, dear?"

"I cashed in a CD," Margery said. "Then Zach left me his life insurance and his condo. He was behind on the mortgage, but Nancie helped me. I paid two months' worth of missed payments, his condo fees, and some late penalties, so I'll be able to sell it once his estate is probated."

"The housing market is bouncing back in Florida," Phil said. "Especially waterfront property."

Whenever two or more property owners were gathered together, you heard that line, Helen thought. It's the Florida mantra.

"Right now there are two interested parties and it isn't even listed yet," Margery said. "One wants to pay cash. While we're on the subject of cash, I want to talk to you and Peggy about your rent at the Coronado."

Helen looked at Phil. They'd expected a substantial increase. It was definitely due.

"I haven't asked for a rent increase the whole time you've lived here," Margery said. "Now I've had all this work done."

Helen braced herself. She and Phil had three units—their two apartments and Coronado Investigations in 2C. Their business was thriving. They could afford more rent. They didn't want to live—or work—anywhere else.

Peggy looked uneasy, and Daniel squeezed her hand.

"When I was in trouble, you all pitched in and helped," Margery said. "I owe you my life and my freedom. So I'm making my promise now, in front of both legal eagles: I won't raise the rent for at least two years."

Everyone applauded. Peggy smiled with relief and Phil poured another round of champagne. They toasted Margery in style.

EPILOGUE

. . . .

H elen talked Trish Barrymore into hiring Jan
Kurtz for Justine's first Gold Cup cat show in the
Kitten Class. "She knows the ropes," Helen said.
"I'll be there to help."

They met at Trish's home at seven o'clock the morning
of the show. Justine's short gray coat was in good condition,
so she got a combing but not a bath. Helen thought the
kitten looked so much like a stuffed toy she expected her
to have a Made in the USA tag. Her coppery eyes sparkled
with feline mischief, and her fur was luxurious with good
health. Her ears were tiny tents on her round head.

"She's perfect," Trish said, and Helen agreed. This
wasn't maternal pride. Justine was a splendid Chartreux.

Trish, in a slim black dress, carried Justine like a stylish accessory in her bejeweled Baby Coach. At the cat
show, Justine gave a surprisingly loud mew of displeasure at the noise and throngs of people. On the bench,
Jan and Helen made sure she was comfortably settled

into her show cage. The midnight blue curtains high-lighted her hypnotic eyes.

"Justine has star quality," Jan said. "Look at the spectators lining up to see her."

Trish basked in the praise heaped on her cat: "Look at those eyes!" "Beautiful fur!" "Adorable!"

If the cat lovers' awed stares and admiring comments were any indication, Helen thought, Justine was a shoo-in for Best Kitten.

The judge in Ring One called the numbers, including twenty-seven, Justine's number. Trish bore her triumphantly through the crowd, confident Justine would come back with her first rosette.

But Justine didn't like the plain wire cage. She hissed at the cats on either side of her.

The judge, a studious woman of forty, seemed to sense that Justine had beginner's nerves. She praised and petted her, then carefully lifted her out of the cage. Justine bit the judge. Not a nip—a hearty chomp on the thumb.

"Ouch!" the wounded judge said.

Trish, Helen and Jan watched in horror from the back of the ring.

"Uh-oh!" Jan said. "Trouble."

"It's just a little bite," Trish said.

"She drew blood," Jan said. Helen saw three dark red drops splashed on the white stage. Justine was quickly returned to her cage and the judge retired to the first-aid area up front.

"I don't know why they're making such a big deal about a little blood," Trish said.

"Cat bites need to be treated right away," Jan said, "and the exhibitors of the next cats get offended if a judge bleeds on their cats. The wound has to be disinfected and covered. Let's hope it's not a deep puncture. Justine's disqualified. Let's get her out of there, Trish, before the judge returns."

"But she's only disqualified in this ring," Trish said, desperate to save her cat's career.

"The ring clerk is required to advise all the other rings of the incident," Jan said. "Do the right thing for Justine. She's clearly not happy about something."

"But I can show her again, can't I?" Trish said.

"She's not barred from future competitions," Jan said. "But if she bites and continues to be shown and is unhappy, Justine will quickly get a reputation as a bad actor. Do you want that for her? She's hissed at the other cats and complained since we walked through the door. Justine is beautiful, but she's telling you this is not the life she wants."

"Please listen to her," Helen said. "You've always done what's right for Justine. Mort would want it, too."

"You're right," Trish said, and sadly carried her cat back to her cage. The other exhibitors averted their eyes. Helen and Jan helped Trish pack up and go home.

Justine ended her show-cat career with that one chomp. Trish blamed the trauma from the catnapping. Jan thought the kitten had never been properly socialized. Helen believed clever Justine had figured out the one way to avoid a life she hated. Justine had the instincts of a true queen: People didn't judge her—she judged them.

Trish decided not to breed Justine. She was spayed and lives happily as a house pet.

Trish Barrymore continued to date Arthur Goldich. The couple married a year after Mort's death and now live in Trish's Fort Lauderdale mansion. Trish has resumed her position as a social leader and gives fabulous parties. Arthur is devoted to Trish and to their cats.

Trish paid for the four red-light-camera traffic tickets Coronado Investigations racked up during the catnapping and gave Helen and Phil a fifty-thousand-dollar bonus, the ten-percent share of the ransom money. "I never expected to see any of it again," she said.

Chatwood's Cheshire Dream—Chessie for short—was the Gold Cup National Champion that year. Dee Chatwood commissioned an oil portrait of the blue-eyed beauty. Chessie retired, and Midnight fathered a coal black kitten, the spitting image of his father, who became a national winner.

Red did not win top honors in the Premiership Class, but she enjoys her retirement. Chocolate and Mystery each produced two stunning Persians. All the cats spend their days petted, loved and pampered.

Jan Kurtz inherited Mort's mansion as well as half his estate. She could never enjoy living in the house where her fiancé died. She sold it to a South American shipping magnate.

As soon as she received her inheritance, Jan quit Chatwood's Champions. Dee begged her to stay on. Jan refused, but promised she'd stay long enough to train her replacement—if she made twelve dollars an hour.

Dee screamed like every dollar was stripped off her skin, but gave in and started advertising for Jan's replacement. But Dee's reputation was known throughout the cat world: She went through six candidates in five days. No one lasted more than eight hours.

Jan, tiring of the drama, gave Dee an ultimatum: She was leaving next Friday, whether Dee had a replacement or not. But Jan loved the cats and wanted to see them properly cared for. She suggested Dee promote Gabby Garcia, the maid, to the head of the cattery. Gabby enjoyed the gentle Persians, but refused to work unless she made twelve dollars an hour, and she wanted an assistant.

Gabby hired her cousin, Graciela. Their other cousin, Rosita, took Gabby's old job as a maid. The Garcia family has made a tidy sum tolerating Dee's tantrums.

Jan began seeing Dr. Bob, the veterinarian she met at the Hasher School Pet Appreciation Day, six months after Mort's death. They dated for a year, then married and moved to North Carolina. Jan breeds and shows prize-winning Persians, and Dr. Bob has a successful small-animal practice and an award-winning cable TV show.

Lexie Deener was convicted of the first-degree murder of Mortimer Barrymore and sentenced to twenty years in prison. The former cat show judge was forced to sell her beloved '86 Jaguar, Black Beauty, to pay her attorney. Because of the classic car's high mileage and the damage done when law enforcement searched it for evidence, Blackie brought less money than expected at auction.

Carol Berman, Mort's executive assistant, received two offers to work at other financial firms, but decided she'd never have another employer as good as Mort. Instead, Carol manages the J. McLaughlin store on Worth Avenue in Palm Beach Gardens. She knows the stock, the store and the kind of women who shop there.

Amber Waves, the catnapper, refused to take a plea offer. She'd had nothing to do with Mort's murder and believed she was owed that five hundred thousand dollars in ransom money. She was sure her sizzling good looks would help convince the men on the jury and the judge to be lenient. Amber's attorney was thrilled that she had a male judge and a majority of men on the jury. But the jury was appalled that Amber had stepped over Mort's dead body to steal his cat, and moved by Trish's dignified and heartrending testimony about her suffering when Justine was catnapped. Justine herself made an appearance and captivated the courtroom. Amber was sentenced to twelve years in prison for extortion, and they were hard years.

After her release, Amber couldn't find work as a fitness trainer or a pole specialist. She dances in a bar as Miss Kitty, wearing cat's ears and not much else.

BSO Deputy Webster Maddow was promoted to sergeant for his work on the Mortimer Barrymore murder case.

Nancie Hays wreaked havoc on the two detectives and the communities who had falsely arrested her clients. Lester V. Boland, the Peerless Point Crimes Against Persons detective who railroaded Trish into jail, was forced to resign. Trish settled out of court with the city for an undisclosed amount.

Millard Whelan, the bristly haired Snakehead Bay detective who conducted the careless investigation of Zachariah Flax's murder, retired without a pension. He bags groceries at a local supermarket. Margery's settlement with the city of Snakehead Bay was enough to replace the CD she cashed in to renovate the Coronado.

Margery Flax held a small, simple service for her ex-husband Zach. Before his body was cremated, she slipped their silver-framed wedding photo into his casket. "That will either make him happy or torment the heck out of him," she told Helen as the casket rolled toward the fiery furnace.

Helen, Phil, Peggy, Elsie and XD Duncan, Zach's barfly friend, attended. Mike, the dealer he'd cheated out of his share of the drug money, did not, though he did call

Margery and tell her that Zach owed him twenty thousand dollars "for a business deal."

"You're welcome to sue me for your money," Margery said sweetly. She has not heard from Mike since.

Later, Zach's ashes were packed in a pink scallop-shell urn. Helen accompanied Margery and the biodegradable urn to the beach at sunset. The urn floated on the pink-tinged water under a flamingo sky shot with molten gold.

"I thought our love would last forever," Margery said, as the ocean carried away the urn. "But our love didn't last. His lies did."

Helen patted Margery's hand. "Lies destroyed my first marriage," she said.

"Dust," Margery said. "That's all that's left—dust and ashes."

"Like the African dust that creates these incredible sunsets," Helen said. "It's beautiful."

"Yes," Margery said. "Yes, it was."

A pink wave swept over the urn, and Zach was gone.

Helen and Phil drove down to Key Largo in the Igloo and spent the week swimming, sipping cocktails on the beach, making love in the lazy afternoons and listening to the local bands at night. They often ate at the Fish House, a restaurant that served locally caught fish. Helen loved the grilled yellowtail snapper. The Fish House's ceiling was strung with colorful lights shaped like flip-flops, pineapples, martini glasses, palm trees and parrots. After lunch on their last full day, Phil said, "Let's take a drive. I want to show you something special."

They drove for more than an hour on the Overseas Highway, the romantic name for US 1 in the Keys, passing restaurants, dive shops and tourist haunts. Helen enjoyed the inventive Keys mailboxes along the roadside: manatees, flamingos, fish and buoys.

Finally, they reached Big Pine Key, some thirty miles north of Key West. "Good," Phil said. "It's close to sunset. That's the best time to see them."

"See who?" Helen asked. But when he turned in to the National Key Deer Refuge, Helen knew the answer.

"Key deer live on Big Pine Key and a few nearby islands," Phil said. "They're the smallest of the white-tailed deer, and they're not found anywhere else in the world. Back in the fifties, there were fewer than thirty Key deer left. Now there are about eight hundred."

They quickly slathered on bug repellant, then softly slipped down a nature trail toward the water. Fat whipped-cream clouds sailed overhead. Helen heard a tiny *snap!* and Phil put his hand on her shoulder. In a mangrove thicket near the water, they saw a doe and her fawn.

Helen was bewitched. The doe was barely bigger than a dog, and the fawn was smaller than Thumbs. The pair delicately stepped toward Helen and Phil. They put out their fists, and the doe and the spotted fawn sniffed them and took a step forward, watching Helen and Phil with big, melting brown eyes.

There was a loud guffaw from the trail, and the deer disappeared.

"They're beautiful!" Helen said.

"They're tough," Phil said. "Survivors. Like you."

"Like us," Helen said, and she kissed him by the fading glow of the setting sun.

Read on for a sneak peek at the next
Dead-End Job Mystery
by Agatha and Anthony Award–winning author
Elaine Viets,

Checked Out

Available now from Obsidian.

"I need your help," Elizabeth Cateman Kingsley said. "My late father misplaced a million dollars in a library book. I want it back."

Helen Hawthorne caught herself before she said, "You're joking." Private eyes were supposed to be cool. Helen and her husband, Phil Sagemont, were partners in Coronado Investigations, a Fort Lauderdale firm.

Elizabeth seemed unnaturally calm for someone with a misplaced million. Her sensational statement had grabbed the attention of Helen and Phil, but now Elizabeth sat quietly in the yellow client chair, her narrow feet in sensible black heels crossed at the ankles, her slender, well-shaped hands folded in her lap.

Helen studied the woman from her chrome-and-black partner's chair. Somewhere in her fifties, Elizabeth Kingsley kept her gunmetal hair defiantly undyed and pulled into a knot. A thin, knife-blade nose gave her makeup-free face distinction. Helen thought she looked practical, confident and intelligent.

Elizabeth's well-cut gray suit was slightly worn. Her turquoise-and-pink silk scarf gave it a bold splash of color. Elizabeth had had money once, Helen decided, but she was on hard times now. But how the heck did you leave a million bucks in a library book?

Phil asked the question Helen had been thinking a little more tactfully: "How do you misplace a million in a library book?"

"I didn't," Elizabeth said. "My father, Davis Kingsley did."

"Is it a check? A bankbook?"

"Oh, no," she said. "It's a watercolor."

Elizabeth sat with her hands folded demurely in her lap, a sly smile on her face. She seemed to enjoy setting off bombshells and watching their effect.

"Perhaps I should explain," she said. "My family, the Kingsleys, were Florida pioneers. My grandparents moved to Fort Lauderdale in the 1920s and built a home in Flora Park."

The Kingsleys might have been early local residents, Helen thought, but this pioneer family hadn't roughed it in a log cabin. The Kingsleys had built a mansion in a wealthy enclave on the edge of Fort Lauderdale during the Florida land boom.

"Grandpapa Woodrow Kingsley made his money in oil and railroads," Elizabeth said.

"The old-fashioned way," Phil said.

My silver-haired husband is so charming, only I know he's calling Woodrow a robber baron, Helen thought.

"For a financier, Grandpapa was a bit of a swashbuckler," Elizabeth said, and smiled.

Helen decided maybe Elizabeth wasn't as proper as she seemed.

"He enjoyed financing silent films. He often went to Hollywood. Grandmama was a lady and stayed home."

The old gal was dull and disapproving, Helen translated. Grandpapa had had to travel three thousand miles to California to go on a toot.

"Grandmama would have nothing to do with movie people. She dedicated herself to helping the deserving poor."

Heaven help them, Helen thought. Their lives were miserable enough.

"Grandpapa put up the money for a number of classic films, including *Forbidden Paradise*—that starred Pola Negri—and Erich von Stroheim's *The Merry Widow*."

Films with scandalous women, Helen thought. Did Grandpapa unbuckle his swash for some smokin'-hot starlets?

"Impressive," Phil said. "Von Stroheim was famous for going over budget. He ordered Paris gowns and monogrammed silk underwear for his actors in *Foolish Wives* so they could feel more like aristocrats."

A tiny frown creased Elizabeth's forehead. She did not like being one-upped.

"When he was in Hollywood, Grandpapa would drink scotch, smoke cigars and play poker," she said. "He played poker on the set with the cast and crew, including Clark Gable."

"Wow!" Helen said.

"Oh, Gable wasn't a star then," Elizabeth said. "Far from it. He was an extra and Grandpapa thought Gable wouldn't get anywhere because his ears were too big. Many men made that mistake. Until Gable became the biggest star in Hollywood."

There it was again, Helen thought, that glimpse of carefully suppressed glee.

"Gable was on a losing streak that night," Elizabeth said. "He was out of money. He'd lost his watch and his ring. He bet a watercolor called *Muddy Alligators*."

"A painting?" Helen said. "What was Gable doing with that?"

"I have no idea, but he was quite attached to it," Elizabeth said. "He thought gators sunning themselves on a mud bank were manly. Grandpapa won the painting with a royal flush, but he didn't trust Hollywood types. He made Gable sign it over to him. Gable wrote on the back: *I lost this fair and square to Woodrow Kingsley—W. C. Gable, 1924.* Gable's first name was William. He changed his stage name to Clark Gable about then.

"Grandpapa admired the watercolor, and was surprised that a roughneck like Gable owned a genuine John Singer Sargent."

"Sargent painted muddy reptiles? I thought he did portraits of royalty and beautiful society women," Phil said.

"He did, until his mid-forties," Elizabeth said. "Then he had some kind of midlife career crisis and painted landscapes in Europe and America. Sargent painted at least two alligator watercolors when he stayed at the Florida home of John D. Rockefeller."

"Sargent switched from society dragons to alligators," Helen said, then wished she could recall her words. Elizabeth's grandmother was definitely a dragon.

"Dragons in training, usually," Elizabeth said, and again Helen caught a flash of well-bred amusement. "Most of his society belles were young women.

"Grandmama refused to display the painting in her house. Grandpapa couldn't even hang it in his office. She said it was ugly. I suspect it also may have been an ugly reminder of his Hollywood high jinks. She banished the alligator watercolor to a storage room.

"Sargent died the next year and Grandpapa had a fatal heart attack seven years later, leaving Grandmama a widow with one son. The watercolor was forgotten for decades.

"Until about five years ago," Elizabeth said. "My father,

Davis Kingsley, inherited the family home in the fifties. Papa was eighty when he found the watercolor in the storage room. Sargent's work was fashionable again. He had it authenticated and appraised. The watercolor wasn't worth all that much, maybe three hundred thousand."

Helen raised an eyebrow and Phil gave her a tiny nod. Three hundred K might not be much to Elizabeth, but the PI pair thought it was a substantial chunk of change.

"But it was worth much more, thanks to what the art world calls 'association.' A painting owned—and signed—by a film star brought the price up to more than a million dollars. The story behind it helped, too.

"Papa told everyone he'd discovered a lost family treasure. My brother, Cateman, and I begged him to have it properly stored and insured, but Papa said it wasn't necessary. 'It's in a safe place,' he'd say. 'Safer than any vault.' But we were concerned. Papa suffered from mild dementia by then.

"He died in his sleep six months ago, leaving his estate to Cateman and me. Papa gave me the Sargent watercolor and my brother inherited the family home. When the will was made five years ago, I was happy with that arrangement. I was a single woman with a comfortable income."

Comfortable. That was how rich people said they were rolling in dough, Helen thought.

"Since then, I've had some financial reversals. That watercolor has become important. I need that painting to save my home, and we can't find it."

"It was stolen?" Helen said.

"Worse," she said. "I believe it was accidentally given away. We've looked everywhere in the house, checked Papa's safe-deposit boxes and the safe, but we've found no sign of the missing watercolor. My brother even hired people to search the house. We can only conclude that my father hid it in one of his books that were donated to the Flora Park Library."

"Who gave it away?" Helen asked.

"Scarlett, my brother's new wife. Cateman recently married his third wife. It's a May-December marriage. He's sixty and she's twenty-three."

Did Elizabeth disapprove of her new sister-in-law? Helen thought Elizabeth had made a face, like she'd bitten into something sour, but it was hard to tell.

"Cateman and Scarlett moved into the family home immediately after Papa's funeral, and Scarlett began redecorating.

"Papa had let things slide in recent years. Scarlett doesn't love books the way he did. I doubt she reads anything but the magazines one finds in supermarket checkout lines."

Yep, Helen thought. Elizabeth definitely doesn't like her brother's new wife.

"Her first act was to get rid of what she called the 'dusty old books' in my father's library, which dates back to Grandpapa's time. Scarlett donated more than a thousand books to the Flora Park Library. Most of the books were of little value. Papa was a great reader of hardcover popular fiction, and the Friends of the Library began selling those while they had the more valuable books appraised.

"The Friends put ten mysteries on sale for a dollar each, and the hardcovers were bought within a few days. But a patron found the birth certificate for Imogen Cateman, my grandmama, in her thriller. She returned it to the library. Then a man discovered the deed to property in Tallahassee in a spy novel."

"The Flora Park Library has honest patrons," Phil said.

"People of quality live there," Elizabeth said. "I would expect them to return family papers."

Elizabeth sat a little straighter. She considered herself one of the quality.

"We concluded that my late father hid valuables in his

books, and the missing watercolor was in a donated volume."

"Why don't you look for it?" Phil asked. "Don't you know the people at the library?"

"Of course I do," Elizabeth said. "But my job as a facilitator for my college alumni association takes up all my time."

Helen had no idea what a facilitator did, but Elizabeth said it so gravely, Helen felt she should have known.

"I could have taken the books back and searched them myself, but that would cause talk.

"I can only give you a small down payment," Elizabeth said. "But if you find the watercolor, I'll pay you ten thousand dollars when it's sold at auction. The library director is a friend and she's agreed that you can work as a library volunteer, Helen, while you discreetly look for the watercolor."

"Me?" Helen said. A library, she thought. I'd like that. I'd get to read the new books when they came in, too.

"If Helen takes this job," Phil said, "how do you know Scarlett didn't keep the watercolor?"

Helen thought her husband would make a fine portrait—eighteenth-century British, she decided. He had a long, slightly crooked nose, a thin pale face and thick silver hair. She dragged herself back to the conversation.

"I showed her a picture of one of the alligator watercolors and she said it was 'gross.' She prefers to collect what she calls 'pretty things,' such as Swarovski crystal."

"What about your brother?" Helen asked. "Does he have the watercolor?"

"Cateman is an honorable man," Elizabeth said. "Besides, he has more than enough money."

Rich people never have enough money, Helen thought.

"He actually hired people to search his house. Why would he do that if he was trying to keep the painting for himself?" Elizabeth asked.

"The search was done after the books were donated to the library?" Phil said.

"Of course," Elizabeth said. The frown notched deeper into her forehead. She was annoyed. "My brother is most anxious to help me find that artwork. He has sufficient means for himself and Scarlett, but he doesn't feel he can afford to support me. His two divorces have cost him dearly."

Now, that's convincing, Helen thought.